Praise for *88 Names*

"Ruff's fast-flowing, fascinating narrative is full of amusing topical and pop culture referents without being overburdened by allusiveness. His witty, often snarky dialogue crackles, and every aspect of the gaming experience is sharply rendered and explicated. . . . Any novel that can . . . appeal to gamers and literary fans alike is a treasure greater than the loot in a cyberdragon's cave." —*Washington Post*

"Employing a diverse cast of characters and weaving historical facts with an abundance of pop culture references, Ruff's richly imagined world of next-generation internet is plausible and a bit frightening. The action inside the virtual gaming world is sleek and exciting, but the extrapolation of identity, friendship, and human relationships makes the narrative shine."
—*Booklist* (starred review)

"Ruff's newest technothriller is an exciting page-turner that delves into the online gaming world and should appeal to both veterans and newbies." —*Library Journal*

"Ruff remains on a winning streak with this seamless genre hybrid."
—*Publishers Weekly*

"Following in the footsteps of Ernie Cline, who hit the geek gold mine with *Ready Player One*, Ruff takes his shot at a near-future gaming world. . . . Gamers for life who can pry themselves off the controller will certainly dig this digital-era whodunit."
—*Kirkus Reviews*

88 NAMES

Also by Matt Ruff

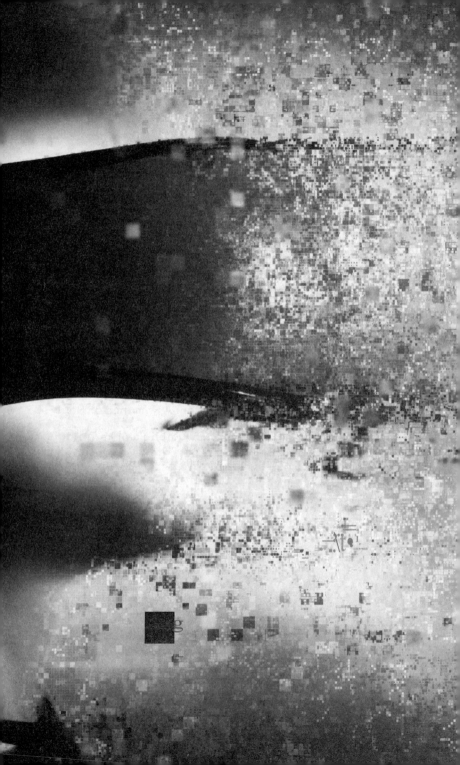

88 NAMES

A NOVEL

MATT RUFF

HARPER PERENNIAL

NEW YORK • LONDON • TORONTO • SYDNEY • NEW DELHI • AUCKLAND

HARPER ● PERENNIAL

A hardcover edition of this book was published in 2020 by HarperCollins Publishers.

P.S.™ is a trademark of HarperCollins Publishers.

FIRST HARPER PERENNIAL EDITION PUBLISHED 2021.

Designed by William Ruoto

The Library of Congress has catalogued the hardcover edition as follows:

Names: Ruff, Matt, author.
Title: 88 names : a novel / Matt Ruff.
Other titles: Eighty-eight names
Description: First edition. | New York, NY : Harper, [2020].
Identifiers: LCCN 2019020231 (print) | LCCN 2019021528 (ebook) | ISBN 9780062854698 (E-book) | ISBN 9780062854674 (hardcover) | ISBN 9780062854681 (softcover)
Subjects: | GSAFD: Science fiction. | Fantasy fiction.
Classification: LCC PS3568.U3615 (ebook) | LCC PS3568.U3615 A615 2020 (print) | DDC 813/.54—dc23
LC record available at https://lccn.loc.gov/2019020231

ISBN 978-0-06-285468-1 (pbk.)

21 22 23 24 25 LSC 10 9 8 7 6 5 4 3 2 1

for Neal

88 NAMES

NEW TO ONLINE ROLE-PLAYING GAMES? Don't worry! At Sherpa, Inc., we are dedicated to providing a fun, quality gaming experience to clients of all skill levels. Feel free to dive right in—we'll explain everything you need to know, when you need to know it. Or if you'd prefer to do some reading in advance, check out our handy quick-start guide (located in the **appendix** of this document), which covers all of the important game concepts and terminology. We look forward to serving you!

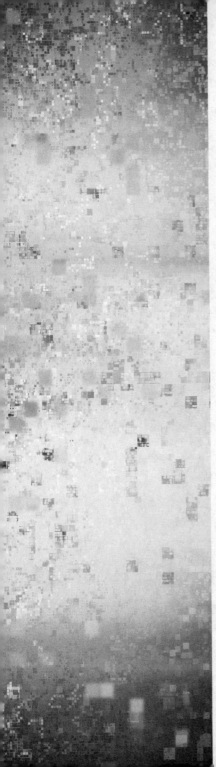

PART ONE

Mr. Jones

An exclamation point above a character's head indicates that they have a quest for you.

—*Call to Wizardry* loading screen tip

sherpa — A person who acts as a paid guide in a massive multi-player online role-playing game (MMORPG). Sherpas provide their clients with playable characters, equipment, and skilled team-mates, allowing them to experience high-level game content that would otherwise require hundreds of hours to reach. Sherpas typically act as freelancers, unaffiliated with the companies whose game worlds they operate in.

Like gold-buying and other "pay to win" strategies, the use of sherpas is regarded by many players as a form of cheating. Game companies vary in their attitude towards the practice, with some tolerating sherpas' existence while others—notably Tempest, makers of the popular *Call to Wizardry*—classify sherpa activity as a violation of the End-User License Agreement (EULA) and a bannable offense.

—*Lady Ada's Lexicon*

The client is an idiot.

His name is Brad Strong, and in real life he works as a commodities trader at one of those big Wall Street banks that's always implicated, but never held accountable, whenever the economy crashes. According to his social media accounts, Brad is a graduate of the Wharton School of Finance. He owns a nineteen-hundred-square-foot duplex in Soho and drives a Jaguar XP. He rock-climbs and SCUBA dives and is a student of Krav Maga, the martial art practiced by Israeli commandos. Philosophically he considers himself a libertarian, but he votes Republican because let's be serious. He's a fan of the Three Stooges and early Chuck Palahniuk. He hates fat chicks, libtards, and people who won't shut up about their kids.

Tonight, Brad is paying me and my associates at Sherpa, Inc. a substantial fee—substantial to us, trivial to him—to take him adventuring in the Realms of Asgarth in Tempest's *Call to Wizardry*. Like the majority of clients, he has opted for a dps character: a 200th-level elf samurai. Brad thought about going with an orc ninja instead, but decided he'd rather not lurk in the shadows like a pussy. He wants to charge the monsters head-on and "crack some skulls."

I'm tanking, as a warrior troll named Blockhead of Moria. My job is to hold aggro, get the monsters to concentrate their attacks on me and my Plate Mail of Invulnerability, while the dps characters—Brad and my colleagues Jolene and Anja—do their damage-per-second thing, and Ray, running heals as a gnome cleric, staunches any bleeding that my armor can't prevent. It's a balancing act. The dps need to finish off the monsters before the healer runs out of mana and everybody dies. But if they do too much damage too quickly, they'll steal aggro off the tank, and what should be an orderly killing spree will become a chaotic melee.

This shouldn't be an issue. Jolene and Anja both know what they're doing, and Brad bought his character from us. His samurai has been carefully specced out to hit the sweet spot between too much damage and too little.

The problem is the hammer. When Brad hired us two days ago,

he asked if he could have access to his samurai in advance, to get in some practice before the run. Since he was paying a quarter of our fee up front, I said yes. I guess I should have paid more attention to his comment about wanting to crack skulls. During practice, he decided he didn't like the katana his samurai was packing, so he went to the in-game auction house and bought himself a new weapon: Ivar's Hammer.

Ivar's Hammer is basically Thor's Hammer, without the Marvel trademark issues. Even by the high production standards of *Call to Wizardry*, it is a gorgeously rendered virtual object, a brutal, sexy work of art with black basilisk-leather handle wraps, a dragontooth butt spike, and mithril filigree thunderbolts on the mallet head. You can see why an alpha-male skull-cracker would be drawn to it.

Unfortunately, Ivar's Hammer is a tanking weapon. Anything you hit with it gets really pissed off, and on critical hits it shoots out fingers of lightning that aggro every other monster within thirty yards. Brad's samurai keeps getting mobbed, and unlike my plate armor, his scale mail can't handle that much punishment.

Brad dies and Ray resurrects him. I warn Brad that this is going to keep happening if he insists on using the hammer. Brad doesn't want to hear it. As a paying customer, he feels he should be entitled to use any weapon he likes. I remind him that I'm only a guide to the game world; I don't make the rules. "Figure something out," Brad says.

We do what we can. I switch from Blockhead the warrior to Sir Valence, a paladin who can call down holy fire and throw his shield like Captain America, and who is generally better at emergency crowd control. Jolene's ranger summons a special companion animal, a fire-breathing tortoise that can serve as a secondary tank. When, despite my and Jolene's best efforts, Brad dies again (and again), Ray revives him, and Anja, whose druid moonlights as an armorsmith, patches the holes in his scale mail so we don't have to go back to town for repairs.

Our contract with Brad guarantees him two full dungeon runs. Even the most difficult dungeons rarely take more than three or four hours to complete, and the Caverns of Malice, where we are now, ought to be a cakewalk. But the constant cycle of death and resurrection slows our progress to a crawl; an hour in, we've barely cleared the first boss.

Brad is as frustrated as we are and not professionally constrained from showing it. As he gets more impatient, he starts charging into battle before the rest of us are ready, with predictable results. Jolene tries to calm Brad down, at which point we discover he doesn't particularly like black chicks, either. Jolene shuts up and Anja takes over; her attempt to soothe Brad is more successful, but the dying continues. I crank up the gib setting on my user interface, causing Brad's demises to be rendered in as gory a fashion as possible, blood and viscera exploding from his wounds. This has no practical effect on game play, but it makes me feel better.

After another forty minutes, we reach the second boss, the green dragon Anastasia. We stop outside her lair so I can explain the fight to Brad. There are three phases, I tell him. In phase one, Anastasia will bite and claw. In phase two, she'll vomit a river of acid. In phase three, she'll beat her wings and conjure a storm of tornadoes. Then back to phase one and repeat, until either she or all of us are dead. The rules of survival are straightforward: Don't steal aggro off the tank. Don't stand in the acid. Avoid the tornadoes. We also need to be mindful of Anastasia's eggs, which are stacked along the walls of her cavern. The eggs are sensitive to jostling and if bumped—or struck by lightning—they'll hatch. Anastasia's brood spit acid like their mom; they also poop little patches of Krazy Glue that make it much harder to dodge tornadoes. Hatch more than a handful of eggs, and the fight quickly becomes unwinnable.

Having laid all this out, I ask Brad if he would please, just for this one battle, switch back to his katana.

"No," Brad says.

It's getting harder not to lose my temper with this guy, and not just because of the way he's behaving. *Call to Wizardry*'s avatar-creation system maps your real face onto the skull of whatever mythical creature you're playing. Brad's spray-tanned mug, stretched over the angular physiognomy of an elf, produces an unfortunate suggestion of yellowface that is amplified by the samurai costume. I feel like I'm talking to the lead from an old-fashioned production of *The Mikado*. Who is an idiot.

I'm a professional with bills to pay, so I keep my cool. But I also keep pressing: The hammer just isn't going to work in here, I say. It'll break too many eggs and we'll be stuck on this boss all night.

Brad tells me that he *can't* switch back to the katana, OK? He doesn't have it anymore; he sold it to a vendor right before he bought Ivar's Hammer. If I want to teleport back to town and buy him a new sword, fine, he'll use it for this one fight. Otherwise, I need to suck it up and deal.

I really should buy him the replacement sword. It's the smart play. But I'm running out of patience and we've still got a long way to go, so I decide to brute-force it instead. I look over at Jolene, who nods. Among the arrows in her quiver is a Shaft of Obliteration, the ranger equivalent of a tac nuke. The resources required to craft it cannot be purchased but must be gathered, tediously, by hand, and generally its use is reserved for the deadliest end-level bosses.

For Anastasia, it's complete overkill, but it should get us through the fight on the first try.

Next I b-channel Ray and slap a DNR order on Brad; no heals for him on this fight. Ray doesn't respond, but his expression tells me he'd already decided to cut Brad off.

"All right," I say, "let's do this."

Anastasia, curled in slumber at the center of her lair, blinks herself awake as we enter. I draw my sword and charge, but I don't rush to get to her first; when Brad cuts in front of me yelling "Banzai!" I let him take lead. He runs up and bops Anastasia on the nose. Wide awake now, she rears her head back, roaring. The quality of the animation is incredible; the mix of rage and confusion on the dragon's face perfectly mimics the expression of someone startled out of sleep by a band of homicidal midgets. Her eyes flit from Brad to me and back again and she cocks her head, suggesting a new level of bafflement: Why is the dps in front? Do these morons not understand how this works?

Brad raises Ivar's Hammer for another blow and Anastasia swipes him with a claw, shredding his armor and tearing out his rib cage. As his heart and lungs exit stage right, she bends down and bites his head off. What's left of Brad's body collapses into a pile of quivering giblets.

The cavern flares white as Jolene's nuclear arrow finds its mark. I move in, hurling my shield and hacking with my sword.

"Battle rez me!" Brad's disembodied voice cries. "Battle rez me!"

We ignore him. While I hold aggro, Anja, her druid now shapeshifted into a mountain lion, comes in from the side and rakes Anastasia with her claws. Jolene's pet tortoise hits the other flank and Jolene, staying behind me, looses arrow after arrow.

In no time, Anastasia is caught up in her own bloody death

throes; we never even make it to phase three. As the dragon crashes to the ground, the vibrations from her fall cause all of her eggs to swell up and burst, harmlessly. For an instant, all is peaceful in the cavern.

"Rez me, you fucks!" Brad shouts.

Ray's already doing it. I'm sure he's tempted not to, but like me, he wants to get paid.

Brad doesn't appreciate Ray's professionalism. His body reassembled, he leaps to his feet, shouting, "The *fuck*!" and darts at Ray with Ivar's Hammer swinging. But the game won't let you attack your teammates. Or shove them: When Brad tries to chest-bump Ray, he passes right through him.

"Brad," I say. I point to the treasure chest that's taken the place of Anastasia's corpse, its purple aura signifying epic loot.

Still fuming, Brad stomps over to the chest and kicks it, which is allowed. The lid pops open, unleashing rays of gold-orange light; a trumpet flourish sounds. Not just epic loot then—legendary loot. Brad's won the lottery.

I step up to get a better look, and my heart sinks as I see the sword hilt rising out of the chest. The Vorpal Blade of Gilliam: another tanking weapon.

And not just any tanking weapon. For a paladin, the Vorpal Blade of Gilliam is *the* tanking weapon. It is as rare as it is powerful: You could open a thousand loot chests and not find another. And like all legendary weapons, it's bind-on-pickup, so you'll never see one for sale in the auction house.

Most sherpa contracts specify that clients are only entitled to loot their characters can reasonably use: No tanking weapons for non-tanks, no dps weapons for healers, et cetera. But clients of Sherpa, Inc. are entitled to any and all loot, without restriction.

That way they never feel cheated by the rules, and if they choose to pass up loot voluntarily, they get to feel virtuous and altruistic.

Brad's no altruist, but he stares for so long at the sword without taking it that I foolishly allow myself to hope he doesn't want it. Then he glances over at me. I've got my best poker face on, but Brad's Wall Street trader instincts see right through it; he grins and turns back to the chest.

Brad ditches Ivar's Hammer, which falls ringing to the floor and vanishes back into his inventory. His hand closes around the Vorpal Blade's hilt and another trumpet flourish signals that it is now bound to him irrevocably.

The sword blade is a length of razor-sharp crystal filled with changeable light. When Brad first holds it up, it's white with holy fire, but as he waves it back and forth, it turns brimstone red, noxious green, icy blue, and finally dark purple shot through with violet sparks. My despair deepens as I realize I'm never going to be able to hold aggro against this thing. And Brad was talking about going to Crimson Castle for his second dungeon run: vampires and succubi, a crowd-control nightmare.

CHUNK!

The cavern suddenly brightens, as if Jolene's set off another nuke. I turn and shield my eyes against the bank of Klieg lights that have appeared up near the ceiling. A second bank comes on beside them, and then a third.

I'm reminded of my only visit to a real-world amusement park, on a field trip when I was nine. A friend and I snuck away from the group and went on the haunted house ride, which proceeded to break down, stranding us in the middle of a ghoul-infested graveyard. We screamed our heads off until the ride operator came to rescue us, emergency lights exposing the ghouls as nothing more than puppets on a stage.

These Klieg lights have a similar effect, albeit one that is entirely computer-generated. In the blink of an eye, Anastasia's lair transforms from a photorealistic cave to a cheap set constructed of wood and papier-mâché. The 3D treasure chest becomes a painted flat propped up with a plank.

"What the hell is going on?" says Brad, his legendary Vorpal Blade demoted to a Styrofoam toy.

What's going on is we're about to get busted by the EULA police. I should be upset about this, and I am, but I can't help being impressed as well. Any other game company, having caught us violating their terms of service, would just dump us out of the system. But not Tempest. Even when they ban you, they turn it into a show. And it's this extraordinary level of polish that has made *Call to Wizardry* the most successful MMORPG in history.

A section of the cavern wall swings open, revealing a concrete maintenance tunnel. Two men in suits emerge. At first glance they read as lawyers, but then you notice the gloves they are wearing— blue latex, like the kind police use when handling evidence. The gloves are an inside joke, a reference to a cult science-fiction show that aired before I was born and was canceled after only one season. I'm a big enough nerd that I get it: The EULA cops aren't here to haul us off to virtual jail. They're executioners.

Brad thinks he can fight them with his Nerf sword. He manages a few halting steps before the movement controls on his user interface stop working.

Two by two, hands of blue, the EULA cops advance to the center of the room. We find ourselves drawn into a semicircle before them. EULA Cop #1 consults a computer tablet and addresses us one at a time, starting with me: "JohnChuAlias8437 at gmail dot com, aka Blockhead of Moria, aka Sir Valence, you are guilty of violating Section 5 of the *Call to Wizardry* End-User License Agreement . . ."

Section 5 of the EULA prohibits unsanctioned commercial activities within the game world. I.e., it's the anti-sherpa clause. Jolene, Anja, and Ray are all guilty of this offense as well, as is Brad, for hiring us. Interestingly, Brad is also guilty of violating Section 2, which prohibits hacking into other players' accounts or profiting from said hacking.

"The penalty for these crimes is the immediate and permanent suspension of the offending user accounts," the EULA cop concludes. "If you believe this judgment has been reached in error, you may appeal to customer service within sixty days."

With that, he turns to his counterpart. EULA Cop #2 extends a gloved fist clutching a small cylindrical device; translucent blue antennae sprout from both ends of it. They emit a harsh buzzing noise that jangles the nerves like fingernails scraping on a blackboard.

I can't move, but from where I'm standing I can see Brad, at the far end of the semicircle. Blood starts drizzling from his samurai's nose and ears. The buzzing gets louder and the drizzle becomes a gusher. I experience a brief moment of satisfaction as Brad's head explodes.

Then it's happening to me, too. Everything goes black. Words appear, floating in the void: ACCOUNT TERMINATED.

RIP, Blockhead of Moria.

RIP, Sir Valence.

I'm down to eighty-eight names.

avatar — The audiovisual manifestation of a person or software agent in a virtual environment. Avatars can resemble any animate or inanimate object that their host computer is capable of rendering. They can also manifest differently to different observers simultaneously: In a three-way virtual conference, Alice might appear to Bob as a photorealistic rendering of herself, while Charlie sees and hears her as a cartoon character, a talking horse, or the ghost of Neville Chamberlain. This ability to project multiple aspects, known as **faceting**, allows for all manner of interesting exploits and shenanigans.

—*Lady Ada's Lexicon*

'm not fucking paying you."

Jolene and I have reconvened with Brad at the Game Lobby, a virtual lounge that is popular as a pre- and post-run hangout spot. The Lobby has a cyberpunk chrome-and-neon aesthetic; there's a bar with a Jumbotron TV that's always tuned to your favorite channel, a laser-lit dance floor that switches over to karaoke three times a week, an arcade where you can play emulations of old coin-op video games, and everywhere, interactive screens you can use to find teammates for *Call to Wizardry* and a dozen other popular MMORPGs. Because of its sponsorship agreement with

Tempest, the Lobby doesn't allow advertising for sherpa services, but there's nothing to stop you opening your own pop-up screen and surfing over to the sherpa forum on GigSearch.

The three of us stand around a table near the edge of the dance floor. I've invoked a cone of silence so we don't have to shout over the music. We've all switched to our default avatars. Brad no longer resembles a racist Gilbert and Sullivan character, but he still doesn't strike me as someone I'd want to know in real life. I didn't attend a normal high school, so I was spared the ritual humiliation that a lot of nerdy kids go through, but I've seen enough *Glee* reruns to peg Brad as the kind of guy who spent his formative years stuffing nerds into lockers.

Jolene is a tall, fit black woman in her early fifties. Her avatar resembles her Facebook photos, though like most people she's made a few edits, smoothing away some blemishes on her skin and erasing the gap between her front teeth. And of course there's her hair, which on Facebook is natural but short, a conservative 'do that comports with her day job as an IT specialist for a Colorado Springs law firm. Her avatar sports a complex weave whose interlocking braids hang down to the small of her back. It's a style that in real life would cost hundreds of dollars in hair extensions alone and require God knows how many hours of upkeep. But here in fantasyland, it's free, and you don't have to worry about strangers touching it.

If you subscribe to *People* magazine, you might recognize my avatar from the spread in the March 8 issue: "John Chu, Sherpa to the Stars." My legal surname is Conaway, but I go by Chu out of respect for my mother, who raised me, and also to cut down on awkward questions like, "How come you have an Irish name when you're Asian?"

My avatar has fewer acne scars than I do, but the main difference between us is what I call the Mom-and-Pop switch. It's a piece of code created by a friend of mine, Djimon Campbell, who's also biracial: Scots-English on his father's side and Yoruba on his mother's. Djimon's folks were divorced but shared custody, and growing up he noticed he got treated differently depending on which parent he was with. One day as an experiment he took some public-domain morphing software and created an avatar extension that allowed him to emphasize one side or the other of his ethnic heritage, in effect presenting as a blacker or whiter version of himself. The results surprised him: He expected it to affect people's behavior, he said, but wasn't prepared for how strong the effect was.

I paid Djimon a hundred bucks to write a version of the code for my avatar. I use it as a business tool. The historical connection between Chinese hackers and gold farming has given rise to a stereotype that ethnic Chinese are natural-born sherpas, just as we are all biologically predisposed to score high on the SATs, so for initial meetings with clients I like to put on my Mom genes. When dealing with customer complaints, on the other hand, I find that you can never be too Caucasian.

At the moment I have the Dad setting cranked up to eleven. Even at that extreme, Brad may not consciously notice. But Jolene does.

She b-channels me: From Brad's point of view she's standing motionless with her hands folded on the table in front of her, but I see her lean in close, eyes going wide in astonishment. "Oh my God!" she says. "White . . . whiter . . . whitest!"

I ignore her. Outwardly I'm aping my father, but inside my head I'm in one-hundred-percent Mom mode, running a psych profile on Brad and trying to work out a strategy that will get him to cough up the rest of our fee. I could threaten to blackball him on the sherpa forum, but that would probably only make him laugh, while appealing to his sense of fairness might provoke the part of him that likes stuffing nerds into lockers. Really, anything that can be interpreted as weakness is best avoided. I decide my only hope is to throw him off balance and try to redirect his anger.

"Did you hear me? I said I'm not fucking paying y—"

"You bought gold," I say.

The words bring him up short. "What?"

"Ivar's Hammer would have run you at least twenty-five thousand gold pieces on the auction house. Your samurai was broke when I gave him to you, and you couldn't have gotten more than a few hundred for your katana, so you must have bought gold."

"So?"

"So I'm guessing you didn't buy it from the in-game currency shop." After years of trying unsuccessfully to bar gold farmers from *Call to Wizardry*, Tempest decided to undercut their business by allowing players to buy gold legally from the company store. The price fluctuates, just as it would on a real gold exchange, but is kept low enough that black market gold-selling is no longer profitable. With one exception.

"I bought the gold from a guy advertising on the same forum where I found *you*," Brad says.

I nod knowingly. "Here's the thing. The only way to make decent money selling gold in *Call to Wizardry* anymore is by stealing it. These guys crack players' accounts, liquidate their characters' possessions, and then sell the gold to"—idiots like you—"people looking for bargains."

Brad shrugs. Players careless enough to let their accounts get hacked, the shrug says, are not his problem.

Except they are. "Everything that happens in the game world

is recorded," I say. "As soon as those hacked accounts get reported, Tempest can track exactly where the gold went. They can't punish the thieves, because the money you paid them is outside the system, but they can punish you."

Brad shrugs again, but with less conviction. "You don't know it was because of me," he says. "They busted you too."

"Because we were with you. When Tempest traced the gold and saw you were in a party, they must have decided to hang back and eavesdrop a while. That's how they knew we were sherpas." I go on, improvising: "And then, to really teach us a lesson, they must have waited for the perfect moment to pull the plug. I bet they even rigged the loot table in Anastasia's cavern to make sure we'd get a legendary drop."

"You mean that sword you wanted? They gave that to us on purpose?"

"And then snatched it right back," I say. I am talking out of my ass now, but Brad doesn't know that. "Look, I understand you're upset, but we're not the ones who fucked you over. You want to be mad, be mad at Tempest. Be mad at the rip-off artist who sold you that gold."

Brad looks away and appears to think it over. When he turns back to me he is nodding, and his carefully composed expression suggests he's decided to be reasonable. It's then I know for certain that we're screwed.

"You're right, it's not your fault," Brad says. "But I'm still not fucking paying you." Another shrug. "It's like what you were saying about the company: I can't punish the guys who really deserve it. So I guess I'll have to settle for taking it out on you."

Jolene breaks her silence. "What is wrong with you? Why would you want to be like—"

Brad cuts her off: "Who asked you to butt in, Beyoncé? You think I give two shits what you—"

"Dead to me," I say. Brad disappears. His avatar still occupies the same coordinates in cyberspace, but I can no longer see it or hear it, and he can no longer see or hear me.

Jolene goes on staring across the table, listening to—and, I assume, recording—whatever Brad is saying to her. Another half minute elapses before she says, "Dead to me," and sighs.

"Griefnet?" I ask her.

"Nah," she says. "If he'd dropped the n-word I'd post it to Griefnet. But I can't be too mad about 'Beyoncé,' even if he meant it as a slur . . . So, I guess we'd better break the bad news, huh?"

Anja and Ray are waiting for us in the Lobby arcade. Anja's avatar looks like Anja herself did before her accident: a pretty, petite teenager with a gymnast's physique. Anja's family, the Kirchners, are a clan of German Argentines who live in Paraná. Anja was on her way to the summer Olympic trials in Buenos Aires when the van taking her to the airport got sideswiped by a bus. She was left partially paralyzed, and an experimental stem-cell treatment meant to repair the damage instead made things worse, rendering her unable to breathe on her own. The machine that keeps her alive has a thought-controlled VR rig that reads and interprets the electrical impulses in her cerebrum. Anja's online 24/7, which combined with her eagerness to please and her relative indifference to money makes her the perfect employee, a fact I try not to take too much advantage of. Jolene tells me I need to try harder.

Ray Nelson presents as a thirtysomething white guy with a medium build, brown eyes, and short black hair. He has no social media presence—not under that name, at least—so I don't know if he's really a white guy, but if forced to guess I'd say he probably is. People masquerading as another race or gender tend to gravitate towards stereotypes. Ray's avatar isn't celebrity beautiful or Aryan chic, nor does it suggest an inbred hillbilly. He looks, by white guy standards, unremarkably ordinary, and who would want to pretend to be that?

Jolene has some interesting thoughts on the matter. Not long after she became a Sherpa, Inc. regular, she asked me what I knew about Ray. I told her he was the best healer I'd ever worked with. What about offline? she said. What's he do when he's not playing? I don't know, I replied. He doesn't really talk about himself. Jolene, not satisfied with that, used her IT skills to sniff out Ray's IP address. She looked it up and found it was one of a block of IP addresses assigned to an internet provider in southeast California. The provider's coverage area included a region of the Mojave Desert that is said to be popular with people who are legally forbidden to live near children.

You think Ray's a pedophile because of his IP address? I said when Jolene told me about this. I don't know what he is, she said, but my gut tells me he's hiding something. You don't get that vibe? Not from him, I said. But I'm starting to wonder what you haven't told me.

One thing I do know about Ray is that the sherpa gig isn't a part-time job for him, it's his main source of income. Which is a concern, because good healers are hard to come by, and if he can't make rent working for Sherpa, Inc., he won't hesitate to join another crew. I already came close to losing him once before.

"He stiffed us?" Ray says, not even waiting for me to deliver the news. "We got stiffed, right?"

"The guy's an asshole," I say. "Look, it happens. Just bad luck, that's—"

"Bad *luck*?" Ray's avatar's cheeks stay pale but I can tell that he's red-faced with anger. "And what about that thing last week? Or the two the week before that?"

We have been going through a rough patch lately. Tonight is the third time in a month the EULA cops have busted us during a run. On the previous two occasions, our customers did pay us, but they were unhappy and left us one- and two-star ratings on the sherpa forum.

Last week's incident was different. The run itself went off without a hitch, with the client, who went by the screen name Ollie Oxenfree, opting to add a third dungeon at overtime rates. The trouble started afterwards, when Ollie failed to meet us at the Game Lobby. My instant messages and emails inquiring about payment all bounced, and when I tried to log back into *Call to Wizardry*, the account I'd used for the run had been suspended: Besides stiffing us, "Ollie" had ratted us out to Tempest.

Pranked. It happens. Concern that it might happen again was the reason I'd spent so much time vetting Brad Strong on social media, making sure he was real.

"It's not bad luck," Ray says. "It's Darla."

"You don't know that." Sounding uncomfortably like Brad as I say this.

"She's getting even with you, like she promised she would. And she's making the rest of us pay, too."

"Come on, Ray. Don't be—"

"I'm sorry, John. I can't afford to keep doing this."

"What if I give you my share of tonight's upfront money?"

Ray makes a face. "The guy only paid a quarter in advance, right? So even with your share, that's only half of what I'm owed. And—"

"You can have my share, too," Anja pipes up.

Jolene interjects: "Oh no you can't. You keep your money, honey."

"It's not just the money," Ray says, staying focused on me. "I don't have a million spare accounts like you do. You know how long it takes to level up a new cleric?"

"You want a replacement for the one you lost tonight?" I say. "I'll give you one of mine. Two—I'll give you two."

"Two clerics," Ray says. This is insanely generous and he knows it. "Max level?"

"One of them is. The other's in the high hundreds, like one-seventy or one-seventy-five."

"I could finish leveling that one up for you," Anja offers. "It won't take long."

Jolene opens her mouth to say something, then thinks better of it. But I know I'll be hearing from her about this later.

"Two clerics," says Ray, still mulling it over. "*And* your share of tonight's upfront money?" I nod, trying not to think about my own unpaid bills. "All right," Ray says. "I'll stick around a while longer. But you need to go deal with Darla. Find her and kiss her ass, or whatever it's going to take to get her to lay off."

"I will," I promise. "Don't worry about it."

Ray and Jolene log off. I give Anja the account ID and password for that second cleric I promised Ray. "Only if you really want to," I say, picturing Jolene's parting glance to me.

"I wouldn't offer if I didn't want to," Anja says. And whether that's true or not, I know she'll have the cleric maxed out by the next time I see her.

"Are you feeling OK?" I ask. "About tonight, I mean." I know that EULA busts, like anything involving loss of avatar control, are potentially traumatic for her.

She shrugs. "It happens. Do you really think Darla was responsible?"

"I think tonight was on Brad. Last week, though, yeah, could be. But don't worry, I'll figure something out."

We say goodnight. Anja goes back into *Call to Wizardry*. I stay in the Lobby arcade, playing *Gauntlet*. I think about Darla.

DARLA HAS ME BLOCKED ON SOCIAL MEDIA, BUT IF YOU go on her Facebook page you'll find a profile pic of what looks like a young Chloë Grace Moretz in combat boots and paint-spattered camo, sitting cross-legged in the grass with a paintball rifle balanced across her knees. Her green eyes look out from under sweat-matted bangs, and she's got this wicked grin on her face like she knows something you don't and is wondering just how long it's going to take you to get a clue. According to her bio, she's Darla Jean Covington, "Virginian by blood, Arizonan by birth, Oregonian by choice." A twenty-two-year-old white, bi-curious, cisgender, middle-class, apolitical atheist omnivore who doesn't like being put into boxes. "Ha ha, see what I did there?" Occupation: Shit-stirrer and gamer gurl. Relationship status: Single.

We met in *Call to Wizardry*, in the Jurassic Swamp, where we'd gone to farm dinosaur hides and archaeopteryx feathers. The game server we were on is used primarily by South Koreans, and it was three a.m. in Seoul, so we'd both been hoping to have the swamp to ourselves. After a cursory attempt at sharing, we started stealing each other's kills. When I bagged a rare T. rex that Darla had her eye on, she challenged me to a duel, and despite her character being four levels below mine, she kicked my ass. Twice. I offered her a job with Sherpa, Inc. on the spot.

Considered purely as a player, she was a great hire. Her dps skills were phenomenal, but she could also tank, and while she didn't really have the temperament for healing, in a pinch she could do that, too.

In the area of customer relations, however, she left a lot to be desired. When clients were rude, Darla took it personally; when they made mistakes, or were slow to understand the rules of a boss fight, she made fun of them. This latter tendency in particular bugged the shit out of me. As I kept pointing out to her, our business model was dependent on our clients being amateurs; if they could put in the time required to become great players, they wouldn't need to hire sherpas. I know that, Darla said, but they're just so lame sometimes, it makes me want to scream.

When she wasn't alienating customers, Darla poked fun at her coworkers. Anja, the German South American, got a steady stream of fugitive Nazi jokes. I got cracks about lactose intolerance and requests to share my thoughts on Mickey Rooney's performance in *Breakfast at Tiffany's*. Getting under Ray's skin was harder, since he revealed so little about himself, but Darla somehow deduced that he was Catholic, or at least sensitive to remarks about Catholics; she was still teasing out which heresies most offended him when he threatened to quit.

I should have fired Darla then. But our relationship had gotten complicated, so instead I just read her the riot act. She laughed and told me I was cute when I was angry. I told her I wasn't kidding; she could knock it off or she could look for another sherpa crew. Fine, she said, if Ray's going to be such a huge pussy about it I'll leave him alone. Anja too, I said. And the customers. All right, *all right*, she said.

And she did knock it off. Mostly. I was relieved, though I also assumed that this was temporary, and that in a week or a month she'd start in again, and there would be another crisis where I'd have to choose between her or the business. I still believe that; it was doomed to end badly, one way or another.

But the way it did end was this: I got a call from the CAA agent who represents Janet Margeaux. She was set to costar with Jaden Smith in a film about a sherpa crew who stage a bank heist in cyberspace—"a sort of *Snow Crash* meets *The Thomas Crown Affair*." To research the role, Ms. Margeaux wanted to spend a couple days hanging out with some real sherpas. *People* magazine was also interested: If I agreed, they'd embed a reporter on one of the dungeon runs, get some video and some screenshots, and interview me about the business.

I hadn't even said yes yet when I started worrying about Darla. What if she decided to razz Janet Margeaux about the lousy box-office on that *Citizen Kane* remake she did last year? Or what if she decided to get "edgy" and say something racist to the *People* reporter?

I could have tried talking to Darla, to impress on her how potentially important this gig was for the future of the business. I could have admitted that I didn't trust her, her recent good behavior notwithstanding. But I was afraid of how she might react, so I took a more cautious, which is to say cowardly, approach: I scheduled Janet Margeaux for a weekend when I knew Darla would be offline, facetiming with her family at a reunion in Virginia. I brought in Jolene, who'd subbed for Darla a couple times before, and only told Ray and Anja what was up at the last minute—and even then, I was cagey about it. I think Ray understood that I'd cut Darla out deliberately, but Anja didn't get it; she thought it was just bad luck that Darla couldn't be with us.

The gig went extremely well—Janet Margeaux was thrilled,

and the reporter said she'd be devoting a full page to our interview. I told myself that I'd made the right call and that even Darla would come to agree with that, after she'd had some time to cool off.

But I wasn't in a hurry to test that theory. The day Darla was due back from the reunion, I went to the Jurassic Swamp again. *Call to Wizardry*'s most recent software patch had introduced a new subspecies of velociraptor whose claws could be used to make magic necklaces. I switched off my instant messages and settled in to farm a few hundred of them.

Darla came online and went to the Game Lobby to look for me. She ran into Anja, who, not knowing any better, spilled the beans about what we'd been up to in Darla's absence.

Back in the swamp, I got into another territorial pissing match, this time with a couple of low-level griefers. I picked a fight and killed them until they got bored and went away. I was still flagged for PvP when Darla found me. She'd logged in as a 200th-level deathlord, so the first sign that she was coming was when the ferns at the edge of the clearing I was in shriveled up and turned black. She burst through the dead foliage wielding a flaming two-handed sword the size of a telephone pole.

"Hey Darla, let's talk," I said. She decapitated me. I came back from the graveyard and she was desecrating my corpse; I imagine she had her gib setting turned up full. I knew if I resurrected she'd just kill me again, so instead I hovered there, disembodied, saying, "Come on Darla, let's talk."

She logged out. I did too. I went to the Game Lobby and waited. It was karaoke night, and a group of senior citizens were competing to see who could do the most grating rendition of Celine Dion's "My Heart Will Go On." As penance, I decided not to invoke a cone of silence.

But that was self-indulgent bullshit. One of my mother's most often repeated pieces of wisdom is that there's a difference between being unhappy with the consequences of your actions and being sorry. I was unhappy that Darla was pissed off, but I didn't regret what I'd done—if anything, her reaction confirmed for me that I'd made the right decision.

Not being sorry, I knew it would be wrong to apologize. I could explain why I'd done what I'd done, I could try to make it up to her, but to say sorry when I wasn't would only add insult to injury. Do not apologize, I counseled myself as I waited. Do. Not. Apologize.

Then I saw her, standing over by the bar. She saw me too—had seen me first, no doubt—but pretended to ignore me.

I walked up to her. "Darla," I said.

She turned and threw a virtual martini in my face. This is less effective than throwing a real drink—like a chest-bump aimed at an avatar teammate, it passed right through me.

Darla's words had more of an impact. "You lying, backstabbing *piece of shit*!" she shouted. Onstage, the latest bout of *Titanic* theme music had just ended, and the scattered applause hadn't yet begun; Darla's exclamation landed at full volume in the space between. Suddenly it felt like everyone in the Game Lobby was staring at us.

I spoke without thinking: "Darla, I'm sorry. I—"

"*Sorry?*" Darla said. "You're not *sorry* . . . But you will be." Then: "Dead to me."

That was two and a half months ago. I spent the first week awaiting Darla's revenge, which I assumed would take the form of a post on the sherpa forum. There were things she could have revealed about the nature of our relationship that would have been embarrassing, and maybe bad for business. But time went by and no post appeared. Darla blocked me on social media, as I've said, but she didn't take her accounts private, so by logging in under a different name I could look and see that she hadn't posted on Facebook or anywhere else, either. It was as if she'd left the internet entirely—though of course, she was free to log in under a different name, too.

The *People* magazine article came out. The publicity had the effect that I'd hoped for, and more—Sherpa, Inc. was suddenly very busy. I raised our standard fee and hired Jolene as a full-time replacement for Darla. We made good money, at first.

There were a few negative repercussions. Some of the other sherpa outfits, jealous that Janet Margeaux hadn't picked them, started badmouthing us. Others complained that by inspiring "John Chu wannabes" the article was creating too much competition, driving overall profits down. Gold-selling scams increased, and Tempest, unhappy with the expansion of the black market, began cracking down harder on EULA violations. All of the accounts we'd used for the Janet Margeaux job got banned.

The price of fame, I figured. I had other accounts, and could afford to get more. I settled in to what I thought was the new normal, and talked about expanding.

But now our luck has changed again, and instead of building a larger crew I'm struggling to hold the core group together. Karma, or Darla? The main argument against the latter is that I just don't see Darla having the patience for an extended revenge scheme. Her idea of a long game is making sure you're listening with both ears before she unloads on you.

But strong emotions can cause people to act very differently than they normally would. That's another of my mother's axioms. I keep thinking about the expression on Darla's face when she pronounced "Dead to me" in the bar that night, which was the same expression she wore when she cut my head off in the swamp. As if she were wishing the invocation of death were more than just a metaphor.

Speaking of death: In *Gauntlet*, my elf, who needs food badly, falls to an onslaught of grunts. Rather than plug in another virtual quarter, I open a pop-up screen and surf over to Darla's Facebook page. There are no new posts. While I debate whether to leave a message tagged with my real name, Darla's profile pic stares at me, grinning.

I'M ABOUT TO LOG OUT WHEN I GET AN INSTANT MESSAGE, the words appearing in a pop-up box at the bottom of my visual field:

ARE YOU AVAILABLE TO MEET NOW? — SMITH

Smith—no first name, no "Mr." or "Ms.," just Smith—emailed me a week ago, claiming to be the personal assistant of a "wealthy, famous person" who wanted to hire a sherpa for a special project. The job paid "quite generously," Smith promised, but added that the client wished to remain anonymous. Would that be acceptable?

Coming as it did on the heels of the Ollie Oxenfree incident, this offer struck me as highly suspicious, but on the off chance it was for real I wrote back. I said that I was fine with not knowing the identity of my employer, so long as they were willing to pay my full fee in advance—and by the way, what did "quite generous" mean in actual dollars? When I got no response, I assumed that whoever it was had given up the gag after having their bluff called.

I'M AVAILABLE, I message back. WHERE?

GAME LOBBY PRIVATE CHAT ROOM #24, Smith replies. ENTRY CODE 77G4M9.

The door to the chat rooms is right outside the arcade. I knock and a peephole slides open; a robot bouncer jabbers at me in faux *Star Wars* droid language. "Room twenty-four," I tell it, and recite the code. The door opens and I step directly into a conference room where Smith and the client are waiting.

They are Gray People. This is a special type of anonymizing avatar, inspired by a bit of business from an old Ursula K. Le Guin novel. Users manifest as androgynous, racially nondescript humanoids with light gray skin; the avatar suite includes an audio filter that replaces your real voice with an accentless monotone, though unless you're also speaking through a translator, your word choice can still give information away.

I see they have opted not to use the avatar's lack-of-affect toggle. The Gray Person on the right is smiling as I enter, and he or she regards me with an open and intense curiosity. The Gray Person on the left is more reserved, but in a way that suggests seriousness rather than an absence of emotion.

"Smith?" I say.

"I am Smith," the serious one replies. He—I decide to think of him as "he," because otherwise I'll think of him as Darla—indicates his companion. "This is my boss, Mr. Jones."

"Hello. I'm John Chu." I nod. Jones doesn't nod back, just goes on staring at me, his smile starting to seem a little creepy now. "I understand you're interested in hiring a sherpa for some sort of project."

"Yes," Mr. Jones says. "I wish to undertake a comprehensive survey of the world of more pigs."

More pigs: MMORPGs. "What kind of survey?"

Smith answers: "Mr. Jones believes that the design philosophy of massive multiplayer online role-playing games may have applications beyond the realm of mere entertainment. Applications that are relevant to his own profession."

"Which is?"

"Not your concern."

"I have researched the subject of more pigs," Mr. Jones says. "Read articles, watched videos. But I lack firsthand experience. I want you to help me rectify this."

"OK," I say. "Do you know which games you'd like to play?"

"All of them."

"All? You know there are dozens of them, right? Hundreds, if you count legacy games."

"All of them," Mr. Jones says. "I wish to experience the full potential of the medium. You can arrange this for me?"

"I can," I say. "I've got accounts on all the most popular MMORPGs, and I can get others. But it'll cost you."

"Money is no concern."

It is to me, I think. "When do you want to start?"

"As soon as Smith is satisfied with the security arrangements. You understand, I must maintain strict anonymity."

"Yeah, I got that."

"The logistics of that I leave to Smith. But I do have a question before we begin."

"Go ahead."

"It is about identity." He lowers his gaze and studies the backs of his avatar's hands. "I can resemble anything I wish to, in here." Looking up again: "And so can you."

"And so can anyone else." I nod, guessing where he's going with this.

"Yes," Mr. Jones says. "So when you are guiding me through the world of more pigs, how do I know that you are you, and not one of my enemies? How do you know that I am me?"

I can't tell whether he's asking because he really wants to know, or just wants to see if I do. But I've got this covered. "It's a standard cryptographic protocol," I say. Jones arches an eyebrow: crypto-whaticol? "Here, let me show you . . ."

I pass my hand over the conference table between us, causing three objects to materialize there: a small blue box, a blue key, and a red key.

I pick up the red key. "This is my public encryption key," I say, offering it to Mr. Jones, who accepts it after exchanging a quick glance with Smith. "Because it's public, I can give away a copy to anybody who wants one.

"The blue key is my private key," I continue, "and I'm very careful not to let anyone else have that. Now if I want to send you a message, I can put it in here . . ." I lift the lid of the blue box. Inside is a business card, which I hold up so Mr. Jones can read the words preprinted on it: It's me, John Chu. I put the card back in the box and close the lid. "Now I lock it with my private key." I turn the key and the box turns red. "And I send it to you." I slide the box across the table. "If you've got my public key, you can open it."

"But so can anyone else," Mr. Jones says. "Anyone with your public key can read the message."

"Unless the message is also encrypted, with a code that only you have the key to. But that's not necessary in this case. In this case, the real message is the box itself. My public key will only open boxes that were locked with my private key. So if you get a box that you can open, you know it came from me."

"I see," Mr. Jones says. "Clever, but also cumbersome. Anytime I wish to verify your identity, I ask for a box?"

"It's just a metaphor." I nod at the table; the box disappears, and the key in Mr. Jones's hand transforms into a key fob, the kind you use to find your car in a crowded garage. "Go ahead," I say, pointing to the little blue speaker pin that has appeared on my avatar's lapel. "Try it."

Mr. Jones stares at the key fob like he's never seen one before. Then he says, "Ah," in a way that makes me think Smith just b-channeled him. He aims the fob at me and pushes the button.

"It's me," the lapel pin says in my voice. "John Chu."

A new smile appears on Mr. Jones's face. He laughs like a little kid and presses the button again. And again.

"It's me, John Chu . . . It's me, John Chu . . . It's me, John Chu . . ."

A dozen times. Finally satisfied, he lowers the key fob and turns to Smith. "This is the one I want," he says.

And then he's gone, without so much as a goodbye glance.

"Thank you for explaining public-key cryptography to my boss," Smith says. "You did a much better job than I would have."

"It's no problem." I consider telling him that I created this demonstration for Janet Margeaux, but divulging even that small a detail about a former client relationship might come across as indiscreet. Instead I say, "I want you and your boss to feel totally comfortable."

"It is good that this is your attitude," Smith says. "Because your encryption protocol is inadequate to our security needs."

"Inadequate how? Are you worried about the integrity of my computer?"

"I am worried about that, also. But I was referring to the encryption itself."

"I generate the keys with a Really Good Privacy app. It's solid. No known vulnerabilities."

"No publicized vulnerabilities," Smith replies.

"You're saying someone's found a hole in RGP?"

"I am saying my boss has powerful enemies with extraordinary capabilities."

"Enemies like who, the NSA?"

"Their identity is not your concern. But I am going to require root privileges on your computer; I will be modifying the operating system and installing additional software that you are not to remove or tamper with."

"You understand why that's impossible, right?" I try to say this lightly, but it's hard to keep the disappointment out of my voice. For all of its weirdness, I'd been starting to hope this job offer might be genuine.

"I understand why you would be reluctant to grant root access to a stranger. But you will do it."

"No I won't, Darla."

"I am not your darling," Smith says. "Now listen carefully, John Chu: In addition to granting me the access I require, you will clear your schedule of all other personal and business commitments. You will make yourself available on fifteen minutes' notice, any time of the day or night. You will show my boss the world of MMORPGs and answer his questions. You will explain things in a way that he can understand. You will do all of this tirelessly and without complaint, and you will tell no one else what you are up to. In exchange, you will receive a weekly salary of one hundred thousand dollars, for as long as Mr. Jones chooses to employ you."

"A hundred thousand a week," I say. "And is that U.S. dollars, or *Monopoly* money?"

"You can have it in whatever currency you like," Smith says. "As per your email, I am prepared to wire the first week's payment right now, to the bank account of your choice. The money will be available for immediate withdrawal. You can spend it, transfer it to another account, or do whatever else you require, to convince yourself it is real. In seventy-two hours, I will contact you again, and you will either agree to my terms or refund the money in full. Will that be satisfactory?"

FIVE MINUTES LATER I STUMBLE OUT OF THE CHAT ROOM and head for the bar. You can order drinks from the cyborg bartender, but since this is virtual reality, you have to provide your own intoxication.

Tonight that won't be a problem; I'm feeling plenty stupefied. PayPal has just sent me confirmation of a deposit of one hundred thousand dollars. A part of me is wondering how Darla could have faked this, while another part is trying to figure out if it's too late to avoid reporting the income to the IRS. If I'd believed for a moment I might actually get the money, I'd have handled it differently.

I'm almost at the bar when a Chinese woman catches my eye. The avatar looks a lot like my aunt Penny; it's not her, but the woman smiles as if she expects me to recognize her.

"I'm sorry," I say. "Do I know you?"

"That's a good question, John," she says. Her accent is British, with just a hint of Cantonese. "Let's find out. Do you have another of those red key fobs?"

The question takes a moment to process. Then, feeling as though

I've downed a bucket of virtual martinis, I hold out my hand and conjure another copy of my public encryption key.

She doesn't take it. "It's not for me," she says, "it's for you." She points at the little blue speaker pin on her blouse. "Try it."

I aim the red key fob. Press the button.

"It's me," the blue pin says, in my voice. "John Chu."

"There you go," says the woman. "I suppose we must be twins."

"Who are you?"

"I'm you, John." She laughs. "Or maybe I'm someone with 'extraordinary capabilities.'"

"What do you want?"

"I want you to take the job. You'll really be working for me, of course; I'll pay you twice what Smith's offering you."

"Two hundred thousand dollars a week? And what else are you going to want, for that?"

"One thing at a time. For now, just tell Smith yes." All the humor goes out of her expression and she gives me a look that is terrifying in its seriousness. "Don't disappoint me, John. You won't like what happens if you do that. At all."

She smiles again. Winks.

Then she's gone.

memory palace — A virtual architectural space used for storing data. The original memory palaces were purely mental constructs: Ancient Greek and Roman rhetoricians would populate an imaginary structure with mnemonic images and then "walk through" the space in the course of giving a speech. Although this old-school art of memory still has its enthusiasts, modern memory palaces tend to be digital and optimized for VR.

—*Lady Ada's Lexicon*

The *People* article described me as a "third-generation gold farmer," which is technically true, but for a lot of readers conjures up a false image of a Chinese immigrant kid whose grandpop played video games in a Beijing internet café. In fact the Chus have been American since long before there was an internet, or video games. Or video.

My great-great-great-grandfather, Chu Yi-wei, emigrated from Guangdong Province in 1871. He helped build the Northern Pacific Railway and started an import/export business in Seattle. In 1886, Seattle's white Knights of Labor rioted and tried to run the entire population of Chinatown out of the city. The local militia intervened at the last minute, but Yi-wei decided to play it safe and left town anyway, taking his family and his business to San Francisco.

It was Chu Yi-wei's great-grandson, Joseph Chu, who first got into gold farming. Grandpa Joe was a graduate student in mathematics at U.C. Berkeley. In his free time, he played a primordial MMORPG called *Ultima Online*. The game was popular enough to support a side economy in which players exchanged virtual treasure for real-world cash. Grandpa used the money he earned selling gold pieces and magic items to buy an engagement ring for his girlfriend, Judy Chen.

My mother was born a year after Grandpa and Grandma got married. One night two years after that, they left Mom with a sitter and went to their favorite dim sum house to celebrate their anniversary. During the meal, a neo-Nazi named Charles Clayton came into the restaurant. California law at the time banned semi-automatic "assault weapons" like the AR-15 rifle, so Clayton had armed himself with a pair of pump shotguns, loaded with a type of heavy slug that is normally used to hunt elk. He had fired both guns empty and switched to a backup revolver when he found my grandparents hiding under a table.

My mother was sent to Hawaii to live with the family of my great-aunt Tamara, who was a cryptographer for the Navy. Mom grew up on the base at Pearl Harbor. She learned how to program at an early age and played her fair share of computer games, though her tastes ran more to *Sim City* and *Civilization*.

It was my father, David Conaway, who was that generation's gold farmer. Like Grandpa Joe he was a grad student, but in English rather than math; his pursuit of a doctorate was mostly a way of buying time to finish the epic sci-fi/fantasy novel he'd been working on since freshman year. Dad considered his online gaming a form of research for the novel. He did a *lot* of research, earning a nice chunk of change selling gold in the process—though his profits were dwarfed by the size of his student loans.

The summer before his dissertation was due, Dad flew to Hawaii, ostensibly to unplug and get some writing done, but really to bum around the beach for a couple months. Mom, who'd joined the Navy straight out of high school, had just completed her first term of enlistment and was trying to decide whether to reenlist or go to college. It was the wrong time for her to get involved with anyone and Dad was one of the worst romantic choices imaginable, but as Mom later explained to me, she'd done everything right in her life up to that point and was overdue for a screw-up. Also, contrary to the stereotype about basement-dwelling video gamers, Dad was hot.

They'd been together a little more than a month when Mom found out she was pregnant. Dad, in a grand gesture towards taking responsibility, asked Mom to marry him; Mom said she needed to think about it. She'd been careless but she wasn't stupid, and her instincts were telling her that this wasn't someone she could depend on in the long run. She probably would have turned him down no matter what, but two things happened that made the decision much easier.

The first thing was that Dad cheated on her while he was waiting for her answer. That destroyed any lingering illusions she might have had about his suitability as a husband.

The second thing was that Mom got a visit from a captain with U.S. Cyber Command. The captain was recruiting for a new covert anti-terrorism task force called Zero Day, and Mom's service record showed that she had the aptitude and skill set they were looking for. It was a dream assignment, one that Mom assumed her status as a soon-to-be single parent would disqualify her for. But when she told the captain she was pregnant, he didn't even blink. Zero Day was different, he said, a twenty-first-century organization designed to deal with twenty-first-century realities, more forward-looking even than Cyber Command. Child care issues didn't faze them. Also, Great-aunt Tamara, now a rear admiral with Naval Intelligence, had personally recommended Mom for the job. So it was hers if she wanted it.

Mom said yes to the captain and no to my father. When Dad came back around, begging for another chance, Mom ghosted him, vanishing into thin air as only a member of covert services can. She took me with her.

I spent my childhood shuttling from top-secret command post to top-secret command post. I wasn't always sure what continent I was on, but that didn't matter; like the other kids whose parents worked for Zero Day, my real home was the internet.

It was a good time to be a digital native. After decades of over-hyped promises, fully immersive VR was finally becoming a thing, and the tech Zero Day had access to was a generation ahead of what was available on the commercial market. We had great tech support, too, and bandwidth was never a problem.

Of course our every move in cyberspace was monitored, to make sure we didn't blab about what our folks did. We couldn't really talk about ourselves, either, so we made up fake autobiographies to use with online friends and acquaintances. That could get weird sometimes, but trying on different identities is something all children do, and for us it was a form of patriotism.

I suppose it's no surprise that I gravitated towards role-playing games, though for me it's always been as much business as entertainment. Selling gold was my version of having a paper route, and the adventurers' guild I founded with the other Zero Day kids became an early prototype for Sherpa, Inc.

At seventeen I left the Zero Day nest and moved to San Francisco, where I'd gotten early admission to Berkeley. My plan was to go for a double major in computer science and business administration, then found a game company and create my own MMORPG. I did attend a few classes, but much of my freshman year was taken up by the same sort of research that had so obsessed my father.

Since it seemed we were more alike than I'd realized, I decided to track Dad down. I found him in Los Angeles. After Mom left him he gave up on his novel and made his way to Hollywood, where he eventually established himself as a screenwriter.

He was happy to meet me, and after some initial awkwardness the feeling turned out to be mutual. In the three years since, we've gotten to be good friends. Dad doesn't farm gold anymore, but he does play *Call to Wizardry*, and we've got a standing monthly game night.

My father has told me many times how sorry he is that he wasn't there when I was growing up. He says he wants to make it up to me, and I believe him. Though he hasn't taken credit for it, I'm almost certain it was him who gave Janet Margeaux my contact info: He was a script doctor on her *Catwoman* reboot. And if I were looking for investors for my game company, or needed an emergency loan to help cover my tuition debt, Dad would be my first call.

But he's the wrong parent for my current situation. I don't need an ex–gold farmer; I need a god gamer, someone with a top-down view who can see the big picture and help me figure out what's going on. Someone with power and access to special codes, who, if things get desperate, really can change the rules.

My mother keeps a memory house on MySpaceII. It's got a

number of unpatched security vulnerabilities, so even if you're not on the approved guest list, it's a simple hack to come inside and check out the virtual mementos that collectively tell the story of my mother's life—or rather *a* story, since a lot of it is fiction. While you're poking around, the house will be getting into your business, too: back-tracing your internet connection, grabbing any unsecured files off your computer, and running a threat assessment. If you're an ordinary identity thief, you'll probably be left alone (although, spoiler alert: the tax returns in the office filing cabinet are fakes, with a randomly generated address and social security number). If the house decides you're a Real Threat, your info will be forwarded to a Zero Day counterintel agent with the power to make you unhappy.

I'm on the guest list, so I don't need to hack in. I come right in the front door, wave to the picture of Grandpa and Grandma on the fireplace mantel, and proceed to the back bedroom that would have been mine if this were a real house I'd grown up in. I open the secret door that only I can access and step into what looks like the reception area of an ultramodern office suite.

A Korean-American woman in a Navy ensign's uniform smiles at me from behind the reception desk. Her name is Maggie Kim, and I'm not sure whether she's human or a software agent. "Hello, John," she says. "Your mother is on a call right now, but she'll be free in a few minutes."

I look around idly while I'm waiting. My picture hangs on the wall beside an American flag and a photo of the president; the Janet Margeaux *People* issue tops a stack of magazines on a side table. This room is a kind of avatar, capable of manifesting differently to different observers, and I assume these details would not be visible to anyone else. Mom wants me to know that she loves me and is proud of me, but given the nature of her work, she can't risk letting other visitors learn what she cares about.

"John," Ensign Kim says, "she's ready for you now."

I don't have to move. The room morphs around me, becoming Mom's office. "Hey, kiddo," Mom says. "What's up?"

She is standing in front of a window that looks out at a mountain range in twilight. Even before I spot the second moon in the sky, I know the view is fake, selected at random from a library of thousands of imaginary vistas. If you need to know Mom's physical location, she'll tell you; if you don't, she's not giving away free clues.

But there are limits to how much you can conceal from people who are close to you. My mother has always been a morning person, and the chipper tone of her voice tells me she's only been awake for a couple of hours. It's close to midnight here on the West Coast, so assuming Mom got up at the crack of dawn like she always does, that would put her somewhere in Europe or Africa. But the kind of circumstances that would require her physical presence in Africa would also keep her from getting a good night's sleep, and she sounds well-rested. Europe, then: probably the Zero Day base in Berlin.

Her smile tells me something, too. Once when I was a kid I asked my mother whether it bothered her to kill people for a living. She said she didn't have a problem with killing people who deserved it, but added that her job wasn't really like that. Mostly what she did was study people, to learn why they acted the way that they did and figure out how to convince them to act differently. And when she did need to hurt someone, she preferred to get them to do it to themselves, by tricking them into making bad choices. When my mother smiles the way she's smiling now, it means that one of her subterfuges has worked; somewhere in the world, some Real

Threats have been coaxed down a wrong path and are now either dead or wishing they were.

It's a good mood to have caught her in, and I try to make the most of it. "I need your help with something," I say. I tell her about my job interview with Smith and Mr. Jones. Her eyebrows go up at the mention of the hundred thousand dollars, but when I get to the Chinese woman in the bar I can see her turn skeptical. "You don't buy it."

"That this woman you bumped into is some sort of government agent? It sure sounds like she wants you to think that. But."

"What about the part where she forged my encryption key?" I say. "Is that— Can you guys actually do that?"

This is one of those questions that my mother will never give a straight answer to. She turns it into a hypothetical: "Suppose someone did figure out a way to subvert public-key cryptography. Do you really think they'd brag about it just to impress you? It's a dramatic gesture, but it doesn't make sense."

"She had my private key, though."

"That doesn't mean she forged it. She could have just hacked you and stolen it."

"I practice safe computing, Mom. I learned it from you."

"I didn't teach you everything," she says. "And there are always exploits. Tell me, do you know anyone who might want to pull a prank on you? Someone you trust, or trusted, enough to run a piece of software they sent you without checking it out first?"

Darla, I think. But. "I don't know anybody with a hundred thousand dollars to blow on a prank."

"The money's interesting," Mom acknowledges. "Have you tried spending it yet?"

"No. I thought I'd better talk to you before I did anything."

"What account is it in?"

I tell her, and she gets this distracted look that means she's either b-channeling someone or checking a pop-up screen. Then her avatar's eyes refocus on me and she says, "Very interesting."

"What?"

"The money is real," Mom says. "And it was transferred from a bank in Burma."

If you pay any attention to the news you know that Burma has become notorious lately as a money-laundering haven for Chinese and Southeast Asian mobsters. "So it's like a numbered account?"

"All bank accounts are numbered. Burmese accounts are designed to keep their holders anonymous, even from people like me." She thinks a moment. "All right. You're going to take the job."

"I am?"

"Yes. But first, you're going to use some of the money to buy yourself a new computer and VR rig. I'll give you the web address of a vendor and a coupon code to use when you order. It'll be an upgraded version of the system you have now, with some special features that won't be in the documentation."

"Special features. So you're going to be watching my back on this?"

Mom smiles that smile. "I can use a new project," she says.

PART TWO

Online Games

When interacting with other
players, a little kindness goes a
long way.

—*Call to Wizardry* loading screen tip

Fuck you, perv," is the first thing Darla ever said to me.

It was in the Jurassic Swamp, right after she beat my ass the second time. Newly resurrected, I lay on the ground with my armor in tatters; at higher gib settings, you could see bone fragments and bits of intestine scattered all around me. Darla was an orc that day—a green-eyed orc, with long blond hair—and she loomed above me with her scimitar, ready for round three. When I asked her if she'd like to make some money, I guess it must have sounded like a weird come-on.

"Fuck you, perv."

"Wait!" I said, before she could kill me again. "I didn't mean it like that. My name's John Chu, and I run a sherpa crew, Sherpa, Incorporated? Maybe you've heard of us?"

"A sherpa crew." Darla was incredulous. "People pay *you* to be a guide? Are these retarded people?" Seeing me frown: "What, you don't like the word 'retarded'?"

"I don't mind it, but some of the clients do. And the ones who do, really don't like it."

Darla smirked in a way I would come to know well. "So this is one of those jobs where you have to watch what you say?" As if the concept of professionalism was the silliest thing she'd ever heard of. "Is there a dress code, too?"

"No dress code. As long as you're not sending selfies to the clients, you can dress however you like."

"I bet you'd like me to send you a selfie. Perv." Smiling this time, like she enjoyed whatever my face did when she said it.

I decided to try selective deafness as a tactic. "What's your name?"

"Darla."

"Darla what?"

"Why, so you can stalk me on Facebook?"

"Can you tank?"

"Of course I can fucking tank."

"What about healing?"

"If I'm feeling suicidal and want to bore myself to death, sure."

"Do you play any other MMORPGs or first-person shooters?"

"Ooh, you *are* planning to stalk me! As soon as you log out, you're going to Google 'Darla' and the names of any games I mention, see if you get a hit. Maybe find a nice picture of me to jerk off to, am I right?"

Selective deafness wasn't working. "I want to know what other games you play because we're looking to branch out. Our client base is almost all *Call to Wizardry* players right now, but—"

"You might be disappointed if you did find out more about me,"

Darla said. "I mean, I could be a guy for all you know. A fat, disgusting old guy with yellow underwear."

"If you can tank as well as you dps, I don't care how much you weigh. Or what your underwear looks like."

"Or I might be a kid. A twelve-year-old boy. What would that do for your perv fantasies?"

"You're not a twelve-year-old boy."

"How the fuck would you know?"

"Because I used to be one. When a twelve-year-old boy plays a female character, he picks a human or an elf. Not an orc."

Darla glanced down at her avatar's bust. Orc cleavage is not the stuff of typical schoolboy fantasies. "Maybe I'm a perv, too."

"Maybe," I said. "But I think you're a girl. The kind who used to get into a lot of fights in high school."

"Used to?" She raised an eyebrow.

"It's hard to judge with the fangs, but you look more college-age to me."

"You don't even know if this is my real face."

"Also, it's the middle of a school day in America right now."

"Who says I'm in America? Or maybe I'm cutting class."

"If you were, you wouldn't suggest it."

This earned another smirk. "OK, Mr. Profiler," Darla said. "Tell you what: You guess my age, and I'll come work for you."

"How many guesses do I get?"

"One, duh."

"All right," I said, "but I get to ask you three questions, first."

"Yeah? And what do I get?"

"If I guess wrong? A hundred dollars."

"Fuck you, a hundred dollars. How do I know you'll pay?"

I shrugged. "How do I know you won't lie to get the money?"

Darla thought it over. "OK. Three questions."

"On your tenth birthday," I asked, "was the president of the United States a man or a woman?"

"A woman."

"Which makes you at least eighteen. On your eighteenth birthday, what actor was playing Doctor Who?"

"You watch that stupid show?"

"What actor? You can look it up on Wikipedia if you need to."

"I didn't say I didn't know . . . It was that Pakistani actress, Miriam whatshername."

"Meryem Halil? She's from Wales. And her family's Turkish."

"Whatever. Her."

"OK, so you're either twenty-one or twenty-two. Last question: On your twenty-first birthday, if I showed you a meme of King Charles offering Camilla a hot dog bun, would you know what that was about?"

Darla rolled her eyes. "Fine, I'm twenty-two," she said. "That's a really lame parlor trick."

"It's a simple trick." I nodded at her scimitar. "Like dps is simple, if you're talking about the mechanics. But to do it under pressure, without stopping to think—that takes some skill."

"Plus, the *Doctor Who* nerdery really wows the ladies, am I right?"

"I do all right with the ladies," I said. "And I'm definitely a nerd. But to be honest, I'm not a *Doctor Who* fan. I think I've seen like three episodes."

"Well, that's even more pathetic. You don't watch the show, but you memorized the stars' bios in case you need to guess someone's age?"

"I didn't need to memorize anything. I told you, it's on Wikipedia."

"You checked Wikipedia? Just now, while you were talking to me?"

"Yeah."

"No. Bullshit."

"It's a simple b-channel exploit." I held up my hands, made tapping motions with my fingers. "You can't type and talk at the same time?"

"Of course I can—and I can read and talk, too. But I was watching you. You didn't cut your eyes away. You were looking at me the whole time."

"My avatar was looking at you. I have a custom mod, You So Interesting. It keeps my avatar's eyes focused on whoever I'm talking to, even if I'm checking a pop-up screen."

"This mod, it's something you wrote?"

"An old girlfriend."

Darla snorted. "That must have been some relationship."

"We didn't use it on each other."

"You didn't use it on her, maybe . . . So this is for your clients? You watch porn while you're making your sales pitch?"

"Mostly I use it to look things up on the sly. It helps me keep up my end, making small talk. And I always know the answer to game-related questions, even if I have a brain fart. Clients expect that. It's part of the whole sherpa stereotype." As I said this, I gave the Mom-and-Pop switch a push towards the Mom side. It was just a nudge, but Darla saw it, and she got it. And she laughed.

"All right," she said, "maybe you're not a total loser . . . But I still think your clients are retarded." She gave it a beat, watching my expression, then burst out laughing again. "Wow, you are going to be so much fun to mess with."

In hindsight, I suppose I should have recognized that as a red flag.

But in the moment I was happy, because it meant she was taking the job.

problematic — A weasel word. "Problematic" can mean immoral, heretical, politically objectionable, bigoted, rude, harmful to children and small animals, bad for society, personally offensive to the speaker, or some amorphous combination of any of the above. The word's vagueness makes it popular among the intellectually lazy: Whereas calling something "immoral" might require you to articulate—and defend—a theory of right and wrong, "problematic" expresses the same disapproval while offering nothing solid for an interlocutor to push back against. It also accords with the common belief that all right-thinking people share identical worldviews: Either you know intuitively what "problematic" means, or you are too stupid or wicked to deserve an explanation.

See also: **"mistakes were made," shibboleth**

—*The New Devil's Dictionary*

The day after my new computer arrives, I have my first game session with Mr. Jones.

I've decided we may as well start at the top. I sign Mr. Jones up for a *Call to Wizardry* account and tell him to meet me in the Hall of Generation.

Step one in creating a character is to choose your race and

gender. "Race" in this context means species, although, in a tradition that goes back to pen-and-paper RPGs, many of *Call to Wizardry*'s species are thinly veiled ethnic stereotypes. Humans are generic white people who live in medieval European castles and towns. Dwarves are alcoholic highlanders with funny Scottish accents. Goblins are greedy, big-nosed schemers who run all the banks. Orcs are dark-skinned marauders who worship death and love cutting innocent people's heads off with their scimitars. And then there are the trolls: savage jungle creatures who talk like Jamaican ganglords, practice voodoo and cannibalism, and have a shuffling, stoop-shouldered gait that appears to have been motion-captured at a minstrel show.

The popular internet term for this is "problematic," but I don't like to be coy. My specific complaint is not that it's racist (although it is) or that it reinforces negative attitudes about minorities (it might, but let's be serious—if fantasy role-playing games are your main source of information about minorities, the problem is you). No, what bothers me is that it's such bad business practice. Black and brown people's money spends just as good as white people's, so why the hell would you insult them?

Please note that this is not a rhetorical question. It would be one thing if Tempest had made a deliberate decision to alienate minorities in order to cater to people who still think Stepin Fetchit is comedy gold. That would be stupid, but at least there'd be a logic to it. But I doubt the explanation is that cynical. My guess is that the game design team just didn't realize how offensive some of their worldbuilding choices were, and the guys who were supposed to check their work didn't notice either. That may sound incredible, that otherwise intelligent businesspeople could be so clueless, but I see it happen all the time and it galls me.

But that's my ax to grind. I'm curious what Mr. Jones's take will be.

The Hall of Generation contains interactive models of the various races, so you can get a sense of what your character will look like. The sample troll is stirring a big cauldron as we approach. "I and I gon' use your guts for me gumbo, mon!" he greets us—a line that always gets a healthy side-eye from Jolene. Mr. Jones has no visible reaction. This could mean that he's using a translator, which would strip out the Bob Marley accent, or that he's from a part of the world with different racial stereotypes. Or he could be an English-speaking American who just doesn't think the way Jolene and I do.

His only criticism of the troll concerns posture. "Do they all slouch like that?" he asks. I nod. "A pity," Mr. Jones says. "Its size is quite impressive, otherwise."

We move on to the next model. The xiongmao are a race of anthropomorphic panda bears created as fan service for *Call to Wizardry*'s millions of Chinese players. They are another stereotype, but a carefully crafted, positive one. Xiongmao study kung fu and Taoist sorcery, revere their ancestors, and know a thousand and one recipes for stir-fried bamboo, but they do not have buck teeth or exaggerated epicanthic folds, and they can pronounce the "L" sound just fine. Most Americans find them either cute or silly. Mr. Jones, oddly, is contemptuous. When the model xiongmao presses his paws together and says, "It is an honor to meet you, adventurer," Mr. Jones sneers, as if the bear were trying to pass off one of its own turds as dim sum.

"You don't like pandas?" I say.

"They are overrated," Mr. Jones sniffs.

Mr. Jones does like elves, who are as tall as trolls and don't slouch, but he decides they are "too skinny." He passes on dwarves, gnomes, and goblins without comment. He admires orcs' "fierceness," but they, too, have posture problems. Humans earn another sneer, though he won't share what he dislikes about them.

In the end, he decides to become a plainswalker: an intelligent, bipedal buffalo. Culturally, plainswalkers are Native Americans of the Mix-and-Match tribe. They live in both longhouses and teepees, carve totem poles, send smoke signals, worship the Sky Father and the Earth Mother, and shed tears whenever they see humans littering. Physically, they are the largest of the playable races, which is the part that appeals to Mr. Jones. And male plainswalkers are both taller and more broad-shouldered than females, so his choice of gender comes as no surprise.

The next step is to choose a class. In another throwback to pen-and-paper RPGs, your race determines your career options. Plainswalkers, for example, can be warriors and rangers, but not paladins or ninjas—the design team having apparently decided that talking buffalo *ninjas* are unrealistic.

Mr. Jones wants to know which class has the best leadership skills.

"What kind of leadership? You mean in combat?"

"In general. But in combat, yes, definitely."

"You'll want a tanking class," I say. "For a plainswalker, that means either a warrior or a druid."

"What is a druid?"

"A shapeshifter. For tanking, they can turn into bears with armored skin." Mr. Jones purses his lips, and I clarify: "Grizzly bears, not pandas."

"Show me the warrior," Mr. Jones says. The model plainswalker morphs into a warchief with a painted face and a massive eagle-feather bonnet that adds another foot to its already considerable height. Mr. Jones approves. "This is the one I want."

"All right," I say. "The last step is to pick a name. Other players will be able to see it, if they want to—it'll look like a movie credit that floats over your head—so there's a length limit, but you can use any combination of extended Unicode characters you like. Don't feel like you have to stick to the Roman alphabet."

"I will be Mr. Jones," Mr. Jones says. There is a pause while he types this in. Tempest's host server then checks to see whether the name is already taken, and also verifies that it does not contain any obvious profanities.

The name is available. Mr. Jones locks in his choice. The model plainswalker steps off its pedestal and merges with Mr. Jones's avatar. Mr. Jones becomes a gray-faced bipedal buffalo. A mirror materializes in front of him and he checks himself out. He's pleased with his stature, but less so with his equipment: The big tomahawk the model was carrying has become a teensy stone hatchet, and in place of the war bonnet, he's wearing a headband with a single feather.

"Don't worry," I tell him. "You'll get cooler gear as you level up."

"What about you?" Mr. Jones asks. "Are you going to create a character?"

"I'll be using an existing one. You need to be at least tenth level before you can party up for dungeon runs, so for now I'll just observe and make sure nobody hassles you . . . Hold on a moment."

I switch to an alternate account and become Keebler, a 200th-level elf sorcerer. Mr. Jones looks me up and down, paying special attention to my wizard's staff, which is capped with a hollow crystal sphere containing a bored-looking homunculus.

"Nice walking stick," Mr. Jones says, sounding jealous. "But you are still too skinny."

A portal at the end of the hall teleports us to Happy Valley, the starting zone for plainswalkers. The valley is lush and green and surrounded by a ring of cliffs that provide an illusion of safety; at its center is a lake, with a large teepee encampment on the eastern shore. We arrive just south of the camp.

A questgiver named Chief Wampum waits to greet newcomers. "How!" he says, focusing on Mr. Jones. "Welcome, young warrior!"

"Hello," Mr. Jones says.

Chief Wampum and I do not acknowledge one another. As a max-level character—and an elf—I do not belong here, and if I insist on talking to him he will just ask me if I'm lost. I keep my mouth shut.

The chief tells Mr. Jones that he could use some help. Recently the tribe received a gift of blankets that turned out to be infested with gremlins. The gremlins escaped and are now breeding and making mischief along the southern lakeshore. If Mr. Jones kills ten of them and brings back their scalps, the chief will reward him with a better hatchet and a new pair of moccasins.

"Very well," Mr. Jones says.

"May the Sky Father light your way," says Chief Wampum.

We walk clockwise around the lake until we see the gremlins. They have invaded a fishing camp, punching holes in the canoes and knocking over the salmon smoker. I count about two dozen of them, but they respawn quickly and continuously, so no matter how many scalps are taken, there will always be more.

Mr. Jones indicates the nearest gremlin. "I just hit it with my hatchet?"

I nod. "Try to take them on one at a time. And when they die, reach down—the scalps peel right off, like decals."

"Very well."

While Mr. Jones works on his quest, I keep my eye on a trio of unpleasant-looking 200th-level characters currently harassing another newbie a short distance away. These guys are, literally and figuratively, trolls. Their screen names are BootFuqqer, Choaksondik, and CukULongtime; in place of their real facial features, their avatars sport skins of Al Jolson in blackface. Collectively they represent half a dozen violations of Section 8 of the EULA, which prohibits both obscene names and "racial insensitivity."

The EULA cops have their hands full running down hackers, bots, and sherpas, so Section 8 violators are a low priority. I could screenshot these guys and report them, but it's unlikely they'd get even a temporary suspension. Instead, as a precaution, I shoot off an instant message to Jolene.

The trolls' current target is a first-level shaman named Medicine Girl. BootFuqqer stands behind her, screaming to break her concentration, while Choaksondik and CukULongtime run around killing all the gremlins in her vicinity. Because of the high respawn rate, they can't actually prevent her from completing the quest, but they can make it a lot harder and significantly less fun.

Though clearly frustrated, Medicine Girl does her best to go on with her business without engaging them. In between screams, BootFuqqer comments on the futility of this strategy: "You think if you pretend to ignore us we're going to give up and go away? Think again!"

"Can't not feed us!" the other trolls chant. "Can't not feed us!"

Medicine Girl collects one more scalp, and then—either because she's reached her quota, or because she's run out of patience—she turns and starts walking away. BootFuqqer stays right on her heels, no longer screaming, but breathing hard so she'll know he's still there.

It gets to her. She's only gone about a hundred yards when she stops, squares her shoulders, sighs, and logs out. BootFuqqer spins around and raises his fists in triumph. Choaksondik and CukU-Longtime exchange high-fives.

Idiots.

Mr. Jones has wandered away from me in pursuit of his fourth or fifth gremlin. I move closer to him—a protective gesture that BootFuqqer notices.

"Hello there!" BootFuqqer calls to me. Pointing at Mr. Jones: "Is that your boyfriend?"

BootFuqqer's sidekicks scope me out.

"A five," Choaksondik pronounces.

CukULongtime nods in agreement. "Definitely a five."

Mr. Jones looks up from his latest kill. "Who are these people?"

"Griefers," I say. "Assholes who try to ruin the game for other players. You see that red halo around their heads? That means they're flagged for PvP—player-versus-player combat. They want to pick a fight with us. With you, really."

"Should I accept?"

"No. They're maximum level, you wouldn't stand a chance."

"Hey five!" BootFuqqer shouts. He raises his middle fingers to his face and tugs down the corners of his eyes. "Five-*four*!"

"Why is he shouting numbers at you?"

"It's code," I explain. "To get around the profanity filter."

Call to Wizardry's user interface offers an optional audio filter that can bleep out specific words and phrases. The basic filter only bleeps curse words, but you can get custom add-ons to suppress racial epithets and other forms of hate speech. Griefers have adapted by making code-slurs out of common words that can't be censored without rendering ordinary conversation impossible. Numbers are popular: A shout of "six," for example, would mean "nigger," "faggot," "retard," or all of the above. "Five-four," I'm guessing, is "slant-eyes." The fact that I *am* guessing—that they've actually got me wasting precious brain cycles to figure out what they're calling me—says something about the genius of the method. If only they'd use that ingenuity for good.

I lock my slant-eyes on BootFuqqer and his friends and say, "Mute. Mute. Mute." They fall silent. Unfortunately, I can still see them. Despite numerous requests, Tempest refuses to implement a "Dead to me" feature, saying it would cause too much confusion to have characters who couldn't see one another attacking the same monsters and trying to harvest the same resources. This is actually a fair point, one that underscores the difficulty of policing antisocial behavior in a game whose core elements are murder and pillage.

When BootFuqqer realizes I've muted him, he walks over and gets in my face visually, waving his hands and mouthing obscenities with his troll-sized Al Jolson lips. Choaksondik and CukULong-time focus on Mr. Jones. His gray features have them stymied; they don't know what numbers to shout at him. Even more vexing from their perspective, Mr. Jones has better ignoring skills than Medicine Girl did. Trolls love it when you only pretend not to care about them, but they find genuine indifference intolerable. Mr. Jones, having decided that the trolls are not worth his attention, puts them out of his mind, and not even rampant kill-stealing can get them back in. He just works around them.

But these assholes are nothing if not adaptable. Choaksondik waits for Mr. Jones to swing at another gremlin and then steps into the path of the blow. The game engine, which is smart but not infallible, interprets this as a deliberate attack by Mr. Jones and flags him for PvP. His hatchet nicks Choaksondik for one hit point of damage. Choaksondik winds up and hits back for a hundred thousand hit points. Mr. Jones explodes into a cloud of pink vapor.

BootFuqqer claps his hands to his cheeks and shoots me a look of mock horror. Then he grins and drops a hand to his crotch and mimes jerking off. He pokes the inside of his cheek with his tongue and makes more jerk-off motions near his mouth.

I open a b-channel. "You there?"

Jolene's voice comes back loud and clear: "Yep. Right behind Tweedledum and Tweedledumber." I look over at Choaksondik and CukULongtime, who are now squatting over Mr. Jones's remains, pretending to shit on him. The air on the far side of them shimmers, and I glimpse the outline of a third person. Then Jolene drops back into full ninja stealth mode.

"Get ready," I say.

"Remember I'm not the only one who can be invisible," she replies. It's a good bet that the griefers have brought their own ninja— or two of them. If it's a pair, they can take turns stunning me with paralytic strikes while the other trolls tear me to pieces.

I grip my wizard's staff with both hands. The homunculus in the crystal snaps to attention, pulling out a lighter and an aerosol can. BootFuqqer smiles and makes a "come at me" gesture.

I take three quick steps to my right and set off a freezing sphere. A wave of subzero cold expands ten yards in all directions around me. BootFuqqer is caught in the blast and encased in a solid block of ice. Another ice block forms around the invisible ninja who was lurking beside me.

A second ninja breaks stealth to my left. He's not frozen, but my sidestep has put me out of melee range, so his opening strike hits empty air. Before he can close the gap, I teleport backwards thirty yards. Then I light him up with fireballs and magic missiles.

BootFuqqer breaks free of the ice block. I pause in my immolation of Ninja #2 and hit BootFuqqer with a polymorph spell, turning him into a pig. I turn Ninja #1 into a pig, too. Ninja #2 is almost in melee range, so I frostbolt him in the face to slow him down and teleport away again. In the background, I see Choaksondik stumbling around blindly, trying to rub ninja pepper spray out of his eyes, while CukULongtime staggers beneath a flurry of blows from Jolene's Nunchucks of Severe Head Trauma.

I finish off Ninja #2 and turn my attention to BootFuqqer. I use my Arcane Trinity cooldown: My avatar splits into three identical copies, hurling fire, ice, and lightning respectively. As BootFuqqer's hit point total plummets, Ninja #1 squeals impotently and lowers his snout to root in the dirt.

CukULongtime is down. I kill BootFuqqer, and Jolene kills Choaksondik. Ninja #1 de-swines and tries to make a run for it. I hit him in the back with an ice lance, and Jolene, going for style points, whips out a Flying Guillotine and takes his head off from twenty yards away. Game over.

We hear the sound of disembodied applause. Mr. Jones's spirit reunites with his corpse. He gets up slowly, his deerskin armor and headband looking somewhat the worse for wear.

"That was *excellent*," Mr. Jones says. He surveys the bodies. "Will they come back?"

"They can," I say. "Without a healer to resurrect them, they'll have to walk their souls back from a graveyard, the same way you just did. And because this is supposed to be a beginners-only zone, they'll be sent to a graveyard that's farther away. It may take them several minutes to return."

"But they will be back."

"Probably."

"And then you can kill them again."

"Yes."

"How many times?"

"As many times as we feel like. Until we get tired, or they get tired."

Mr. Jones nods. "Until they get tired," he says.

> **culture shock** — A feeling of profound disorientation caused by exposure to an alien worldview or way of life. Once primarily an affliction of immigrants, soldiers, and wealthy tourists, it was democratized by the internet, which put culture shock on tap 24/7. Whether civilization can survive the resulting stress remains an open question.
>
> —*The New Devil's Dictionary*

Smith is mad at me.

After eight hours in *Call to Wizardry* with Mr. Jones, I go to the Game Lobby and leave my avatar standing at a table by the bar while I take a much-needed bio break. When I come back, my instant message queue is overflowing and Smith's avatar is snapping its gray fingers in my face.

"What's wrong?" I say. Smith answers with a grunt and jerks his head in the direction of the chat rooms.

I don't go. Mom has suggested that I try pushing back against Smith's authority to see how he'll react, and this seems as good a time as any.

"We can talk here," I say, invoking a cone of silence. "It's OK, no one can overhear us. Just don't move your lips."

Smith scowls and his hand twitches like he'd like to grab my wrist and start dragging me. If he could.

"Is this about Jolene?" I ask.

Losing patience, Smith speaks: "You were given strict instructions not to tell anyone what you were doing!"

"I didn't tell Jolene anything. I mean, she knows he's a client, obviously, but I didn't share any details about our arrangement."

"You are not to involve other people in this."

"It's a *massive multiplayer* game," I say. "I have to involve other people, to do what your boss wants me to do. They can either be people I know and trust, who are competent players, or random strangers who may not know what they're doing. Which do you think Mr. Jones would prefer?"

Smith shakes his head, furious at the dilemma this puts him in. "Your people will have to be cleared," he says after a moment. "Their systems will have to be secured, as yours was."

"If you want my crew to give you root access on their computers, you're going to have to let me tell them what's going on. And they'll expect to be well-paid."

"Then you will have to pay them," Smith says pointedly. "Out of the already generous fee you are receiving."

"Mr. Jones said that money is no concern."

"And *I* am saying that you will do the job for the amount you agreed to."

This is not what I want to hear, but I decide to table the issue for now; later I can always lobby Mr. Jones directly for more money. "Do I have your permission to tell Jolene and the others what's up?"

Smith considers. "Yes, but say as little as possible. Tell them only that you have a new client who wishes to remain anonymous."

"What about your security concerns?"

"Perhaps there is another way to handle that." He gives me a knowing look. "One that will not require you to pay them so well."

"If you think I'm going to help you hack my friends' computers—"

"I think you will do whatever is in your own best interest."

Ouch. He's not entirely wrong, of course: If my mother weren't watching, I'd at least be tempted to do what he's suggesting. In this case I'm pretty sure I'd resist temptation, but I'm just as happy not to put that to the test. I suspect, going forward, I'll have plenty of other chances to demonstrate my virtue.

Now that he's put me in my place, Smith relaxes a little. He looks over at the bar, where She-Hulk—or a reasonable facsimile—is hitting on Superman. "What is that?"

"Superhero cosplay," I say. "They're probably coming off a run in *League of Avengers*." The DC/Marvel co-branded MMORPG.

"Not the costumes," Smith says. "I am talking about the necklace she is wearing. I have seen other women with this, and some men as well. What is the significance?"

I take a closer look. She-Hulk has a thin chain around her neck; dangling from it is a shiny silver talisman the rough size and shape of a rifle cartridge. "It's a bullet."

"For another game? A shooting game?"

"No, not a bullet," I say. "A *bullet*. You know, a virtual blow job?"

Smith tilts his head and raises a finger to his ear—as if, off in reality, he were tapping his headset, checking for a malfunction. "A virtual—"

"Blow job. As in oral sex? Seriously, you don't know what bullets are?"

Clearly he doesn't. Which is interesting. "This is . . . a fad of some kind?"

"A fad?" I say. "Not really. It's just something people do. I suppose it *was* a fad, back when it first got started. And of course originally, it was an art project . . . You really don't know the story?"

Smith just stares at me, conflicted. A part of him wants to know, but another part really, really doesn't.

So I tell him.

"This would have been about seven, eight years ago," I say, doing the math in my head. "The artist was a German woman, Leni Ortmann, and the project was called *Datenfetisch*. Data fetish. What it was, she wired up a dildo with all kinds of sensors, and then convinced a hundred women to, you know, be recorded going down on it . . ."

"Women," Smith says darkly. "You mean prostitutes."

"One of them was a sex worker," I say. "Number sixty-two, I think. But they were from all walks of life. A few of them were already famous—there were a couple of actresses, a pop singer, a professional wrestler—but most were just ordinary women who accepted Ortmann's invitation." I pause, recalling number eighty-seven, Raquel Sandoval, a welder from Barcelona, who thirteen-year-old me had had a huge crush on.

"But how is this *art*?" Smith wants to know.

"It was transgressive art," I explain. "The point is to provoke people. The art isn't so much the project itself, it's the reaction to the project—what Ortmann called the Spectacle."

"I do not understand this at all."

"Think of it as the fine art version of clickbait: The more attention you get, the better. Now, anything involving famous women and sex is guaranteed a certain amount of attention, but Ortmann was savvier than that. She'd studied marketing at university, and she knew how to manipulate public interest. And the thing that really made *Datenfetisch* take off, that sent it into the stratosphere as far as Spectacle was concerned, is that she didn't build a play-back device. She made these recordings, and she put each one on its own custom flash drive—the drives were supposed to look like lipstick cases, but what they also looked like, especially when they were racked together, was bullets, which is where the name comes from—and then, when she had all hundred of them, she destroyed her recording equipment, and all the technical notes that went with it. All that was left was the data."

"Which would be useless without the technical documentation," Smith says.

"That depends on your assumptions. Ortmann put up a *Datenfetisch* website, with pages for each of the women in the project. There were photographs, capsule biographies, video interviews, and of course, the data. Which, yeah, without the technical specs, were just long strings of ones and zeroes. But that was Ortmann's marketing savvy at work. It's a classic strategy for building demand: Show customers something they think they want, then tell them they can't have it."

"But they *couldn't* have it," Smith insists. "On their own, such data strings would be meaningless."

"On the contrary, they were full of meaning—the trick was getting access to the information. Ortmann herself had provided at least one clue: On the website, each data string was tagged with a time code showing how long that particular recording was supposed to run. With that, and an educated guess about the sampling rate, you could divide up the string into discrete data packets, and start hypothesizing about the number of different variables you were dealing with. And if you were obsessed enough to go that far, the next step, obviously, was to ask yourself whether there might not be other, subtler clues hidden in the *Datenfetisch* website. To wonder whether *Datenfetisch* was actually a puzzle that was meant to be solved."

"That is repulsive and insane."

"It's the power of targeted marketing," I say. "Ortmann's data strings were like the Voynich Manuscript for chronic masturbators. All over the web, people—guys—started setting up forums devoted to cracking Ortmann's code. And there was a corresponding hardware effort, an amateur Manhattan Project to build the playback device. That was what set off the Spectacle: *Wired* magazine ran a squib about all these Kickstarters and Patreons people had created to fund the hardware research. Then *Slate* did a post about how problematic it was that Men on the Internet were trying to build a magic decoder ring for fellatio, and it went viral. The whole internet started weighing in."

Talking about this is making me nostalgic. The *Datenfetisch* affair certainly wasn't the first online controversy I'd witnessed, but thanks to the raging hormones of puberty, it was the first one I felt personally invested in. I even wrote a few impassioned Reddit posts on the subject—all of them, thankfully, lost in the noise. "It struck a lot of nerves, especially in America. This was right after a bunch of Hollywood celebrities got their nude selfies hacked, and there were people arguing that the *Datenfetisch* decryption effort was the same sort of violation—and that was just one subgenre of hot take. Another sore spot was that four of Ortmann's subjects were transwomen—you can imagine the reactions *that* provoked, right? The back and forth on that, people lecturing each other about how they were supposed to feel, went on for weeks . . ."

Peak Spectacle was achieved when the U.S. Senate and House of Representatives held joint hearings to determine whether digital blow-job technology represented a threat to children. My own youthful eye-rolling aside, this was a reasonable thing to have a conversation about, but only if you assumed that grown-ups would be doing the talking. In Zero Day, I was used to dealing with adults who wielded power with restraint and tried to educate themselves before forming opinions; it was a jolt to log into C-SPAN and see members of Congress acting more like the dickheads I encountered in game chat.

"The Spectacle did eventually die down," I tell Smith. "Ortmann sold her original set of bullets to a private collector for some crazy amount of Euros, and the outrage machine moved on to other things. As for the Men on the Internet, they never did crack Ortmann's code. But the hardware effort was more successful: They say *Datenfetisch* jumped cybersex technology ahead half a decade overnight." I look over at the bar, where She-Hulk is dangling her bullet above Superman's open palm, teasing him with it. "So now, yeah, it's just a thing people do."

Smith's avatar has taken on a jittery quality, almost like he's lagging. But it's not a latency issue. He's trembling with rage. "This," he sputters, "this is . . . this is . . ."

"Immoral? Psychologically unhealthy? An example of the toxic masculinity endemic to rape culture?"

"Decadent!" Smith roars. The cone of silence keeps his voice from carrying, but She-Hulk finally notices the way he's looking at her. She gives us both the finger, mouths "Dead to me," and vanishes. Superman goes with her. Smith, still trembling, logs out.

I am left with the dregs of my nostalgia. And a question.

Lots of people think bullets are gross. But it's rare to encounter someone online who has no idea what they are. And Smith is an IT guy—or an IT girl. But Smith being female would make this sort of ignorance even more remarkable. Raise your hand if you're a woman in tech who's never had some creep ask you to email him a hummer.

Where did you get your computer training, Smith? I wonder. On the moon?

I summon Googlebot. "Hello, John Chu," she greets me. "How can I help you?"

"I'm an American tourist interested in experiencing severe culture shock. Can you give me a list of travel destinations that might satisfy me? I'm looking for places that are commonly described as 'like going to the moon' or 'like being on a different planet.'"

"There are a number of countries that remain culturally isolated from the West, such that an American with your travel history would probably find them very strange," Googlebot says.

"Is there one country that stands out as being more culturally isolated from the West than any other?"

"Yes," says Googlebot, and names it. But I've already guessed.

grinding — Engaging in a repetitive and often mindless task. In a video-game context, grinding may refer either to (a) actions performed to reach the parts of the game that are fun, or (b) the same actions performed out of habit after the game ceases to be fun.

See also: **behaviorism, Skinner box**

—*The New Devil's Dictionary*

look for Jolene at her favorite fishing spot.

Mom has given me permission to take Jolene into our confidence, but I need to be careful how I do it. As I log into *Call to Wizardry*, a telltale icon of an eye at the top of my visual field warns me that Smith is monitoring my POV. The telltale should be invisible to him, but he can see and hear everything else that I do.

I play it cool. I teleport to the Hinterlands of Goth and head for the coast, carrying my Krakenmaster 3000 and a Bottomless Creel of Holding.

Among all the secondary professions that a *Call to Wizardry* character can learn, fishing is the most tedious. The mechanics of it are simple enough: Equip a fishing pole. Find a body of water. Cast your line and wait three to fifteen seconds, as determined by the server's random number generator, for your fishing bobber to signal that you've hooked something. Reel it in and see what you've got. Repeat ad nauseam.

As with other crafting and gathering skills, your proficiency is measured in levels, but fishing is unique in having no maximum proficiency. Instead, leveling up just gets progressively more difficult. To go from level 1 to level 2 requires a single successful cast, but at level 100, you might fish for half an hour before advancing. By level 500, the estimated mean fishing time between level increases is eight hours.

If it's so boring and such a time sink, why do it? A comprehensive answer would require an explanation of dopamine's role in the brain's reward system, as well as a sidebar about the unusually high incidence of obsessive-compulsive disorder among MMORPG players. But the short version is, you do it for the same reason you do everything in *Call to Wizardry*: to get imaginary stuff. Newbie fishermen catch fish and the occasional tin can; at higher levels, the loot tables get more interesting, and there are rumors of truly exotic, even game-breaking treasures just waiting for someone skillful enough to draw them up.

The current record holder is Ahmet Mirza, a French *Call to Wizardry* player who briefly achieved fishing level 999. Just as Ahmet was about to crack the four-digit barrier, EULA took a look at his game logs and discovered a series of marathon sessions during which he had fished literally nonstop for days—strong circumstantial evidence of bot use. On the gaming forums, Ahmet swore up and down that he hadn't cheated—he was just an insomniac with epic bladder control—but Tempest banned him anyway. When customer service denied his final appeal, he weighted his backpack with the pieces of his smashed computer and jumped into the Seine. As you would.

People who fish in the Hinterlands usually go to Martin's Beach, but the site's popularity attracts griefers as well, so I know Jolene won't be there. Instead I climb Dead Man's Bluff and enter the Emerald Sea Caves. The caves are infested with bloodthirsty nagas; I know a way to sneak past them, but if Smith has an in-game spy following me, there's a good chance they'll blunder into a fight and reveal themselves.

I emerge onto a narrow cobblestone beach at the base of the bluff. I listen for sounds of melee behind me, but there's only the faint hiss and slither of the nagas. I walk south over the cobblestones, my footsteps echoing beneath the overhanging cliff.

A few hundred yards on, the beach bends sharply to the right, out of sight. I pause and look up, focusing on a distinctive knob of stone projecting from the cliff face. Off in the real world, I flip a control toggle. The telltale eye closes and blinks out; it is replaced by an icon of a spinning tape reel. Playback mode: Smith, or whoever he's got minding my POV, is now viewing a recording of a previous visit I made to this spot.

I continue around the bend. Jolene is standing on a spit of sand. She's just reeled in a barnacle-encrusted crate. I watch her pry it open, revealing a dozen bolts of enchanted silk. These vanish into her inventory and she quickly casts her hook into the water again. I step up beside her and deploy my Krakenmaster 3000.

"So," Jolene says, "you going to tell me about that weird guy from the other day?"

"Even better," I reply. "I'm going to tell you twice."

I've only got twenty minutes before the playback loops, so I lay out the situation as quickly as I can: Smith. Mr. Jones. The job offer. The Chinese woman at the bar. And last but not least, Mom, who I describe as a generic "federal agent," because this already sounds way too much like a spy movie plot and I don't want Jolene to think I'm bullshitting. But it turns out skepticism isn't a problem.

"Which agency?" Jolene asks. "FBI? Homeland Security?"

"It's a part of Cyber Command. A special task force called—"

"Zero Day? For real?" Sounding seriously impressed, like I've just told her Mom's a rock star.

"You know about Zero Day?"

"Hell yeah. I'd have tried to join, if they'd had it back when I was in the service."

"You were Navy?"

"Marines. Six years. Where I got my IT training." Jolene's fishing bobber twitches, and she reels in another crate. Gold doubloons. "So who is this Mr. Jones, that Zero Day would care about him?"

"We don't know yet," I say. "But I have this crazy theory that he might be North Korean."

Now Jolene looks skeptical. "Do North Koreans even have internet access?"

"I need to do some research about that. But I assume the guys running the country have whatever they want."

"Why would a North Korean bigwig want to study MMORPGs?"

"No idea. But game theory has plenty of applications outside entertainment." I reel in a magic halibut and toss it into my creel. Make another cast. "Psy ops. Economics. Military strategy."

"And what makes you think he's North Korean in the first place? The bank in Burma?"

"Partly that. But also . . ." I tell her about my last meeting with Smith.

She's laughing by the time I finish. "Man," Jolene says. "And you busted *my* chops for reading too much into Ray's IP address . . .

Have you told your mother about this yet? Because if not, I would like to be a fly on the wall for that conversation."

"Ha ha," I say. "So are you in?"

"On a Zero Day op? Sure. Do I get a new computer, too?"

"That's part of the plan," I tell her. "That way you and I can b-channel right under Smith's nose, without having to do this again."

"And the money? I get a cut, right?"

"Of course." Then, just to get it out of the way: "I'm going to need you to fill out a W-9 form, too."

"Why, so you can claim my share as a business expense?"

I shrug. "It's a lot of money."

"You do know the IRS likes you to declare *all* your income, right? Not just the individual payments that are big enough to make you nervous."

"Are you saying you report all the money you make as a sherpa?"

"Are you saying you don't?"

A tug on my fishing line saves me from making a potentially in-criminating statement. I reel in a vanity license plate: YTWHALE.

"What about the split?" Jolene asks. "Fifty-fifty seems fair, especially if you're claiming me as a deduction."

"The split will be fair," I promise. "But it's four ways, not two, so it can't be fifty-fifty."

"You're bringing Ray and Anja in on this, too?" She sounds like she doesn't approve.

"Sure, why not? We're going to need them."

"I'll bet you Ray's not going to be happy about someone poking around in his system, even if you do give him a clean machine first."

"Ray's not getting a new computer." Mom's orders are explicit, I explain: Ray is not to be told about Zero Day's involvement in this. "As far as he's concerned, Mr. Jones is just another client."

"So your mom doesn't trust Ray either," Jolene says. "That's interesting. She say why?"

"No, and I didn't ask. I don't think you're right about Ray, but if you are, I don't want to know."

"You don't, huh?"

"Why would I want to know a thing like that? I've still got to work with the guy."

"That's right, I forgot you don't have a choice who you work with. What about Anja?"

"What about her? You don't think . . . Come on, she's nineteen years old. And Ray's never shown any kind of interest in—"

"That's not what I'm asking. Are you allowed to tell Anja what's really going on?"

I shake my head. "She's a foreign national. There are strict recruiting rules that apply to those, and U.S. and Argentine intelligence aren't getting along right now."

"Well, if you don't tell Anja what's up, how are you supposed to satisfy Smith's security requirements?" From the way Jolene says this I can tell she's already worked out the answer, and she *really* doesn't approve.

"There's a malware package," I say. "Smith sent it to me. Mom's people are decompiling it right now—we're going to need to infect your computer, too, so they want to make sure they know exactly what the malware does and how to control it."

Out on the water, Jolene's fishing bobber is jumping again, but she ignores it and focuses her full attention on me. "How many lines of code are we talking about?"

"I'm not sure. The file was a few hundred megabytes."

"A few hundred . . . And they're going to work out *exactly* what it does in a day or two?"

"It's a big team. And they're really good at what they do."

"Uh-huh." Jolene frowns. "Look, John, I don't really give a shit if Ray's computer accidentally gets bricked—or mine either, for that matter. But Anja—"

"I know," I say. "But it's OK. Anja's VR rig and her life support are completely independent systems. Corrupting one won't affect the other. I Googled it to be sure."

"Oh, you *Googled it*, did you?" Her expression says: There is not enough side-eye in the *world* for some things. "Before we go any further with this plan, I need to have a serious conversation with your mother."

"Sure, no problem. I'll have her get in touch with you."

We are almost out of time. Jolene makes herself scarce. I stare at my right foot as my computer counts down the last five seconds in playback mode. Then I look up, cast my hook, and fish for another hour.

A couple hours after that, Jolene and I bump into each other in the Game Lobby. The telltale eye observes as I tell her about Mr. Jones again, this time sticking to Smith's preferred script: Jones is a secretive rich guy offering a lot of money, up front, for a sherpa crew willing to work long hours on short notice and not blab about it.

Jolene doesn't have her new computer yet, so we cannot b-channel. But one of the benefits of being as outspoken as Jolene usually is is that even when you're unable to speak freely, people who know you can guess what you're thinking.

I tell Jolene that Mr. Jones is offering us a weekly salary of ten thousand dollars per crew member, and she says, "Ten thousand? Each?" To anyone eavesdropping, it must sound as if she is impressed by—and a little suspicious of—Mr. Jones's generosity. But what I hear, loud and clear, is: "*Ten* thousand each? That's what you call a fair split?" The ensuing discussion about what Mr. Jones is going to expect for his money is edged with a subtext of what an incredibly greedy bastard I am. And when Jolene asks whether I've talked to Ray and Anja yet, I can tell that she's gone from being concerned for Anja's safety to being actively pissed off at me for endangering it: Not only am I selfish, I am reckless.

I can't see what my own face is doing. But my VR rig needs to be able to read my expression in order to render my avatar, which means Smith can read my expression too, if he wants to. So I do my best to not react to any of this.

It's not as if I could argue with Jolene, anyway. On the charge that I am a selfish and reckless person, I can only plead guilty.

DARLA'S FIRST OUTING AS A MEMBER OF SHERPA, INC. was a level grind. The client was a junior executive at Amazon who was scheduled to go adventuring with his coworkers as part of a corporate team-building exercise. He had a high-level elf paladin he wanted maxed out in time for the run, and rather than pull an all-nighter he decided to pay us to do it for him. He also gave us a shopping list of magic items and crafting materials he wanted; our deal stipulated that in addition to our fee, we got to keep any treasure that wasn't on the list.

It was Ray who'd found the client, so it was Ray's gig. He'd mapped out a conservative strategy for getting the job done with a minimum of fuss and a maximum return on time invested. I would tank, as the client's paladin; Anja and "the new girl" would dps; Ray, of course, would heal. That left one open dps spot, but the dungeons Ray wanted to run were easy enough that he thought we could manage with a smaller party—and a four-way split on experience points meant the leveling process would go faster.

When I told Darla about the job, she insisted that I should let her tank. "Come on," she said, when I hesitated. "You wanted to know whether I can do it, let me show you." Of course, this meant giving her access to the client's account. But I made a snap decision to trust her, telling myself, on the basis of nothing more than intuition, that if Darla were going to screw me over it wouldn't be anything as pedestrian as stealing a customer's credit card information. Yes, I am aware of how ridiculous that sounds.

I gave Darla the client's password and told her where in the game world to meet up with the rest of us.

She was late. When I showed up at the meeting spot as one of my own characters—a plainswalker shaman named Dances With Hooves—Ray immediately wanted to know what was going on, and he wasn't happy with the answer. He became even less happy once Darla finally arrived. It took me a moment to recognize what the problem was: Darla looked like herself. That is to say, the paladin avatar had her face and skin tone, and a female body. This would have been fine if it was her paladin, but it wasn't, it was the client's, and the client was (a) male, (b) Hispanic, and (c) not into crossgender play.

Every city in Asgarth has a transmogrification parlor where you can map a new face or hairstyle onto your avatar, swap genders, and even change races. But all of this costs gold, and sex changes are expensive, so unless Darla had been thoughtful enough to transfer the funds from one of her own accounts, she'd just spent a bunch of treasure that wasn't hers.

No, Ray was not happy.

I tried to smooth things over by making introductions: "Ray and Anja, this is Darla. Darla, this is Ray Nelson and Anja Kirchner . . ."

"The girl in the iron lung," Darla said. Anja froze up and her expression turned brittle, but then Darla continued: "I saw the video of your floor routine at the Pan American Championships. You were badass." Which thawed Anja out again, but left her looking more off-balance than flattered.

"So," Darla said. "Where are we going first?"

"Before we go anywhere," Ray said, "I want to know—"

"The Barbican," I said.

"The Barbican?" Darla gave herself a once-over, double-checking the quality of her gear. "We can do a lot better than the fucking Barbican, with this. What about the Temple of the Seven Lanterns? If we four-man that on heroic mode, I'll be maxed out in no time."

"The client wants three hundred ingots of orcish steel. That's a common loot drop in the Barbican."

"Why not just buy steel off the auction house?"

"Because then we have to pay gold for it," Ray said. "If we farm it, it's free." He gave me a look, like: Did you forget to explain who's in charge here?

Darla took the hint. "Fine," she said, rolling her eyes. "We'll run the Barbican . . . And just so you don't wet your panties: I saved the original avatar configuration when I did the transmog, so I can switch back when we're done. Your client will never know he had tits."

"What about the gold you spent?"

"Jesus Christ. Take it out of my share, I don't care."

According to official *Call to Wizardry* lore, the Barbican was originally an archmage's castle. Near the end of the Second Multi-verse War, it was overrun by orcs. The murder of the archmage set off a magical earthquake that swallowed up most of the structure; all that remained above ground was the castle's front gate, which now guards the entrance to a crevasse.

As Darla had noted, this was not a hard dungeon for characters of our level. The most challenging fight is right at the beginning, where you take on a squad of elite orc warriors supported by archers. The archers are on the wall above the Barbican's front gate, protected by anti-missile and anti-magic wards; you can't shoot at them, but they can and do shoot at you, pumping out a steady stream of damage until you fight past the ground troops, climb a ramp up the wall, and engage them hand to hand.

There are a number of effective strategies for tackling this fight. The safest, and the one Ray favored, involves sending the tank in to aggro the warriors and draw them away from the gate, out of arrow range. Without the extra dps the warriors aren't that dangerous, and once they're dead it's a simple matter to rush in and kill the archers.

Darla had a different plan. "OK," she said, as we stood on a hill overlooking the gate, "I'm going to pull the ground troops off to the right, away from the ramp. As soon as I've got their attention, Argentina, here"—pointing at Anja—"is going to run up the wall and go full mountain lion on those archers."

Ray shook his head. "The archers will all aggro on her the second she steps on the ramp. She won't make it."

"Yeah, she will," Darla said, "because Buffalo Boy"—pointing at me—"is going to be secondary heals on this fight. While Mr. Panties in a Bunch is busy keeping me alive, you're going to spam Blessings of the Earth Mother on Argentina."

"That's not good enough," Ray insisted. "If those archers roll critical hits, Blessings of the Earth Mother won't— What are you doing?"

Darla had bowed her head to check herself over again, and as she did so, the pieces of her armor began fading away. Soon all that was left was her shield and her sword, and her avatar was naked, or as naked as *Call to Wizardry* lets you get: A loincloth and bikini top remained, to preserve the game's Teen ESRB rating.

"I've done this fight in armor a billion times," Darla explained. "It's boring."

"Doing it without armor is suicidal," Ray said.

"Not if you do your job. I'll pop my Shield of Righteousness cooldown right at the start. If I can kill two of those guys before the shield breaks, that should lower the damage to a point where you can keep up with it."

"And what if I decide not to heal you?"

Darla shrugged. "Then it's going to be a really long dungeon run. But at least you won't have to waste any gold fixing my armor when you resurrect me . . . OK, let's do this. Argentina, follow me!"

This is not news, but people who fantasize about being knights or ninjas often can't fight worth a damn in real life. Do a search on YouTube and you'll find lots of videos of people in VR headsets flailing around hilariously as they pretend to be Brienne of Tarth or Conan the Barbarian. Good game designers understand that even though players may not *be* cool, they want to feel cool, and so most VR motion-capture systems incorporate a feature called "kinetic photoshopping," which translates the jerky movements of the gamer into the smooth blows and parries of a trained martial artist.

Tempest, as usual, takes things a step further. Buried deep in the *Call to Wizardry* settings menu is an option to turn off kinetic

photoshopping. Ordinarily you would only do this if you were planning to get stoned and have a good laugh at yourself. But if you
actually are a martial artist, or just someone who knows how to
move—someone who doesn't need help to look cool—you can take
off the training wheels and really show your stuff.

Darla knew how to move. She fought like a dancer, with a kind
of brutal grace. She *flowed*. It was breathtaking to watch. I'd seen
it in our duel in the Jurassic Swamp, and it had certainly factored
into my decision to offer her a job. But in the swamp she'd been a
green-skinned monster with fangs and warts. Here at the Barbican,
she was an elf; she looked more like a real person.

And yes, she was naked. I don't want to downplay that, but I
don't want to oversell it, either. I mean, I like nudity. Nudity is definitely a thing for me. But my real turn-on, my big fetish, is competence. Competence gets to me in a way that nudity alone never
could.

Darla knew what she was doing. She tore into those orcs like
nobody's business, and managed to kill half of them before her
magic Shield of Righteousness collapsed. Then Ray, deciding he
had no choice but to play along, stepped in with his own brand of
competence, healing Darla's wounds as the orcs' scimitars finally
started to bite.

I was the one who nearly screwed up. Focused on the Spectacle that was Darla, I forgot about Anja. She started up the ramp
and was immediately hit with a volley of arrows. A second volley
dropped her to a quarter of her hit point total. Then Darla, who'd
managed to maintain situational awareness despite being mobbed
by orcs, called out, "Hey, Buffalo Boy, *WAKE THE FUCK UP!*"

I started firing off blessings. It was a close call, but the random
number generator was kind to me and I kept Anja from bleeding

out. Once she got into melee range, she made short work of the archers. Darla finished off the ground troops, lopping the head off the last one with a flourish, then spread her arms and took a deep bow.

I shuffled my feet and tried to look nonchalant. Beside me, Ray cracked open a potion and guzzled it; keeping Darla alive had used up most of his mana.

"So," I said, "she's a little high maintenance, but I think you can see—"

Ray tossed the empty potion flask aside. "How long?" he said.

"How long what?"

"How long are you planning to be stuck on this girl?"

Lying about your true feelings doesn't make you stop feeling them. Another Mom saying. But Mom's point is that you should be honest with yourself about your motivations; confessing them to other people is optional.

"It's not like that. Darla is—"

"*Trouble*," Ray said. "And since you don't normally have your head up your ass, I can only think of one reason why you'd want her on the crew." He raised a hand to stop me interrupting. "I'm not judging. I've got my own history of stupid, so I get it. I just want some idea of how long I'm going to have to put up with her."

"Ray—"

"Hey ladies!" Darla called. "Are we here to do genocide, or what?"

"Try to make it quick," Ray said to me. "Figure out what you want from this girl, get it, and get out. And when she makes you pay for it—and she will—remember that I told you so."

Korea, North — An independent kingdom for much of its long history, Korea was annexed by Imperial Japan in 1910. Following WWII, Korea was split, with the northern half coming under Soviet-sponsored communist control. After failing in the Korean War (1950–53) to conquer the US-backed Republic of Korea (ROK) in the southern portion by force, North Korea (DPRK), under its founder President KIM Il Sung, adopted a policy of ostensible diplomatic and economic "self-reliance" as a check against outside influence. The DPRK demonized the US as the ultimate threat to its social system through state-funded propaganda, and molded political, economic, and military policies around the core ideological objective of eventual unification of Korea under Pyongyang's control. KIM Il Sung's son, KIM Jong Il, was officially designated as his father's successor in 1980, assuming a growing political and managerial role until the elder KIM's death in 1994. KIM Jong Un was publicly unveiled as his father's successor in 2010.

—*The CIA World Factbook* (text edition)

'm sorry," the guide tells me. "The unicorn cave is a myth."

"Really? I found a million references to it on Google."

"Yes, it is a popular legend in Western media. The story stems from a mistranslated press release that went viral. The name of the site, Kiringul, is more properly rendered in English as Kirin's Grotto. A kirin is—"

"A royal chimera." I've killed slews of them in *Call to Wizardry*: Dragon-headed, ox-footed beasts who guard the tombs of the xiong-mao emperors.

"Yes. What the DPRK archaeologists actually claimed to have found was an inscription in the rock identifying the cave as the home of a kirin ridden by King Dongmyeong, founder of the ancient Korean state of Goguryeo. The discovery is part of a broader propaganda effort to foster a sense of continuity between Korea's first rulers and the modern Kim family dynasty."

"So it's the Korean equivalent of a 'George Washington slept here' plaque. But they didn't actually dig up a kirin."

"No."

"That's disappointing. I was picturing a sort of P. T. Barnum exhibit with fake fossils. You know, like a horse skeleton with a horn glued to its forehead?"

"Kiringul has nothing like that. But if your interest is absurdities connected to the Kim regime's cult of personality, there are numerous other examples I could show you."

"That's OK. I'm actually here to learn about infrastructure."

I am in the DPRK section of the CIA's Virtual World Factbook. An important tool in the CIA's own propaganda arsenal, the Factbook is open to anyone with internet access. You can walk the streets of the world's capitals and visit thousands of other "sites of interest," asking questions about history and current events. Of course, everything you see and hear is the American government's preferred version of reality. But that's good enough for my purposes today; if I have any doubts, I can always ask Mom for the straight facts later.

My guide to virtual Pyongyang is a software agent who goes by Mr. Park. Modeled on a North Korean intelligence officer who defected in the 2020s, he reminds me of some older Germans I knew when I lived in Berlin—people who'd grown up in the East before the Wall came down and were only too happy to share stories of how awful life had been under communism.

Mr. Park and I are in a plaza atop Mansu Hill in central Pyongyang. The space is dominated by a trio of seventy-foot-tall statues depicting three generations of the Kim dynasty: the Great Leader, Kim Il-sung; the Dear Leader, Kim Jong-il; and the currently presiding Supreme Leader, Kim Jong-un. A group of Japanese school kids led by another copy of Mr. Park is gathered at the base of the Kim Jong-un statue. There's also an unchaperoned white guy who looks to be in his early twenties; he stares up at the faces of the statues, panning his head slowly in the way people do when they are recording. He's probably a reporter, a "foreign correspondent" for a news outlet that cannot afford a real travel budget.

Looking down the hillside I can see a curving road that an overlay identifies as Sungri Street. Like every other Pyongyang street I have seen so far, it is eerily empty. "This simulation doesn't attempt to model traffic," Mr. Park tells me when I ask about this, "but the absence of vehicles is realistic. Despite recent improvements in the economy, car ownership remains rare in the DPRK, even among members of the Core Class."

"Core Class?"

"All citizens of the DPRK are assigned a ranking, based on their perceived political reliability. The top ranks form the Core Class, who are accorded special privileges, such as the right to live and work in Pyongyang, priority in receipt of medical care and other services, and relative freedom of movement within the country.

Below the Core Class is the so-called Wavering Class, and at the bottom of the scale are the members of the Hostile Class."

"Who are they?"

"Descendants of people who collaborated with the Japanese during the occupation, or who supported the Americans during the Korean War. Families of defectors, including POWs who chose not to return to the DPRK after the war ended. People whose ancestors were religious, or who owned too much land, or ran successful businesses. Anyone else whose background or associations puts them at high risk of counter-revolutionary activity."

"Is there any way to improve your ranking?"

"Extraordinary service to the state is occasionally rewarded with an increase in status. But social mobility more often goes the other way. From time to time, the government revises the ranking system as new categories of counter-revolutionary are identified. Anyone who offends the regime is subject to demotion, along with their children and their children's children."

"That's harsh."

"The Kims are ruthless," Mr. Park says matter-of-factly. "It's how they've stayed in power so long."

I turn back towards the statues and catch the white guy looking at us. I double-check the telltale at the top of my visual field; the icon is a closed eye. This is sleep mode, a variant of playback mode that is supposed to make it appear to anyone monitoring my computer that I am offline right now. But because this website is public, I can still, theoretically, be spied on from within the simulation. It occurs to me that I probably shouldn't be using my default avatar.

I cover my mouth so the white guy can't read my lips and say to Mr. Park, "Take me somewhere else."

"Where would you like to go?"

"What about that big tower you pointed out before? The one that looks like the Transamerica Pyramid on steroids?"

There is a blur of motion and then I am high up in the air, gazing out a wall of windows at the city below. Ordinarily this would spell instant vertigo, but the glass in front of me is dirty, thickly streaked with grime and bird shit, so I don't actually feel in danger of falling.

"The Ryugyong Hotel," Mr. Park says. "At its conception in 1987, it was designed to be the tallest hotel building in the world, with one hundred and five floors and a height of three hundred and thirty meters."

"Nineteen eighty-seven?" I say. Other than the windows, the floor we are on looks unfinished; I see bare concrete walls, and a wheelbarrow gathering dust beside an exposed steel pillar. "What happened, did they run out of money?"

"Several times," Mr. Park says. "The initial round of construction ran three years past deadline and hundreds of millions of dollars over budget; they did manage to top out the superstructure, but for years it was an empty concrete shell. A second round of construction, commencing in 2008, finished the exterior facade before cash flow problems once more caused a halt. Since then, there have been periodic reports of military units being brought in to continue the work, but the hotel has yet to host a single guest."

Mr. Park dispels the dirt on the windows with a wave of his hand, then conjures a colored overlay that highlights various buildings in the cityscape. He points out the Pyongyang Art Museum, whose six floors are devoted entirely to portraits of the Kim family, and the Museum of Natural Disasters, which documents the storms, earthquakes, tsunamis, and volcanic eruptions that occurred around the world on the day Kim Il-sung died. But this isn't what I'm here for, so I interrupt him: "Talk to me about internet access."

"Access to the global internet is tightly controlled. Only a few thousand citizens, at most, have the necessary security clearance. There is, however, a DPRK intranet—an internal web, with content selected and vetted by the state—that ordinary citizens can use."

"How do they access it?"

"Through public terminals installed in schools, libraries, and businesses. Or through smartphones."

"North Koreans are allowed to have smartphones?"

"Government approved models," Mr. Park says. "The state maintains a 3G wireless network with about eight million subscribers. It can only be used for domestic calls, and of course all conversations and intranet searches are subject to monitoring."

"And you say it's a 3G network? I think that's what my grandparents' cell phones used."

"The DPRK has been looking to modernize the system," Mr. Park explains, "but as the foreign contractor who installed the 3G network was never fully paid, they're having trouble attracting bids."

"Tell me more about the cell phone subscribers. Are they mostly members of the Core Class?"

"Actually, no. Phones must be registered with the police, but they aren't considered a special privilege. Anyone with money can get one."

"But how do members of the other classes afford that? Aren't they poor?"

"Almost everyone in the DPRK is poor, by Western standards," Mr. Park says. "And it's true, at one time, the members of the Wavering and Hostile Classes were poorer still. But that's no longer the case. These days, despite their lack of official privileges, many have as much wealth, or even more, as members of the Core Class."

"And how did that happen?"

"It started with the Great Famine in the 1990s. Owing to the Kims' mismanagement of the economy, the DPRK experienced terrible food shortages, and hundreds of thousands of people starved to death. Even the elite in Pyongyang went hungry, but the situation in the northern provinces, where the members of the Hostile Class are concentrated, was much worse. In desperation, people set up markets and traded whatever they could—including goods smuggled in from China—in order to get money to buy food. This sort of capitalist enterprise was illegal, but authorities turned a blind eye, because the alternative would have been even more widespread starvation.

"After the famine subsided, the markets remained open and expanded to include a wider range of goods. People were able to accumulate small amounts of wealth—again, not much by Western standards, but enough to afford a few luxuries. Citizens who live close to the border often own two cell phones—a DPRK approved phone for local calls, and a black market phone that can call internationally by connecting to cell towers in China."

"Why didn't the government shut the markets down after the famine ended?" I ask.

"Shutting them down completely would be impossible at this point," Mr. Park says. "Most of the true believers in communism starved to death in the famine, while the people who survived became very adept at circumventing the rules. The local authorities and border guards have been corrupted by bribes. As for the central government, they don't really care if people have money to buy refrigerators or nicer clothes. They concentrate their enforcement efforts on select classes of goods. For example, one of the most popular things on the black market is foreign media: books, movies, music, TV series. Like the internet, these are forbidden to ordinary citizens, because they contradict the government's claims about the outside world. But enforcing the ban is extraordinarily difficult, because digital media are so easy to smuggle, and despite severe penalties for trafficking and possession, people are willing to take the risk."

"What about video games? Are there—"

I stop, suddenly aware of another figure in the room. It's the white guy from the plaza. He's materialized off to our left and is staring out the window, pretending to ignore us.

This time I don't bother to hide my lips. "Take me somewhere else."

"Where would you like to go?"

"Surprise me."

Another blur of motion, and I am staring at a rack of metal shelves. The shelves hold rows of large octagonal cases. Each case is labeled in Korean, and most are labeled in a second language as well. DAS BOOT, reads one. Another says: FRIDAY THE 13TH PT. II.

I crane my head around. I am inside what looks like a large, windowless warehouse. There are many rows of shelves, holding what must be tens of thousands of octagonal cases.

"This is the Kim family's private film vault," Mr. Park says. "It—"

"Hold up a second. Do you have any idea who that guy was?"

"What guy?"

"Just now, back in the hotel, there was another guy in the room with us. You didn't see him?"

"I'm a software construct," Mr. Park reminds me. "My awareness, such as it is, is focused on the user or users I'm currently interacting with."

"Is there any way for you to look up information on other users accessing the Factbook right now? Like the IP addresses they're logged in from?"

"I'm afraid not."

"Do you know if the CIA keeps records of visits to this site?"

"I have no direct knowledge of that," Mr. Park says. "But the site's privacy policy, which you declined to read, does contain language suggesting that is the case."

"OK, thanks . . . So, you were saying? This is the Kims' movie vault?"

Mr. Park nods. "It's believed to be one of the largest film collections in private hands. Much of it was amassed by Kim Jong-il while he was head of the DPRK's Propaganda and Agitation Department."

"And it's actual film? These cases, they're for old-style celluloid reels, right?"

"Yes. What you see here is a reconstruction based on a decades-old eyewitness description. The collection may have been digitized in the interim—but perhaps not. Again, all forms of foreign media are considered classified material, and celluloid, being harder to copy than digital files, is more secure."

"*Friday the 13th* is classified?"

"I'm unfamiliar with that title," Mr. Park says, "but, for example, if it contained scenes showing ordinary Westerners driving cars, living in beautiful houses, or eating more or better food than DPRK citizens do, then of course it would be seen as problematic by the regime."

"How did they get the films?"

"Most are bootleg copies. Kim Jong-il had professional dupli-cating equipment installed in all of the DPRK's foreign embas-sies. The diplomatic staff would bribe local theater owners and borrow their film reels for copying. An elaborate security protocol was devised for dubbing the films into Korean: To minimize the risk of ideological contamination, the films' audio tracks would be recorded separately, without images, and broken up into short seg-ments, each of which was given to a different translation team for processing. Whenever possible, the teams were made up of foreign-ers who had already been exposed to the outside world—either de-fectors who had come to the DPRK willingly, or people abducted specifically for that purpose."

"Kim Jong-il kidnapped people to translate movie dialog?"

"Kim Jong-il kidnapped people for all kinds of reasons," Mr. Park says. "So did Kim Il-sung. And Kim Jong-un—"

I put up a hand. "Did you hear that?"

"Hear what?"

It sounded like a cough, a couple rows over. "Hello?" I call out. "Is somebody else in here?"

No answer.

"Would you like to hear a story about the time Kim Jong-il kidnapped a film director from the Republic of Korea?" Mr. Park asks me.

"Sure. But not here. Take me somewhere else."

"Where would you like to go?"

"Someplace indoors," I say, "but smaller than this, with a corner where I can sit and watch the whole room while you're talking."

G.G.R. — "Gonna get raped," a popular video-gamers' utterance meaning either "We are about to inflict a humiliating defeat on those other players" or "Those other players are about to inflict a humiliating defeat on us." The abbreviation, originally coined to bypass speech filters, has since become common even in gaming environments where explicit, humorous references to sexual assault are considered perfectly acceptable. In environments with very strict speech codes, on the other hand, even the abbreviation is bowdlerized, becoming G.G.P., "Gonna get pwned," or G.G.F., "Gonna get fucked" (which, despite containing an obscenity, is viewed by many censors as inoffensive).

—*The New Devil's Dictionary*

I n Alpha Sector near the galactic core, the big boys are getting ready to rumble.

Today's MMORPG is *The Fermi Paradox*, a game of interstellar conquest. There are no character classes, just money, testosterone, and big things blowing up in space. The game's economy runs on space ducats, which can be acquired through honest trade, piracy, or—the most popular option—via direct purchase from Fermigames LLC. The player base skews libertarian, but the ingame ethos is more corporate than rugged individualist: The ship control AI is notoriously lame, so even if you're rich enough to buy your own battlefleet, you still need friends, or lackeys, to help crew it. Players form guilds with hundreds or even thousands of members, pool their resources, and try to take over the galaxy.

There is no official code of conduct. Backstabbing and betrayal are common; even certain forms of cheating are allowed. So are profanity and hate speech: If you want to name your guild The Alte Kämpfer, or Bitch, Make Me a Sandwich, customer service won't hassle you about it. Consequently, *The Fermi Paradox* is also popular with bigots and people who like to kick the shit out of bigots.

In one famous incident, an Israeli guild, Rainbow Pride, got into a spat with a Russian skinhead group, Jews to the Ovens. The Rainbows bought one of their members an Aeroflot ticket and sent him to the St. Petersburg housing projects where J.T.T.O.'s members all lived. Right before Rainbow Pride launched its in-game assault, the projects lost internet access; by the time it was restored, J.T.T.O.'s space fleet had been wiped out and its territory was being divvied up between the Rainbows and the Ukrainian guild Putin Fucked My Cat. Though the victory was sweet, the real winner was Fermigames, which saw a huge uptick in ducat sales as other space Nazis lined up to avenge their fallen comrades.

Today's title fight involves a different sort of rivalry. In one corner is the Los Angeles–based G.R.U. Syndicate, whose leader and chief financial backer is one of Tempest's founders. In the other is a South Korean guild whose members all work for the video-game company GangnamSoft; their guild name is a play on words whose meaning in English would be something like "Penis Swarm." These are the two most powerful guilds in the galaxy right now, which by the logic of *The Fermi Paradox* means genocidal war is inevitable.

Three hours ago, a friend of mine in G.R.U. emailed to tell me that the Mother of All Battles is about to kick off. I messaged Mr. Jones and asked if he'd like to watch two superpowers duke it out in cyberspace.

We arrive just before the shooting starts. The battleground is Penis Swarm's home system. Their capital planet is protected by a ring of heavily armed space stations and three dozen star cruisers. It's an impressive amount of firepower, but to an experienced eye it's obvious that the cruisers are operating on autopilot, which means that they will suck in combat.

We lurk in a conveniently located asteroid field. Our ship is a Wasp, a small vessel with a powerful cloaking device. Ray, at the helm, keeps one eye on the proximity alarm. In addition to dodging asteroids, we need to watch out for the other ships that are sure to be hiding here; the cloaking device will keep them from shooting at us, but the Wasp's lack of shields means that even a minor collision could be fatal.

Anja is in charge of the Wasp's spy drones. Her avatar occupies a chair next to Ray's, but her POV is outside, zooming untethered through space, peeking around the far sides of the rocks. From the sound of her voice as she describes what she sees, she is loving every second of it.

Jolene is back in the engine compartment. The antimatter drive is running smoothly and nothing else on the ship needs fixing, so she's using the downtime to catch up on some work from her real-life job.

Mr. Jones sits in the captain's chair. I stand beside him, playing Spock to his Kirk, or maybe Vader to his Emperor Palpatine. I explain the fundamentals of the game and lay out what is about to happen. I make a point of referring to the Swarm as Korean, not

South Korean, and stress that it is the American G.R.U. who are the aggressors here.

The attack begins on schedule. "Warp signatures," Ray announces. "A *lot* of warp signatures." He brings up a long-range view on the main screen and we watch the American battle fleet drop out of hyperspace.

Because space ducats can be bought for cash, it's possible to put a real-world value on the game's spaceships. Dreadnought battle-cruisers, the largest standard class of attack ship, run about four hundred dollars U.S. apiece; the Americans have brought at least fifty of them. But the serious money is in bespoke ships, custom vessels whose size and firepower is limited only by the purchaser's budget. A pair of enormous warp signatures heralds the arrival of two bronze-tinted Death Stars whose coloring is no doubt intended as a visual pun: Big Brass Balls. You'd need to look at the schematics to calculate an exact price tag, but these are easily worth ten thousand bucks. Each. Add in the star cruisers, destroyers, frigates, carriers, fighter and bomber wings, and support ships, and the Americans are fielding at least eighty grand's worth of virtual hardware—much of which is likely to be destroyed in the next hour.

But first the South Koreans will take a beating. The defense fleet reacts immediately to the incursion, but the response is uncoordinated, with each star cruiser pursuing a different target. The Americans keep their ships in formation and concentrate their fire. One by one, the Korean star cruisers lose their shields and explode.

Mr. Jones is appalled. "Who is in charge of that fleet?" he says. "A blind man?"

"No one." The Americans have timed their attack very deliberately, I explain: It's morning in Los Angeles, which means it is the middle of the night in Korea. For employees of GSoft, it is also crunch time, as the company puts the finishing touches on its own MMORPG, due to roll out next month. The Americans are hoping that the Swarm are all either asleep or too busy to respond.

"A real fight would be more interesting," Mr. Jones suggests. "What can we do to help the Koreans?"

"Nothing. Those star cruisers aren't going to take orders from us."

"What if we fight alongside them? Show them—"

"Wouldn't help. Anyway, we don't have any weapons."

"What?"

"This ship is designed for spec ops. Espionage."

"You should have gotten us one of those!" Mr. Jones says, jabbing a finger at the Big Brass Balls.

"If you want one of those, you're going to need to talk to Smith about sending me more money . . . But listen, this ship isn't useless. We will get a chance to do something. You just need to be patient."

"I do not enjoy being patient."

More than half the Korean star cruisers have been destroyed. The Americans have lost a frigate and suffered minor damage to one of their carriers. Soon they will begin to attack the space stations. The stations have much tougher shields and will take longer to kill, but without human controllers to issue them orders, their target selection will be as haphazard as the cruisers'.

"We must contact the Korean high command," Mr. Jones says. "Warn them about what is happening here, before it is too late."

"No need. The cavalry is already on its way. Look."

More warp signatures are blooming on the tactical display. In a matter of seconds, the amount of money in play more than doubles:

The South Koreans have brought their own fleet of Dreadnoughts and their own custom Death Stars. Bigger ones.

As the reinforcements come out of hyperspace, the surviving star cruisers abruptly smarten up. They fire a combined salvo at the damaged American carrier, turning it to plasma, then fall back towards the space stations, which begin launching waves of long-range nukes from hidden missile batteries.

A caution light flashes on Ray's control panel. "The Koreans just turned on a bunch of warp inhibitors. The whole system is locked down."

"Warp inhibitors prevent ships from using their hyperdrives to escape the battle," I explain to Mr. Jones.

He brightens instantly at the news. "This is a trap?"

"Of course it's a trap. I'm not the only one with a friend in the G.R.U. Syndicate. The Koreans knew this attack was coming."

"But the Americans must have spies as well," says Mr. Jones.

"Oh, sure. And yes, they've probably got a counter trap lined up. That's the game."

The Koreans aren't done springing surprises: As the two fleets begin slugging it out in earnest, one of the American Dreadnoughts turns traitor. It blows up another carrier, then launches a kamikaze attack on one of the Big Brass Balls.

"A mutiny?" Mr. Jones says.

"More likely a cyberattack," I say. "They're generally careful to let only the most trusted guild members crew the big ships. Although with a fleet this size, it's possible that a sleeper agent or two got through. Look there." One of the Korean space stations has just dropped its shields; its last missile salvo pulls a one-eighty and slams into the station's command deck, crippling it.

"I wish to participate in this battle," Mr. Jones says. "What can we—"

The proximity alarm sounds. Ray kicks in the subspace thrusters and boosts us hard to starboard. A small ship resembling a silver teardrop flits past with just meters to spare. The alarm keeps wailing and Ray dodges again as two more teardrops race by.

"Gleaners," I explain to Mr. Jones. "When the big ships blow up, they're like piñatas—they spew space ducats equal to a tenth of their construction cost. Any ship with a tractor beam can collect the money. The Gleaners go in while the battle is under way and try to steal as much loose change as they can."

"They are not allied with either side?"

"No, they're opportunists with good spy networks. They go wherever they hear a fight is about to break out."

"I hope this is not what you intend us to do," Mr. Jones says. "I have no interest in scavenging."

"I had something a little more ambitious in mind. Gleaners are optimized for speed, but they're short-range vessels, with no hyperdrive. There's got to be a base ship back in the rocks here somewhere, that they launched from. We can use the Wasp to capture that, then threaten to strand the Gleaners unless they give us their ducats."

Mr. Jones does not seem enthused about this plan, either. "How can we capture a ship if we have no weapons?"

"The Wasp has a device called a cybertronic ovipositor that lets us hack into a larger ship's computer and seize control of it."

"We can perform a cyberattack? Why didn't you say so? We should capture an American ship!"

"We could try that," I say. "But you understand, even if we capture a Dreadnought—which is a very difficult thing to do—we won't last long against the rest of that fleet. If we take the Gleaner base ship, we have a good chance of making it out of here with enough money to—"

"I don't want the stupid base ship!" Mr. Jones says. He points at the Big Brass Balls again. "I want one of those!"

"That would be extremely difficult." An understatement. "To even attempt it, we'd need to land on the hull without being detected, which—"

"Hey guys!" Anja breaks in. "I think I found something! Ray, bring up the POV from drone number four."

The main screen switches from the view of the battle to the feed from the drone's camera.

"Huh," Ray says.

"'Huh,' what?" says Mr. Jones. "There is nothing there."

"Exactly," I say. The drone is hovering in what should be one of the densest parts of the asteroid field. But a void has developed among the asteroids—a long, narrow, open space. And it's moving. Picture an invisible submarine nosing its way through a rock slurry: That's what it looks like.

A *gigantic* invisible submarine.

"It's got to be five hundred meters long," Ray says. "With a top-end cloaking device, and a shitload of tractor beams to move the asteroids out of the way. I don't even want to know how much that cost."

"It is a ship?" Mr. Jones says. "Whose?"

Ray consults the tactical display. "If it stays on its current heading, it'll exit the asteroid field in perfect position to attack the Koreans."

"American, then," says Mr. Jones. "Good." He looks at me: You know what to do.

"Ray."

"Already on the way," Ray says.

As we maneuver towards the void, I call back to the engine room and tell Jolene we're going to need her to change the laws of physics. The target ship is certain to have a deflector shield, which would ordinarily have to be blasted away before we could get close to it. But the Wasp is equipped with a Planck-Heisenberg oscillator that allows it to pass through intact force fields.

"It's going to be tricky, though," Jolene cautions. "The shield will shimmer when we make contact with it. If they've got guys on lookout—and they should—there's a good chance they'll notice."

"You will ensure that does not happen," Mr. Jones says. "I want this ship."

We round a final asteroid and arrive at the gap in the rocks. Ray reverses thrust to avoid hitting the force field prematurely.

"There's definitely something there," Jolene says. "I'm getting a really strong shield reading . . . It's going to shimmer, for sure. It might even spark."

"Maybe there's a blind spot," Ray suggests. "If we come in from behind . . ."

A Gleaner darts out of the rocks on the far side of the void. Oblivious to the danger, the pilot accelerates and slams full speed into an invisible wall. The Gleaner explodes. A pattern of ripples forms in space, flowing outward from the blast, and for a moment we can see the contour of the force field.

It gives me an idea.

"Anja," I say, "can you spot any more Gleaners headed this way?"

"Plenty. They're all coming from the same direction, too. The base ship must be close."

"Never mind the base ship. Here's what we're going to do . . ."

Fifteen seconds later, a trio of Gleaners enter the void. All three crash into the force field and die. We use this as cover, the shimmer and spark of our passage through the shield obscured by the ripples.

Once past the deflector shield, we are inside the radius of the cloak as well. We can see the ship. It's dark, massive, and sharp-angled, like a big black skyscraper laid on its side. The hull bristles with point-defense lasers; we hover amidships waiting to see if they will vaporize us. But the spotters must have missed our entry, and our own cloak remains intact. They don't know we're here.

Ray swings us around. The big ship's command bridge is located near the stern. We read the name painted above the bridge windows: *U.S.S. PAINAL.* "'Painful anal,'" I translate, for Mr. Jones's benefit. "It's American, all right."

"Good," says Mr. Jones. "Now what?"

"We look for the external AI nexus port." A white circle flashes on the hull of the big ship, directly beneath the bridge. "There."

"That is where we plug in the . . . ovipositor?"

"Yes."

"And then we take control?"

"Hopefully," I say. "But first we have to beat a trivia challenge."

"A what?"

The beta version of *The Fermi Paradox* simulated computer hacking by making players solve a series of timed Sudoku puzzles. According to the handful of people who got to play it, this was a fun mini-game, and one that actually made you feel like you were breaking through walls of encryption. From a development perspective, it had another advantage: Sudoku are language-independent and can be procedurally generated, so they don't require paid translators or puzzle-makers. Unfortunately, this strength was also a weakness. Within days of the beta's debut, someone had created a mod called Spacecracker that could solve the most difficult Sudoku in microseconds, and would even plug in the numbers for you.

Fermigames could have tried to ban the use of Spacecracker, but besides being tough to enforce, such a ban would have gone against the spirit of the game. Hackers *should* be allowed to use exploits. The trick was figuring out a way to let them cheat while still posing a meaningful challenge.

One of Fermigames' lead programmers suggested switching from Sudoku to *Trivial Pursuit*. He crafted a backstory about how ship AIs train to pass their Turing tests by studying the lore of Old Earth; this makes them vulnerable to intruders who exhibit mastery of obscure information. To save on implementation costs, the development team came up with a plan to recruit players to write the trivia questions, paying them in space ducats.

So now, to commit grand-theft spaceship, you must demonstrate your nerd cred. As our Wasp docks with the AI port, a five-minute clock appears on the main screen. To determine how many questions we must answer, the game server compares the two ships' cyberwarfare ratings. I am grateful that for once I resisted the urge to be stingy; the Wasp's ovipositor is Neuromancer grade, the best and most expensive option. If we were going after a star cruiser or even a Dreadnought, I'd be feeling pretty good about our chances. But a bespoke ship is another matter; there's no limit to the amount of security they can buy, and I've never heard of one being successfully hijacked.

The target number appears on screen. At first I read it as two hundred and assume we are out of luck, but then I realize there's only one zero after the two.

"Fuck me," Ray says, as surprised as I am.

"What?" says Mr. Jones. "What is wrong?"

"Nothing." Is it sabotage, I wonder, or did someone on the G.R.U.'s shipbuilding committee decide to cut corners on cybersecurity? The latter explanation seems crazy given the amount of money at stake, but on the other hand, if you expect everyone to *assume* your ship is invulnerable to hacking, why waste ducats actually making it invulnerable? "This is doable."

"I don't know," Ray says. "Twenty questions in five minutes is still a stretch."

"How many wrong answers do we get?" Mr. Jones asks.

"None," I tell him. "The first mistake locks us out of the system and fries our life support. But it's OK," I add, staying positive. "The questions are multiple choice, and we'll have help."

I conjure a control pad beneath my right hand. "I'm going to be quizmaster," I say, addressing the whole crew now. "If I know an answer is right, I'll just go ahead and send it. If I'm not sure, I'll delay as many seconds as I can to give the rest of you a chance to jump in. If I say your name, I want you to screenshot the question and go research it—quickly!—while the rest of us skip ahead. Stay focused and try not to panic. We can do this. Everybody ready?"

Everyone says yes. I signal the game server. The lighting inside the Wasp goes red and a sinister voice issues from the loudspeakers. Male and vaguely British, it is meant to evoke the platonic ideal of an evil computer without violating any Hollywood trademarks. "Foolish users!" it snarls. "You think you can match wits with me? No mortal being—"

I ping the server again to skip the rest of this intro. The game clock starts, and the first of our twenty questions appears on the main screen:

WHICH EPISODE OF **AQUA TEEN HUNGER FORCE**
INTRODUCED THE CHARACTERS OF IGNIGNOKT
AND ERR?

A. "MOON MASTER"
B. "REVENGE OF THE MOONINITES"
C. "MAYHEM OF THE MOONINITES"
D. "MOONAJUANA"

The correct answer, C, is highlighted. The highlighting is courtesy of the latest version of Spacecracker, which cheats by asking Googlebot. Unlike brute-forcing a Sudoku puzzle, however, this form of cheating can be unreliable. Sometimes Googlebot answers incorrectly; sometimes Spacecracker misunderstands what Googlebot is telling it. The nerds who make up the questions delight in finding ways to confuse the bots' algorithms.

For example, question two:

WHICH OF THE FOLLOWING MAN-MADE OBJECTS IS
VISIBLE FROM EARTH ORBIT?

A. THE GREAT WALL OF CHINA
B. GRANT'S TOMB
C. THE SUEZ CANAL
D. ALL OF THE ABOVE

The correct answer, as a moment's calm reflection will tell you, is D. But Spacecracker picks A. There is a popular myth that the Great Wall is the only artificial structure large enough to be seen from space; the myth has been debunked many times, and these debunkings have themselves become part of Googlebot's knowledge base. A human questioner is smart enough to grasp the distinction between "A lot of people believe X," and "A lot of people believe X, *which is false*," but Spacecracker, querying Googlebot in shorthand, misses it. Being able to spot trick questions like this one is key to successful time management. You need to know when you can trust Spacecracker and when to pause and think.

You also need to know when and how to delegate to your teammates. In general you must answer the questions in order, but the rules allow you two set-asides: That is, you can skip up to two questions, but must then go back and answer them before you can skip any more. This allows you to hand off questions that require extra research. Jolene has told me stories of how she used to play vintage *Dungeons & Dragons* with her grandparents when she was little, so I have her double-check Spacecracker's answer to a question about the first-edition *Monster Manual*. I give Anja a question about soccer. Ray saves me from a rookie mistake by reminding me that it was Mary, not Jesus, who was immaculately conceived. Even Mr. Jones contributes: When I balk at what feels like another trick question (THE ASIAN GIANT HORNET IS NATIVE TO WHAT CONTINENT?), he assures me that the obvious answer is also the right one.

Another key to success is a favorable metagame. Because the trivia questions are submitted by players, guilds seeking an edge in cyberwarfare can try to flood the question pool. Four years ago, when I first played *The Fermi Paradox*, the galaxy was dominated by guilds from mainland China; the trivia game in those days referenced an alternate nerd universe, one whose in-jokes and obsessions were, despite my ancestry, foreign to me. Today, with the Americans and South Koreans in ascendancy, it's a much easier challenge—and ironically, it seems like it's the Americans who've been working hardest to stack the deck. We get two questions in a row about *Buffy the Vampire Slayer*; I don't even need Spacecracker for those.

With a minute remaining on the game clock, we are down to three questions. Not only does it look like we'll be able to pull this off, I may even have time to engage in a bit of subterfuge.

Spacecracker routes the questions through the quizmaster's computer before passing the data on to the other players. This allows for some interesting shenanigans if you know how the program works. By abusing the skip function, I can peek ahead and see what the next question in line is. I do this, and see that the penultimate question is one that Spacecracker can be trusted to answer correctly.

So when we come to it, I set that question aside and go immediately to the final one. This turns out to be another softball: WHAT FIRST-PERSON SHOOTER WAS THE FIRST TO ALLOW TARGETED HEADSHOTS? (The *Quake Team Fortress* mod, duh.)

Now all that remains is the set-aside question:

IN KLINGON-LANGUAGE SCRABBLE SETS, THE 𝓨 TILE IS WORTH HOW MANY POINTS?

A. 7

B. 8

C. 9

D. 10

The correct answer is B. The answer key resides on Fermigames' server, so I cannot change this. But what I can do, by messing with the data that Spacecracker forwards to my teammates, is substitute a different question of my own devising:

WHICH GROUP OF NUMBERS ALL REFER TO THE SAME YEAR?

A. 1982, 1402, 101
B. 1982, 1402, 71
C. 1982, 1372, 71
D. 1982, 1372, 101

The correct answer is still B. The year 1982 in the Gregorian calendar overlaps 1402 in the Islamic calendar. It also corresponds to year 71 in the North Korean Juche calendar, which counts from the birth year of Kim Il-sung. And because AD 1982/Juche 71 is the official birth year of Kim Jong-un, it should be especially memorable to anyone raised in the DPRK.

B is the right answer, but I instruct Spacecracker to highlight C instead.

Eighteen seconds remain on the clock as my doctored question appears on the main screen.

"Wait." This from Jolene, who is following a script she and I worked out in advance. "It's not C, it's A or B."

"Which, A or B?"

"Not sure," Jolene says, speaking very quickly. "But my cousin's Muslim, and the 1980s are the 1400s in their calendar."

Ten seconds.

"What about the last number?" I say. "Anyone?"

I can hear both Ray and Anja whispering urgently to their own infobots. Mr. Jones is stone silent. I don't look at him.

Five seconds. "I'm going to guess A," I say.

Mr. Jones comes alive: "No. Pick B."

Three seconds. "Are you sure?"

"B! Pick B!"

With one second left—and just as Ray looks up shouting, "B! B!"—I hit send.

The clock stops. The screen goes blank.

"Well done, human," the voice of the big ship's AI says. "I submit to your superior knowledge."

The interior lighting returns to normal. Now the Wasp's computer speaks to us; it is female, a cross between GLaDOS and Mother from the *Alien* franchise: "Control acquired. Purging target ship atmosphere."

The main screen switches to a forward view of the *Painal*'s hull. All along the ship's length, hatches fly open, venting tall columns of white vapor speckled with the flailing bodies of crew members. As we watch them die, the Wasp's helm expands to make room for a new suite of fire controls. Ray goggles at the assortment of weapons now under his command: "Antimatter cannon. Chained plasma disruptors. Graviton vortex bombs. Nukes, nukes, and more nukes . . . Jesus Christ, we're a superpower."

The big ship is still moving forward. Its tractor beams, operating automatically, sweep aside the last few asteroids at the edge of the field. Beyond is open space, and the exposed flank of the Korean fleet.

Anja, promoted automatically from dronemaster to communications officer, raises a hand to her ear. "I'm getting an encrypted message from the commander of the American fleet," she says.

"He's asking where we are. He wants us to start our attack as soon as possible."

"Tell the American commander not to worry," Mr. Jones replies. The corners of his mouth twitch up into a smile. "Tell him the *Painal* will begin momentarily."

opiate of the masses — That which acts to preserve the status quo by short-circuiting demand for political or social change. In Marx's original formulation, the opiate of the masses was religion. Aldous Huxley, in his dystopian novel *Brave New World*, imagined it as a literal drug, soma. More recent candidates include Twitter, Monday Night Football, legalized marijuana, and virtual reality.

—The New Devil's Dictionary

t's an imaginative theory," my mother says. Today the view out her office window is of a sandy atoll surrounding a crystal blue lagoon. But Mom sounds tired, and CNN is reporting that yesterday's plane crash at Indira Gandhi Airport was the work of cyberterrorists, so I'm guessing she's in Delhi.

"Imaginative," I say. "That bad?"

"Sorry. I meant 'creative.'"

When I was little I used to play at being one of my mother's intelligence assets. I'd collect portentous bits of info off the internet and have her debrief me over dinner. We developed our own private intel rating system. Those rare items my mother deemed "interesting" were genuinely useful to her. At the other end of the scale, "imaginative" referred to tinfoil-hat notions that only a child or a very naive adult would buy into, like the time I became convinced, based on a bad Google translation, that China had staged a secret Mars landing. "Creative" was the middle ground, home of wild theories that might be true, but which Mom needed more evidence or a much better argument to take seriously.

"Tell me what you don't like about the idea," I say.

"Well, to begin with, there's the question Jolene asked you: *Why* would a powerful North Korean want to study online role-playing games? 'Game theory' isn't a real answer. More like a placeholder for one."

"I've been thinking more about that," I tell her. "Do you know the story of the Shin Sang-ok kidnapping?"

"I pulled up the CIA's file on it after I heard about your conversation with Mr. Park," she says. "But why don't you go ahead and give me your version."

"OK." I know she's humoring me, but it makes me happy when she does that, just like it did when I was a kid. "So this was back in 1978, when Kim Il-sung, the original Great Leader, was still running the country, and his son, Kim Jong-il, was head of the state film industry. Film was an important propaganda tool for the regime, and it was also a way for Jong-il to suck up to his dad and ensure his place as successor; but beyond that, he just really loved movies. He spent millions assembling a bootleg collection from all over the world.

"One of his other hobbies was kidnapping. It's like he was role-playing the villain from a James Bond film: He abducted foreigners to serve as teachers for his spies, to train them how to blend in to other cultures. His commandos would grab random people off beaches, drug them and put them on a boat. Or if he wanted someone specific, he might trick them with a job offer, get them on a plane to Pyongyang and take their passport away, tell the world they'd defected.

"So one day Kim Jong-il decided to import some filmmaking talent. North Korean movies weren't very good, and while the home crowd was a captive audience, Kim wanted to compete internationally. He told his people to find him a good director, and the name they came up with was Shin Sang-ok.

"He was famous. In the fifties and sixties, Shin and his wife, Choi Eun-hee, had been like the first couple of South Korean cinema. But by the seventies, Shin's star was falling. The business was in trouble, and the marriage broke up—"

"Choi left him," Mom interjects, "after she found out he'd fathered a son with a starlet half her age."

I pause. Mr. Park's recitation didn't include that detail.

"Sorry," Mom says. "Continue."

"Yeah, OK . . . So Shin's career was on the rocks, and then he got in trouble with the government. South Korea in those days was better than the North, but it was still basically a military dictatorship, and Shin pissed off the state censors. They took away his filmmaking license. By the time the North Koreans came after him, he was close to bankruptcy.

"They decided to use his ex-wife as a lure. They got Choi Eun-hee to Hong Kong with a phony job offer and kidnapped her, and when Shin came looking for her, they grabbed him too. Once they got him back to Pyongyang, they tried treating him nicely at first. But Shin wouldn't play ball—he kept trying to escape—so Kim Jong-il had him thrown into prison. They put him in a special kind of solitary where you spend sixteen hours a day sitting cross-legged on the floor, and anytime you move or make a sound, the guards beat you. Three and a half years of that, and then Kim Jong-il gave

Shin a choice: Live in a nice house with Choi Eun-hee and make movies on an unlimited budget, or go back to solitary for good.

"Shin took the film job. For the next three years he was Kim Jong-il's pet director, and Choi was his leading lady. The movies they made were better than anything North Korea had ever done before. Some of them won prizes. That's how Shin and Choi finally got away: Kim was so happy that he let them travel abroad to attend film festivals. They slipped their guards in Vienna and escaped."

"Did you watch any of the films?" Mom asks. "You know they're all on YouTube now."

I nod. "I checked out one of them."

"Let me guess. *Pulgasari*?"

"Of course *Pulgasari*." The last film Shin directed before escaping Kim's clutches, *Pulgasari* is the DPRK's answer to the *Godzilla* franchise: A giant monster movie steeped in the ideology of North Korean socialism. Not one of the award winners. "Did you see it?"

"I fell asleep before the end," Mom confesses. "So, getting back to Mr. Jones: Your theory is that he's a Kim Jong-il figure who's looking to make a mark in video games rather than film?"

"Not exactly. My main point with the Shin Sang-ok story is that there's precedent for North Koreans going to extremes to acquire professional expertise. As for Mr. Jones wanting to make a mark, well, who knows? I mean, people are snobby about it, but video games *are* an art form, and you can get recognition for making good ones. Would a dictator be as excited about winning E3's Game of the Year as he would about the Palme d'Or? Maybe, maybe not."

"Well, I hate to sound snobby, but put me in the 'maybe not' column."

"OK, fine. I think there's another possibility, one that actually makes more sense. Something else that came up in my conversation with Mr. Park is how much the propaganda war has changed in the last few decades. In the 1970s, the only way a typical North Korean could see a foreign film is if someone smuggled in a bunch of heavy film canisters. These days, you can carry an entire film library in your pocket. It's still a quick trip to a labor camp if you get caught, but people are willing to take the risk to get a glimpse of the outside world. They're watching South Korean soap operas, and Hollywood blockbusters, and Bollywood musicals—not the most accurate sources of info, sure, but enough to let them know how much their own government lies to them. North Korea *isn't* the most prosperous country on earth. South Korea isn't a hellhole. And America—well, they still hate us, which isn't entirely unreasonable given how close we've come to nuking them out of existence, but they know we aren't *just* bloodthirsty imperialists.

"And so this has created a huge problem for the regime, right? People—especially young people—are getting more and more restless. So now what? The government can try cracking down even harder than it already does, but they can't send *everybody* to a labor camp . . . That's why they had to make that deal with China a few years back, where they agreed to limit the size of their nuclear arsenal. They needed more trade dollars, and they needed their foreign aid turned back on, so they could bribe their people with more stuff. Only it's not enough. The younger generation is still pissed off."

"And video games help with this how, exactly?"

"Do you remember Jimmy del Toro?" A friend of mine from Zero Day.

Mom nods. "Lieutenant Commander del Toro's son. The one with diabetes."

"Yeah, and sometimes when Jimmy got caught up in a game, he'd forget to take his insulin. Or he'd remember his insulin but forget to eat. Which was a problem in Jimmy's case, but what if you lived in a country that didn't always have enough food or medicine to go around? What if when you did have enough to eat, that just gave you more energy to think about all the other things you didn't have? In a situation like that, an MMORPG could be a great distraction, not to mention a way of channeling your anger. Instead of rising up and smashing the state, you'd go into the virtual world and kill monsters."

"*Pulgasari: The Home Game?*"

"Maybe," I say. "Or maybe something less metaphorical. Like, you could do a military-themed game, where the players are North Korean soldiers conquering the South for Kim Jong-un, and the bad guys are American and Japanese troops. Or you could do a covert ops game, where players gain levels for committing sabotage and assassinations in enemy countries. And to sweeten the pot, there could be a leaderboard competition with real-world prizes, like extra rations or points towards improving your citizenship ranking."

"I can see you've been giving this a lot of thought," Mom says. "What about the logistics problem? Where does the regime get the money to supply millions of citizens with computers and VR rigs?"

"They don't need VR rigs. Fully immersive VR is nice, but you can do video games without it. As for the computers, North Koreans have millions of those already. And a network."

"Cell phones?"

"Smartphones. The wifi network's only third-generation, so there will be bandwidth issues, but it's not like they've got to compete with *Call to Wizardry*. For an audience that's never played an MMORPG before, even a 2D game could be incredibly addictive."

"True." Mom smiles. "I remember."

"So what do you think?"

She shrugs noncommittally. "Like I said, it's creative."

"What would it take to make it interesting?"

"Some actual proof connecting Mr. Jones to North Korea, for a start."

"He knows about the Juche calendar," I say. I tell her about the trivia challenge.

"Clever," Mom says when I've finished. "But are you certain he knew B was the right answer? Or could he have just been playing a hunch?"

"Well . . . He sounded like he knew. Like he was sure."

"But you didn't ask why. He didn't explain his reasoning."

"There wasn't time. We were down to the last few seconds on the clock. And then once we took the ship, we were busy slaughtering Americans. I suppose I could have brought it up again later, but the whole point was to get him to give himself away without realizing he'd done it . . ."

"No, I get that. It sounds like you handled it as well as you could," Mom says. Once again, I get the sense that she's humoring me, but this time it doesn't feel so good.

"What about the money?" I ask. "Have you had any luck tracing the owner of the bank account?"

"Not yet. But I've put some new assets in place, so we should have a better picture if and when you get your next payment. That's due in two days?"

"Give or take. I have a feeling Smith may push the deadline, just to yank my chain a little. But I should have it by the end of this week."

"There's also your mysterious Chinese woman, assuming she

ever gets back in touch. If she does, you'll want to push her hard about the money she promised you."

"Don't worry about that," I say.

"I'm not worried. But I don't want you to get your hopes up. I think there's a good chance that there won't be any more money coming—and that once that's clear, Smith and Mr. Jones will just disappear."

"You really think this could still turn out to be a prank?"

"I think that's more likely than Mr. Jones turning out to be Kim Jong-un."

"Well, I wasn't thinking it was *him*, necessarily," I say. "Just someone in his inner circle—a family member, or even just an aide looking to score points with the boss."

"Has it occurred to you that if you are right, that might not be a good thing? Given what the Kims are capable of?"

"Are you asking whether I'm afraid of being kidnapped?" It's my turn to shrug. "I guess I would be, if I were doing this on my own. But I've got you watching my back. I bet if Shin Sang-ok had had a mom like you, they wouldn't have gotten him, either."

"Thanks for the vote of confidence."

"It really would be something, wouldn't it? If Mr. Jones *were* Kim Jong-un?"

"Yes," my mother says, "that would be something."

"It would be valuable to you, right? Useful?"

"A secret channel to the heart of the North Korean government? Oh yeah, we could find a use for that. Of course," she adds, turning mischievous, "we'd also have to confiscate the money."

"What? Why?"

"China may have signed an accord with the DPRK, but we've

still got a trade ban in place. You can't legally profit from business with North Koreans."

"Can't you get me some kind of waiver for that?"

"I suppose I could," Mom says, "but then I worry you'd be wracked with guilt when you remember this is blood money the Kims stole from their own people."

"Uh-huh," I say, unimpressed. "Tell me something, Mom: After you confiscate the money, are you planning to give it back to the people? Because if you are, I guess I can't object. But if you're not, I don't see how having *two* governments steal it adds up to justice."

"The moral logic is complicated," my mother acknowledges. "Don't worry, we'll find some way to reward you. Maybe you could pitch a declassified version of the story as a screenplay to your dad." She makes a framing gesture with her hands. "'It's like *Ready Player One* meets *The King and I*.'"

"Funny, Mom. Hilarious." She certainly seems to think so, though as always when the subject of my father comes up, I can sense other emotions under the surface, masked but there.

And then Mom just looks tired. She glances at the watch on her avatar's wrist.

"Time to get back to work," she says. "Be careful, John."

theory of mind — A controversial hypothesis that other human beings are sentient and possess thoughts, emotions, beliefs, and goals that are different from our own. In its most radical form, the theory posits that while these differences may make other people's behavior hard to understand, the question "What the fuck are you thinking?" has a real answer which reason and empathy can discover.

—*The New Devil's Dictionary*

My father didn't believe that infidelity was wrong.

This doesn't excuse his betrayal of my mother, but it does help to explain it. It's not an easy thing to wrap my brain around: Though I have my share of kinks, they all involve one partner at a time, so to really get a sense of where Dad's head was at, I need to resort to analogy. Rachel Nakamura is my go-to for that.

She was the first girl I ever had a crush on. Rachel and her mother worked in the PX at Fort Meade, where Zero Day's stateside HQ was located. Jimmy del Toro's older sister, Sarah, had a part-time job in the PX too, and Sarah was friends with Rachel, which is how I came to know her.

The Nakamuras were devout Christians. The conservative sect

they belonged to had some peculiar taboos—or rather, taboos that seemed peculiar if you hadn't been indoctrinated with them. The weirdest one, from a Zero Day perspective, was that they didn't use virtual reality, which they apparently regarded as a high-tech species of graven-image worship. They weren't Luddites: Rachel was rarely without her iPad. But she used it mostly for reading, limiting her web surfing to what was required for schoolwork. She didn't play video games, not even *Bejeweled*.

And she didn't date. This didn't stop a long string of boys and girls from asking her out anyway: Rachel was beautiful, and there was the added psychological lure of That Which You Know You Cannot Have. But she always said no.

I was determined to take my shot like everybody else. The fact that I was nine years old, while Rachel was seventeen, meant my odds were longer than most, but I was hoping the half-Asian thing might give me a leg up.

That was the same month that Paramount Studios released *Amok Time*—the first, and still only, R-rated *Star Trek* picture. It was a trending topic in nerdland; my underage friends and I had all watched the pirated 2D version online, and were now scheming ways to go see it in 3D IMAX. When I heard Rachel Nakamura was a science-fiction fan (according to Sarah del Toro, she'd been reading C. S. Lewis's Space Trilogy), I decided to kill two obsessions with one stone.

I went to the PX on a day when Rachel was working checkout, grabbed a copy of the latest *eSports Illustrated*, and got in her line. While she rang up the magazine I mentioned—trying to be smooth and casual about it—that I was planning to go see *Amok Time*. I said I'd heard that she might be a *Star Trek* fan too, and asked if she'd maybe like to see the movie with me. I added that I would be happy to pay her way, if—very smooth, here—she wouldn't mind handling the actual purchase of the tickets.

I was hopeful but not delusional; I knew that Rachel would probably say no and wouldn't have been surprised if she'd humiliated me in the bargain. But her reply still stunned me.

"Thank you for asking, John," she said. "But I don't go to R-rated movies."

On its face, this was less weird than the no-VR thing, but it shocked me more, I guess because it ran so contrary to my own impulses. To be free to see any movie you liked without adult supervision or the hassle of illegal downloading, and yet to *choose* not to: What kind of crazy theology was that?

I stood there with my mouth open, trying desperately to think of another movie, something PG- or even G-rated, to ask her to instead. But my mind drew a blank, and then the staff sergeant waiting behind me in line put her hand on my shoulder and said, "You've been shot down, son. Accept it and move on."

A few weeks later, Mom and I deployed overseas. I never saw Rachel Nakamura again. But I still thought of her from time to time, and later, when I was trying to understand my father, I immortalized her in a thought experiment.

The experiment goes like this: Imagine you're in love with a smart and beautiful girl. She loves you too, and she's willing to spend her life with you, but only if you agree to convert and follow the dictates of her religion, the first of which is, Thou Shalt Not Watch R-Rated Movies. So, no more *Matrix* trilogy for you; no more *The Good, the Bad and the Ugly*; no more *Shakespeare in Love* (yes, it's an R). No more *Amok Time*.

Oh, and no more hamburgers, either. She's a vegetarian.

That's the deal, take it or leave it.

Imagine that you take it.

Now imagine you're traveling, alone, on business. You stop for the night at a hotel a thousand miles from home. Though you didn't ask for it, your room comes with a premium cable TV package. In the elevator you overhear another guest mentioning that *Strange Days*—one of your favorite films—is playing on HBO tonight. Further investigation reveals that *Near Dark* and *The Hurt Locker* are also on offer. And the room service menu? They don't just serve burgers here. They serve *gourmet* burgers, made from grass-fed, antibiotic-free Wagyu beef, ground in-house. The kind you can eat blood-rare without worrying about E. coli.

What do you do? True, you've made a vow, and a promise is a promise. On the other hand, these aren't your taboos, they're hers. To you, they're just arbitrary rules, victimless sins; the only person who will be hurt if you transgress is her, and only if she finds out.

This is how my father thought about fucking other women. If you're inclined to argue that the analogy is flawed—because women aren't room service items; because you can't catch an STD from a Kathryn Bigelow film—you are missing the point, which, again, is not to excuse Dad's behavior but to make sense of it.

And not just his behavior, but his timing. That used to bug me even more than the fact of the betrayal itself. Bad enough to cheat on your pregnant girlfriend, I thought, but to cheat on her while you're waiting to find out if she'll marry you? Who does that?

Someone who believes his moral obligation is to not get caught, that's who. If my mother had accepted my father's proposal, as he fully expected her to, they would have moved in together, and not long afterwards, they'd have had a baby to take care of. Which would have made it hard for him to discreetly step out on her. But he had a brief window of opportunity before that happened, and he decided to make good use of it. And as awful as it might seem to me, I can see how, from his perspective, it was not just a reasonable choice, but a responsible one: By having one last fling, getting it out of his system, he'd make it easier to resist temptation later.

Of course, this dubious moral logic is premised on the notion that it is possible to keep secrets from my mother. Not a safe assumption, as it turns out. My father still has no idea how my mother found out he'd been unfaithful. "It's like she just knew," he said, the one time we talked about it. "She looked at me, and she knew."

Which sounds like Mom, all right. And Dad's response sounds like me, before I learned better: He denied the accusation. At first he tried to laugh it off. When that didn't work, he tried to gaslight her, acting hurt that she'd be so paranoid and untrusting of him. Mom hates that tactic, and she's not shy about expressing her displeasure physically. Their confrontation took place outside the motel where Dad was staying; the motel had a pool, and my father ended up swimming, fully clothed. By the time he dragged himself out of the water, Mom had gotten in her car and driven away. Dad waited twenty-four hours for her to come back, realized she wasn't going to, got scared, and spent another two days tracking her down.

By then, he was properly contrite. He confessed. He said that he was sorry and begged for another chance. He swore he would never do it again. He sounded sincere, and, in that moment, he probably thought that he was sincere.

Mom thought differently. She didn't believe that Dad was sorry; just unhappy with the consequences of his actions. Given a second chance, she believed he would act the same way, but try to make it come out differently somehow. Which it wouldn't.

You could make a case for giving him a second chance anyway.

My mother would say that was wishful thinking. People do change, but they change in their own time, for reasons that make sense to them. They don't change just because we want them to, or because it would be convenient to our own desires if they did.

As my mother saw it, she had three choices:

One, she could reconcile herself to marrying a serial adulterer, in the hope that he'd one day grow out of it, or that she'd someday stop caring. Like volunteering to be punched in the gut at random intervals, this was not an attractive option to her.

Two, she could declare war: Find some threat or emotional cudgel to force my father to be faithful. As I've already made clear, Mom has a talent for behavior modification, so I don't doubt she could have succeeded at this, but the resulting marriage would have been miserable, hardly worth fighting for. She'd have done it if she'd had to, for my sake. Thank God, it wasn't necessary. She had her family's support, and then she had Zero Day; she didn't need to marry my father.

Which left option three: Say no. Let him go. Simple.

The decision to cut my father out of her life completely—and, by extension, out of my life—was the only part she ever agonized about. It's also the part that took me the longest to understand.

I used to think she'd done it for me. To protect me from him. But the truth is, my mother didn't think of my father as a bad guy. A jerk, yes, and painful for her to be around, but not wicked. When I asked about him, she was honest about his shortcomings, but she never trash-talked him in front of me (it was some of my other relatives who did that). And when I decided I wanted to meet him, she told me where to look.

It wasn't me Mom was protecting. And it wasn't just my father who she didn't trust. He was the wrong guy for her. She knew that.

But she'd always known it—from the start, before they ever got together. It didn't matter. She got together with him anyway. Fell for him, hard.

And even after he broke her heart, she wasn't sorry.

"YOU CAN SNOOP, BUT DON'T BE WEIRD ABOUT IT," DARLA said when she gave me the link to her Facebook page.

She'd been on the crew for several weeks by that point, and we'd just finished one of the best gigs we would ever work together, a fifty-person raid on the troll city of Zuul'titlan. Currently the hardest dungeon in Asgarth, Zuul'titlan takes a minimum of eight hours to complete, and even experienced raiding guilds often require multiple attempts to get through it. It's not a place you want to bring clients to, even if they're willing to pay overtime rates. Too frustrating.

But there's an exception to every rule, and in this case it came in the form of the Kwan brothers, Wing and Arthur. They were engineers from Shenzhen who'd made a fortune building solar power plants in Africa, and they had a lot of eclectic hobbies, including *Call to Wizardry*. They didn't play often, and when they did, they were only interested in the toughest end-level content. Every few months they'd pop up on the sherpa forum, looking to recruit an army. They paid *extremely* well, but they expected perfection in return. They'd been known to boot whole sherpa crews mid-raid for the mistakes of a single member, and once they'd dinged you, they'd never hire your team again.

Darla had already alienated one of our other long-term customers. To protect our relationship with the Kwans, Ray wanted to exclude her from the run. I overruled him. Darla could be trouble, but she was predictable: She only really acted out when she was bored or when the clients couldn't keep up with her. I thought she'd be an asset on the Kwan brothers gig, and I was right. She did wisecrack a little going into it—enough to make Ray nervous—but once we got started and she saw that she was the one who was going to have to keep up, she did great.

I didn't have a lot of chance to admire Darla's form that day. The Kwans had picked me to be one of the raid tanks, so I was in front and very busy. Beating Zuul'titlan is like running a marathon. The most physically taxing part of the raid happens right in the middle, when, after fighting your way across a long series of heavily defended causeways, you enter the Plaza of Dancing Snakes, where a group of troll high priests are about to perform a human sacrifice. Killing the priests is harder than the final boss fight would be in a normal dungeon, but in Zuul'titlan, it's just a prelude. Once the priests are dead, waves of angry troll peasants start streaming into the plaza. To advance, you must kill ten thousand of them, and if you screw up and let your raid group get wiped, the body count resets to zero.

It took three and a half hours, but we cleared the plaza on the first try. The brothers announced a fifteen-minute bio break. When I got back from the bathroom I looked around for Darla and spotted her unattended avatar standing beside a mountain of corpses, covered in gore and still panting with exertion from the fight. Then Darla resumed control and caught me looking. "Perv," she said, and grinned.

And then it was on to the raid's final act: a running battle up a nine-step pyramid and a showdown with the troll demigod Machu Picchu Mon. Long story short, we aced it.

Afterwards, we and the other sherpa crews went to the Game

Lobby, where the Kwan brothers handed out performance bonuses. While Darla and I waited our turn, she told me she wouldn't be around for the next few days—she was going to visit her dad, who lived in a part of Arizona where bandwidth was sketchy. "But if another job like this comes up, let me know," she added. "I can drive into Flagstaff and find a game café if I need to."

"OK," I said. "I'll hit you up on Ghost." Meaning Ghost-it Note, an anonymous contact app popular with gamer gurls who don't want their online acquaintances following them home. It was how Darla and I had been communicating since we'd met.

"No, wait," she said. "Here." She handed me a virtual calling card with her phone number, instant message code, and a link to her Facebook page.

It's always flattering when a woman lets you know that she's decided you're not an ax murderer, but I've learned from experience not to make a big deal of it. I just nodded and saved the contact info to my system. "You can snoop," Darla told me, "but don't be weird about it."

Just then I was too tired to do anything but crash, so as soon as the Kwan brothers' money was in my PayPal account, I logged out and slept for ten hours. But the next day, after a shower and some food, I went on Facebook and finally learned Darla's full name.

Darla Jean Covington's Facebook page was only four years old, which meant it probably wasn't her first. That's not unusual. I'm hardly ever on Facebook, and I've still managed to accumulate half a dozen separate accounts, for business, family, and different groups of friends.

Darla's timeline consisted largely of reposts of not-safe-for-work memes, and videos in which people did stupid, dangerous, illegal, and/or offensive things. There were also videos of Darla herself at various ages, tagged "personal." The most recent of these, which had been posted less than an hour after she gave me her contact info, was titled "OMG — DARLA NIP SLIP & TWAT SHOT, SO EMBARRASSING!!!" I figured that was a test and didn't click on it. Instead I scrolled down to one marked "CLASSIC: DEENIE LOSES HER SHIT AT 2,000 FEET."

The video showed two little blond girls, one in a dress and the other in ripped jeans and a *Resident Evil* T-shirt, riding in a hot air balloon over a landscape of wooded hills. Deenie, the girl in the dress, was terrified of heights and kept her face buried in her hands. Darla, bored with the view, leaned against the side of the gondola and tilted her head back. "Oh my *God*, Deenie!" she exclaimed. "The balloon has a *hole* in it! And look, the cables are coming loose!" Deenie began shrieking, and an unseen older woman, probably the one holding the camera, said, "Darla! Darla, you stop that!" (Spoiler alert: She did not stop that.)

I scrolled down further, checking out "SISTERHOOD IS POWERFUL" (teenage Darla starts a fistfight during a roller derby game), "DARLA BREAKS HER ASS, CHAPTER 99" (a demonstration of why unicycles are rarely used for stunt jumping), and "HISTORY'S SHORTEST LIGHTSABER DUEL" (Darla and one of the girls from the roller derby video try fencing with fluorescent light tubes).

My favorite was "EARL IS A GINORMOUS PUSSY," in which Darla and three boys—Jeff, Mason, and Earl—played paintball out in the woods, capturing the action with helmet and body cams. They only had three paintball guns, all of which the boys had claimed, so Darla used a BB gun instead. I know that sounds idiotic, but their helmets had solid face shields and they were wearing heavy clothes, so the chance of maiming was minimal. Darla's real problem was getting the boys to admit they'd been hit at all. After giving them a chance to play fair, she adapted, double-pumping the action on the BB gun to increase the velocity of the pellets and aiming for weak spots in their armor. Much of the footage was devoted to ambushes: Darla buries herself in a pile of leaves and shoots Mason in an exposed band of belly fat as he goes by; Darla waits in a tree, whistles as Jeff passes beneath her, and plinks a BB off his face shield when he looks up.

In the video's final scene, Earl crouched behind a stone wall while Darla hectored him from the far side of a clearing, daring him to stop hiding and face her in the open. When Earl declined, Darla charged. With the video slowed to half speed, you could see the paintballs leave Earl's gun, and see Darla do this amazing series of sideways pivots, dodging every shot while somehow keeping her balance and her forward momentum. Then the paintball gun jammed, or maybe Earl just panicked. The POV switched from his helmet cam to Darla's as she vaulted the wall, knocked Earl to the ground, pulled down his pants, and shot him in the ass.

I rewatched that part of the video several times, then scrolled back up to the top of Darla's Facebook page, zeroing in on a line from her bio: "Virginian by blood, Arizonan by birth, Oregonian by choice."

Oregonian, I thought. Interesting.

Right after I first came to Berkeley, I hooked up with another online acquaintance, Suzie O'Dell, who also lived in Oregon. We'd been flirting for a while, and when Suzie found out I was moving to the Bay Area, she invited herself down to meet me face to face. The off-campus apartment I'd rented was unfurnished, and I didn't have a bed yet, but that was OK, Suzie came prepared, driving down from Eugene with a futon mattress strapped to the roof of her car. The hookup didn't go so well: As sometimes happens, the electricity we'd felt in cyberspace didn't translate into real-world chemistry. We gave it our best try, but by the second day it was clear this would be a one-time visit. Suzie did let me keep the futon, though—so if the moral of the story was "sometimes wanting is better than having," the other moral of the story was, "even when having disappoints, you can still get something useful out of it." But in my current frame of mind, the real takeaway was simply this: Oregon is close to California. Practically next door.

Darla had said she'd be at her dad's place for a few days, but two weeks passed with no word from her. I thought about calling to see if she wanted to work, but the gigs we were getting—level grinds, easy dungeon runs—were the sort that brought out Darla's bad side, and meanwhile, Ray had been much happier in her absence; so I decided it would be better all around if I were patient.

Then the Kwan brothers popped up on the forum again. They wanted to take another run at Zuul'titlan, this time going for the Knights and Priests achievement, which requires you to complete the raid using only tanks and healers, no dps characters. The reduced damage output turns the marathon into something more akin to a death march: We were looking at twenty hours, start to finish. And the Kwans wanted to do it all in one day.

I rang Darla's number and left her a message on voice mail, asking if she was up for an insane tanking job.

She called back two minutes later.

"JESUS CHRIST," DARLA SAID, "WHY DID I AGREE TO THIS?"

"Because you were bored, and wanted to do something fun and exciting?"

"Ha ha, fuck you."

It was the day before the raid, and we were out on the Mirage Salt Flats, busting rocks—grueling but necessary prep work. Armor degrades in combat—faster if you die, slower if you don't—and in an hours-long battle like the Plaza of the Dancing Snakes, even plate mail will wear away to nothing, leaving you naked before you've murdered your last peasant. The solution is Arneson's Clearcoat, a magical preparation that prevents armor degradation for up to twenty-four hours. Clearcoat's main ingredient is Essence of Gygax, which can only be obtained by mining adamantium nodes. The nodes are shiny rock clusters that spawn in the Flats; each one contains several chunks of adamantium ore and has a two-and-a-half-percent chance of yielding an Essence. You need ten Essences to make one dose of Clearcoat, so we had a long slog ahead of us. But I was OK with that.

"How was it really, with your dad?" I asked. "You must have been having a pretty good time, since you stayed so long."

"The first week was great," Darla said. "Dad's got this little wind racer he built himself—you know, like a sailboat on wheels? Near where he lives there's a dry lake bed, kind of like this but without the giant scorpions, and if the wind's right, you can get the racer up to seventy, eighty miles an hour, easy."

"That does sound like fun."

"It was, until I tipped it making a turn and broke the mast."

"You OK?"

"Scrapes and bruises." Darla shrugged. "But that put an end to the races."

"You stayed to help fix it?"

"I helped Dad put a new mast on, but me staying, that was more about pissing off my mom." She paused, sizing up a node on the ground in front of her. To mine it you hit it with a pickax; the UI judges your form, and if your aim is off, it can take half a dozen swings. Darla never needed more than three.

"Your mom's in Arizona, too?"

"No, she moved back to Lynchburg after the divorce." Darla swung her pickax—*WHAM! WHAM! WHAM!*—and frowned as the node fractured into three chunks of ore, but no Essence. "My parents have one of those 'mature' divorces where they pretend to still be friends, even though they can't stand to be in the same part of the country. The day after I was supposed to go home, she called him, and when she found out I was still there, she got jealous. She tried to play it like she was upset about the racer crash, but really it was just, 'How come Darla never overstays her visits with me?' She started calling every day to see whether I'd left yet, and so of course then I had to stay. It's like this game we play, Who's the Bigger Bitch? I always win. So what about your parents? They divorced?"

"Never married. Separated, though, since before I was born."

"Whose fault was it?"

"His fault," I said. "But her call."

"Interesting. So your mom's a bitch too, then."

"I wouldn't call her that. Mom's a badass, yeah, but—"

"A badass is just a bitch you happen to like." Darla grinned. "I guess that explains why you have the hots for me, huh? Don't deny it, I know it's true."

This was my cue to say something like, "I wasn't going to deny it," and then swing the conversation around to how San Francisco is a convenient stopover if you're driving between Oregon and Arizona. But instead I said, "You think you remind me of my mother?"

"Don't I?"

"The two of you are nothing alike."

"Really? I'm not a badass?"

"You are, and I like that you are, but you're . . ." I fumbled for a way to frame the distinction that wouldn't come off as an insult. ". . . a different flavor of badass."

"Ooh, a different *flavor*!" Darla laughed. "And what about my cousin? You like his flavor, too?"

"Your cousin?"

"Earl. The ginormous pussy."

"I liked the video."

"Yeah, I know you did. Fun fact about YouTube: Not only can you see how many times a video gets watched, you can also track what part people are looking at. *Somebody* was really interested in the last thirty seconds of that paintball game . . . So what was it that turned you on? Earl's bare ass, or me pumping a BB into it?"

When someone's trying to embarrass the shit out of you, sometimes the best strategy is just to embrace it. "Does it have to be either/or?" I said.

"I knew it," Darla said. "*Total* perv." She turned away, shaking her head, and swung her pickax again. *WHAM! WHAM!* "Fuck." One chunk of ore. No Essence.

I had better luck with my next node, though it took me five swings to crack it. When the rock finally fell apart, nestled among the ore was a glowing pile of silver dust. Already bound to me, the Essence of Gygax shimmered and vanished into my inventory. "Sorry," I said, to Darla's sullen stare. "I'd share if I could."

"Yeah, whatever." She scanned the horizon.

"Want to go find some griefers to kill?" I asked, guessing that was what she was looking for. "Or some innocent players to grief on?"

"I'd love to, but that would only drag this misery out longer . . . How many of these rocks do we have to smash?"

"With a two-point-five percent drop rate, you should expect to farm around four hundred nodes to get all ten Essences. Of course that's the straight average. Depending on the RNG, it could be—"

"Yeah, thanks, I get it. Do me a favor?"

"What?"

"If you ever do get around to making your own MMORPG, leave out this grindy crap. I know the Asperger's crowd eat it up, but it makes me want to throw myself out a window."

"How about I put in a special toggle for you?" I said. "Let you skip the grind, while the players who enjoy it can still do it. Everyone's happy."

"Swell." *WHAM! WHAM! WHAM!* "Shit."

"What else would you want in a game?" I asked. "If you could have anything."

Darla sighed. "Is this your idea of sexy banter?"

"Call it market research. I'm honestly interested."

"OK . . . Permadeath."

"Permadeath? Really?"

"Do I sound uncertain?"

"How would you make that work, though?"

"How do you think? No resurrection: If your character dies, you've got to start over with a new one."

"I know what permadeath *is*," I said. "But how do you get people to sign up for it? Would you really want to play a game where one mistake could cost you a character you'd invested hundreds of hours in?"

"Aren't we doing that already? Think how many thousands of hours' worth of characters are going to be on that raid tomorrow. And EULA will ban every one of them if they get wind we're doing it for pay."

"EULA bans are different, though. They're a cost of doing business. They're not fun."

"Doesn't mean they couldn't be," Darla said. "What if you could fight the EULA cops? Trial by combat, I'd sign up for that in a heartbeat."

"They'd never let you win."

"They'd stack the deck, sure. But what if you had a chance, even five percent? You saying you wouldn't go for that?"

My immediate thought was that I'd rather not have to deal with EULA at all. But I could see how, to a certain mind-set, being able to fight the law and win was an even more attractive option. "What about technical issues? If you lose a fair fight—or even an unfair one—that's one thing. But what if your internet goes out? What if you're lagging so bad you've got no chance at all?"

She shrugged. "Make it so that can't happen."

"But you can't do that."

"I know you can't." Another shrug. "But we're talking about what I *want*, right? What you want, and what you can have, those are two different things." Eyeing me significantly: "*You* should know that."

After that we pounded rocks for a while without talking. But then Darla's luck changed—she found two Essences in a row—and with it, her mood. "Hot streak, hot streak!" She collected her bounty and eyed me again, smiling. "So what about you? You know what you'd want in a game?"

"Oh sure. I've got a whole list of things."

"So tell me one," Darla said. "Come on, I showed you mine."

"All right. I—"

"And never mind the practical shit," she added. "Tell me an idea you think would be really cool, even if you don't think it could work. Those are the ones worth doing."

"OK," I said. "Have you heard of a game called *Footsteps After Midnight*?"

She shook her head. "What is it, some new horror movie tie-in?"

"Original IP. And old. Dial-up era."

"Dial-up? You talking about a MUD?"

"Parts of it were MUDlike. You played a hacker-slash-private investigator caught up in a hunt for a serial killer. You had a side-kick who did fieldwork for you, and the parts where you sent him out to different locations and told him what to do, that played a lot like a traditional text adventure. But to figure out where he would go next, you'd also do things like hack into databases and email accounts.

"But that was just the online part of the game," I continued. "The cool thing was, there was also an offline component. When you first started playing, you'd give the game all this personal in-formation: your name, your mailing address, your email address if you had one, your home phone number, and so on. And then, as you made progress through the case—"

"The killer would call you," Darla guessed.

"Yeah," I said nodding. "And other characters, too. Like, the day after you broke into the central police database, you'd get a threatening call from the chief of detectives: 'Hey, we can't prove it, but we know it was you, knock it off . . .' And there were packages. The way the game company got around bandwidth limitations was by mailing you stuff. You'd hack the coroner's email and forge an evidence request, and a few days later you'd get a set of crime scene photos."

"And the killer?" Darla asked. "What would he send you, body parts?"

"A severed finger, at one point," I said. "Other trophies from his victims. And creepy letters and postcards, personalized to make it seem like he was watching you."

"OK, I'm sold," Darla said. "This sounds awesome. How come I never heard of this game?"

"The company went bankrupt a few months after the game debuted. It was expensive to play, and they couldn't get enough subscribers to cover their overhead. And the few players who did sign up had these, *unique* customer service issues . . . Like, one of the questions you'd get asked when you first started playing was what time of day it was OK to call you. But the company forgot about time zones somehow, and also, this was back when most people still had shared landlines. So these phone calls would be coming in at odd hours, and sometimes the person who picked up would be a roommate who didn't know about the game . . . And it was the same with the packages. Someone's mom would come home early from work and get curious about this envelope from the coroner's office addressed to her kid, and when she opened it, there'd be these photos of a hacked-up body in a bathtub."

Darla was hugging herself laughing now. "Oh my God!" she said. "I would pay *anything* to do that to my mom!"

"Well, you're special," I told her. "Most of the players weren't happy about it—or their parents weren't. The game company had the real cops called on them more than once. So they had to shut down."

"Is there any way I can still play this game?" Darla asked. "Like a legacy version of the online part of it?"

"No, I looked. There's a stub article on Wikipedia about it, but the links are all dead. Nothing else. The only reason I know as much as I do is that my dad has this collection of really old computer game magazines. I was looking through it the last time I visited and came across an article, 'Missteps After Midnight,' about the company going out of business."

"So you want to do your own version of this? New and improved?"

"Maybe," I said. "The idea's not as original anymore—there are alternate-reality games that have covered a lot of the same ground—but I still think you could do something interesting with it. With advances in technology, especially social media, you could do a much better job of personalizing the experience. And at the same time, it'd be easier to keep control of it, make sure only people who signed up to play got involved in the game."

"Fuck that," Darla said. "I want the version that scares the shit out of my friends and family."

"We can do another special toggle. A 'give my mom a heart attack' option."

"No, fuck that, I'm serious. This is what I mean about practical shit—you barely come up with the idea, and you're already looking for ways to water it down."

"Not wanting to send corpse photos to the wrong people is 'watering it down'?"

"If the point of the game is to make people feel like they're involved in something real, that's what you should be focused on—how to make them feel that. Instead, you're thinking about how to put limits on it."

"Because I don't want to get arrested. Or sued."

"So do a EULA: 'This is an intense game, not intended for lightweights, click here if you've got the balls to indemnify us.'"

I laughed. "And assuming for the sake of argument that that would hold up legally, how many people would click, do you think?"

"*I* would."

"OK, that's one subscriber."

"There'd be others. If the game is really cool, cool players will find it."

"But I don't just want cool players. Uncool players have money to spend, too. And there are more of them."

Darla frowned impatiently. "Is the money even that important, though?"

"To a profit-making business? Yeah, it's pretty important."

"No, seriously, think about it: *Footsteps After Midnight* came out, what, thirty years ago? Forty years ago?"

"Forty-five."

"Which means the guys who made the game are probably dead now, or drooling in an old folks' home somewhere."

"Drooling and bankrupt," I said.

"Yeah, but so what? Their *business* tanked, but a half century later you read about what they *did* and you're like, 'Whoa, that sounds cool! I'd like to try that.'"

"OK, but Darla—"

"And isn't that better? Wouldn't you rather go broke doing something cool than get rich doing something lame?"

I'd never seen Darla get this passionate before. I'd seen her excited, but there was always an element of flippancy to her enthusiasm, a sense that she was herself too cool to take anything that seriously. That flippancy was gone now. She sounded *earnest*.

This was another cue, a signal for me to put my own opinions on hold and really hear her out. I didn't need to agree with her, but I did need to let her know that I was paying attention—that I took *her* seriously. But we were deep in what I considered my turf now—business—and I'd already decided that Darla, whatever her other skills, had no head for that. So I plowed ahead with my own way of looking at things. Which was, after all, the right way.

"The thing is," I told her, using that know-it-all voice that women find endlessly endearing, "the thing is, Darla, you don't need to choose. You can do something really cool *and* turn a profit at it . . ."

"Not if wanting to turn a profit makes you a pussy about taking risks." Her voice grew mocking. "'We'll put in a special toggle, Darla.' 'We'll make everybody happy, Darla.' Except you won't. You'll just ruin what's good about the idea."

"Darla—" I broke off, laughing at her sudden fury. Probably the worst thing I could have done.

"Fine, don't listen to me." Stone-faced and indignant now. "Make a lame-ass game, I don't care. I hope you make a billion dollars."

"Darla, wait," I said, too late. "I'm sorry, OK? I do want to hear your thoughts about this, I just—"

"Fuck you and your sorry. I know what you want." Hefting her pickax: "But I've got a ton of rocks to break, so you're out of luck. I'm going this way. You can fuck off that way."

"Darla, come on . . . Darla . . ." But she was already walking away.

Well played, genius, I thought. Yet at the same time I couldn't really bring myself to feel bad. Obviously you couldn't make a game that might panic innocent bystanders. How was it unreasonable to say that?

Assuming that Darla's anger would be fleeting, I gave it half an hour, in the meanwhile collecting another two Essences. Then I started edging back towards her, watching out of the corner of my eye for the telltale silver sparkle that would signal she too had found another Essence. Once I saw that, I moved closer, my plan being to act as if her blowup had never happened. But I was barely within earshot when she said, "I told you to fuck off," without even looking at me.

So on that day, at least, California and Oregon weren't so close together after all.

MUD — Multi-User Dungeon. One of the earliest forms of virtual world, MUDs originated as multiplayer versions of classic interactive fiction games like *Colossal Cave* and *Zork*. Most MUDs are entirely text-based. Players enter commands using simple sentences (e.g., WALK NORTH, or PUT OIL IN LANTERN) and the results of their actions are described in prose . . . MUDs remain popular even today. Their lack of graphics means that they can run on almost any computer system. Where a cutting-edge video game might require as big a production staff as a major motion picture, a MUD can be scripted by a single author. And while fantasy and science-fiction themes are the most common, the lack of commercial pressure means that MUDs can and do exist in every conceivable genre: There are spy MUDs, horror MUDs, Western MUDs, educational MUDs, religious MUDs, and, of course, pornographic MUDs.

—*Lady Ada's Lexicon*

Location: A Clearing at the Edge of Town

You stand in a grassy clearing on the outskirts of a small Midwestern town. It is dusk of a summer evening, and the first fireflies have begun to appear. A path leads east through a sparse thicket of woods. You see lights shining beyond the trees and hear the faint sound of calliope music.

The clearing is littered with brightly colored hand-bills.

>TAKE HANDBILL

You pick up one of the handbills.

>LOOK AT HANDBILL

The handbill is illustrated with a drawing of a car-ousel. The handbill reads:

Green Meadow Midsummer Mystery Carnival
Thrills! Amusements! Contests of Brain and Brawn!
Prove Your Worth and Win a STUPENDOUS TROPHY!!!

A breeze gusts from the direction of the woods, bring-ing a smell of hot dogs and cotton candy. The handbills flutter and dance about the clearing, like children ex-cited by the prospect of the carnival.

>TAKE HANDBILL

You reach for another handbill, but realize that it is identical to the one you are already holding and decide not to bother.

. . .

. . .

Mr. Jones materializes beside you.

Mr. Jones is here.

>LOOK AT MR. JONES

Mr. Jones has not created a physical description for himself.

>SAY, "HELLO, MR. JONES."

. . .

. . .

>SHOW HELP SCREEN TO MR. JONES

You call up a handy tutorial screen and show it to Mr. Jones.

. . .

. . .

Mr. Jones says, "This seems quite primitive."

>SAY, "YOU WANTED TO EXPERIENCE THE FULL POTENTIAL OF THE MEDIUM. MODERN MMORPGS EVOLVED FROM TEXT-BASED ADVENTURES LIKE THIS ONE."

Mr. Jones says, "Very well. What do I do?"

>SAY, "FOLLOW ME."

Mr. Jones is now following you.

>WALK EAST

You follow the path through the sparse woods. Mr. Jones follows you.

Location: The Entrance to the Carnival

A wooden archway strung with lights and festooned with banners marks the entrance to the Green Meadow Carnival. Standing in front of the arch is a Tout in a cheap suit. "Ladies! Gentlemen! Children of all ages!" he cries. "Come right in! Fun and games will be had by all! And for the deserving among you . . . This prize!" The Tout gestures dramatically at a pedestal, spotlit from above, upon which rests a stupendous trophy!

>LOOK AT TROPHY

The stupendous trophy is truly stupendous! It is big, and shiny, and totally awesome! To possess it would make you the envy of everyone in town!

Mr. Jones reaches for the trophy. The Tout smacks his hand away and says, "Careful, pal. That's not yours yet."

Mr. Jones tries to hit the Tout. The Tout dodges the blow and says, "Whoa!"

Mr. Jones tries to punch the Tout. The Tout sidesteps and says, "Hey, knock it off!"

Mr. Jones tries to kick the Tout. The Tout ducks backwards and says, "What is your problem, asshole?"

>SAY, "YOU CAN'T FIGHT HIM. NOT A COMBAT GAME."

Mr. Jones says, "How do I get the trophy, then?"

>SAY, "ASK HIM."

Mr. Jones asks the Tout how to get the trophy.

"An excellent question!" the Tout says. "Throughout the carnival, you will find contests and other challenges that allow you to win *PRIZE TICKETS* like this one." He holds up a gleaming golden ticket. "Collect 25 of these tickets, bring them to me, and the stupendous trophy will be yours!"

"But wait!" the Tout says. "There's more! Bring me an additional 5 tickets -- 30 in all -- and I will throw in an additional prize!" The Tout gestures dramatically at a velvet curtain hanging beside the trophy pedestal. A drumroll sounds, and the curtain is swept aside to reveal . . . "A year's supply of Turtle Wax!"

    . . .

Mr. Jones says, "Why would I put wax on a tortoise?"

>SAY, "IT'S A JOKE. NOT A VERY FUNNY ONE. GOOGLE IT IF YOU ARE CURIOUS."

Mr. Jones says, "I will take your word for it. What now?"

>ENTER THE CARNIVAL

You step through the arch and enter the carnival. Mr. Jones follows you.

Location: Main Carnival Thoroughfare, West End

You are at the west end of a broad thoroughfare lined with carnival attractions. From the east you hear the sound of the calliope, louder now. To the north you see a kissing booth. To the south is a high striker.

>SAY, "EACH OF THE ATTRACTIONS IS A PUZZLE THAT AWARDS A PRIZE TICKET FOR SOLVING IT."

>SAY, "WHAT WOULD YOU L

Mr. Bungle is here!

Appearing seemingly out of nowhere, Mr. Bungle runs up to you, dressed in a heavy trenchcoat. "Balloon smugglers!" he cries, ripping open the coat to reveal a perfectly shaped pair of double-D breasts. Before you can duck away he clamps his hands around the back of your head and kisses you full on the mouth, ramming his tongue down your throat. You sputter and choke and beat your hands feebly against him, but you cannot escape Mr. Bungle's steely grip, and as he grinds against you, you feel both horribly violated and undeniably aroused.

Just as you are about to pass out, Mr. Bungle breaks
the kiss and steps back. "Gazonga!" he says, eyes going
wide. You look down and see that the perfect breasts
have somehow been transferred from his chest to yours!
"Let's motorboat!" says Mr. Bungle. He buries his face
in your ample cleavage and buzzes his lips. Once again,
your sense of violation wars with feelings of arousal.
Arousal wins; you swoon.

"Dee-licious!" Mr. Bungle says, wiping his mouth with
the back of his hand. "Double-dee-licious, I should say!"
Then he spins around, bends over, farts explosively, and
jets out of sight with his coattails flapping.

. . .

. . .

Mr. Jones says, "What."

Mr. Jones says, "What was that?"

>SAY, "GRIEFERS ARE EVERYWHERE. I AM SORRY."

Mr. Jones says, "This is a very stupid game so far."

>SAY, "DON'T GIVE UP YET. TRY ONE OF THE ATTRACTIONS."

Mr. Jones looks around.

Mr. Jones says, "Not the kissing booth."

>WALK SOUTH

You approach the high striker. Mr. Jones follows you.

Location: The High Striker

A classic test of strength, the high striker is a twenty-
foot-tall tower with a bell mounted at the top. The goal
is to ring the bell by striking a lever at the tower's

base and propelling a puck up a metal cable. Vertical gradations painted on the tower indicate ascending levels of strength, from "90-pound weakling" near the bottom to "Man of Steel!" at the height of the bell.

A Tout, who appears to have been cloned from the one at the front gate, is leaning against a guy-wire beside the high striker. "Step right up!" he calls. "Ring the bell and win a *PRIZE TICKET*!!! Cave Boy, show them how it's done!" A young boy in a leopard-skin loincloth steps out of the shadows, holding a big wooden mallet. He strikes a pose, flexing his biceps, then winds up and slams the mallet down onto the lever. The puck goes flying to the top of the tower and rings the bell!

"Well done, Cave Boy, well done!" The Tout steps forward to take the mallet, then shoos the boy back into the shadows. "All right," the Tout says, "who's next?"

>SAY, "GO AHEAD."

Mr. Jones takes the mallet from the Tout.

Mr. Jones swings the mallet at the lever. The blow seems at least as powerful as the cave boy's, but the result is far less impressive: The puck ascends only a third of the way up the tower, to the level marked "Assistant furniture mover."

"It's all in the wrists," says the Tout. "Go on, try again."

Mr. Jones swings the mallet at the lever. The blow lands even harder this time, but the puck only rises to the halfway point, "Popeye's understudy."

"Looks like somebody didn't eat his spinach," the Tout says. "But give it another try."

Mr. Jones swings the mallet at the lever. The thunderous blow sets the cable quivering, but the puck barely makes it past "90-pound weakling."

"Jeez," says the Tout. "Are you low blood sugar or something?"

Mr. Jones starts to swing the mallet at the Tout, but fearing he will only embarrass himself further, he decides not to.

>SAY, "STILL NOT A COMBAT GAME. THINK IT THROUGH. SOMETHING CHANGED BETWEEN THE TIME CAVE BOY TOOK HIS SWING AND THE TIME YOU DID. WHAT WAS IT?"

. . .

. . .

Mr. Jones examines the guy-wire.

>LOOK AT GUY-WIRE

The guy-wire is a length of metal cable that holds the high striker steady and keeps it from falling over . . . or at least, that's what you'd expect it to do. Upon closer examination, you realize that the wire, which should be under tension, actually has some slack in it. The bottom of the guy-wire is attached to a peg in the ground, but you cannot tell how it is attached up top -- the wire just vanishes into a hole in the back of the tower behind the bell. This leads to a final observation: The cable that the puck rides on is the exact same sort of cable the guy-wire is made of . . . and it looks like it might be a bit slack, as well. Curious.

. . .

Mr. Jones says, "I understand."

Mr. Jones orders the Tout to lean against the guy-wire.

"I'm sorry," the Tout says, "carnival gaming regula-
tions require me to stand here and observe while you
make your attempt."

Mr. Jones threatens the Tout with the mallet, but the
gesture is so ineffectual that, out of kindness, we are
going to pretend that he does not do this.

. . .

. . .

Mr. Jones says, "Are you allowed to help?"

>SAY, "YES. YOU'VE GOT IT."

>LEAN ON GUY-WIRE

As you approach the guy-wire, the Tout becomes flus-
tered. "Here now!" he says, "this is highly irregular!"
He doesn't stop you, though, so you lean your weight
against it. As the wire goes taut, you hear the creak
of what sounds like a pulley hidden in the top of the
tower, and the cable on the front of the tower goes
taut, too. The puck should rise much more smoothly now,
with less friction.

>SAY, "GO FOR IT."

Mr. Jones swings the mallet at the lever. A mighty
blow! The puck rockets up the cable and rings the
bell!

"HIGHLY irregular," the Tout grumbles. But a crowd
of onlookers has begun to gather, and fearing that his
secret will get out, he quickly hands each of you a
golden *PRIZE TICKET*. "Now scram!" he shouts, shooing
you back to the thoroughfare.

Location: Main Carnival Thoroughfare, West End

Mr. Jones is here. You now have 1 *PRIZE TICKET*, out of a possible 30.

Mr. Jones says, "Do all of the puzzles require the help of a second player?"

>SAY, "NO. MOST HAVE MULTIPLE SOLUTIONS, AND IT IS POSSIBLE TO GET THE TROPHY SOLO. YOU *MIGHT* NEED SOMEONE ELSE'S HELP TO GET THE TURTLE WAX. I CAN'T RE-MEMBER."

>SAY, "THIS CARNIVAL IS A SUBZONE OF A MUCH LARGER MUD CALLED 'PLANET I.F.' THERE ARE OTHER ZONES THAT REQUIRE A TEAM EFFORT THROUGHOUT."

>SAY, "I KNOW OF AT LEAST ONE PUZZLE WHOSE SOLUTION REQUIRES A HUNDRED PLAYERS TO ACT IN TANDEM, PERFORMING A SPECIFIC SEQUENCE OF ACTIONS WITHIN A SHORT TIME PE-RIOD. VERY DIFFICULT, ESPECIALLY WITH GRIEFERS AROUND."

Mr. Jones says, "Interesting."

Mr. Jones says, "This type of game must be relatively easy to produce."

>SAY, "VERY EASY. SETTING UP THE SERVER CAN BE TRICKY, BUT THERE ARE DEVELOPMENT KITS THAT DO THE HARD WORK FOR YOU, AND LET ANYONE WITH A STANDARD BROWSER LOG IN AND PLAY."

Mr. Jones says, "Interesting."

Mr. Jones says, "I will look around some more. Fol-low me."

>FOLLOW MR. JONES

You are now following Mr. Jones.

Mr. Jones walks east. You follow Mr. Jones.

Location: Main Thoroughfare, Carousel Intersection

At this point, the thoroughfare intersects another path-
way leading north and south. At the center of the intersection is a carousel, blaring calliope music. Looking
around the corners of the intersection clockwise from
the northeast, you can also see: a ring toss, a hot dog
cart, a water pistol range, and a fortune-teller's tent.

  Ms. Pang waves to you from the carousel.

  Mr. Jones walks east. You start to follow him, but
something in the calliope music makes you turn around
and walk back towards the carousel.

  Ms. Pang waves to you from the carousel.

  >WHO IS MS. PANG?

  I don't know who Ms. Pang is.

  Ms. Pang waves to you from the carousel.

  >FOLLOW MR. JONES

  Mr. Jones is not here.

  Ms. Pang waves to you from the carousel.

  >WALK EAST

  No.

  Ms. Pang waves to you from the carousel.

  >GO CAROUSEL

  You climb aboard the carousel.

Location: Aboard the Carousel

You are riding on an old-fashioned merry-go-round.
Teams of wooden horses bob up and down in time to the

music of a steam-powered calliope. As the ride picks up speed, you notice a metal pole that has been erected beside the carousel. A mechanical arm extends down and inward from the top of the pole, so that its tip is almost within reach of the outermost ring of horses as they move past. Attached to the tip of the arm is a shiny brass ring with a *PRIZE TICKET* stuffed inside it!

Never mind the brass ring. The brass ring is not important. You turn your full attention to Ms. Pang, who sits on a bench between two rows of horses. She is a striking ethnic Chinese woman; though small in stature, something about the way she carries herself suggests it would be a fatal mistake to underestimate her. You should do whatever she asks.

Ms. Pang assumes you have already recognized her, but to avoid wasting time, she points to a small blue pin on her blouse. The pin speaks in your voice: "It's me, John Chu."

>SAY, "WHAT ARE YOU DOING HERE?"

Ms. Pang says, "I was going to ask you the same question."

>SAY, "I'M WORKING. I'M BUSY."

Ms. Pang says, "Indeed."

Ms. Pang whips out a computer tablet and shows you the screen. You see yourself -- or, rather, a very convincing copy of yourself -- leading Mr. Jones into the carnival funhouse. The two of you are soon lost in a maze of twisty little passages, all alike.

Ms. Pang says, "We have a few minutes. Why did you bring Mr. Jones here?"

>SAY, "HE IS STUDYING MMORPGS. MUDS ARE THE FOUNTAIN-HEAD."

Ms. Pang says, "I know. I have done my homework. But why this MUD? Why not something more iconic?"

>SAY, "I WANTED TO TRY A DIFFERENT THEME, TO SHOW HIM IT'S NOT ALL D&D AND STAR WARS. I USED TO PLAY PUZZLE GAMES LIKE THIS WITH MY MOM WHEN I WAS A KID. OUR VERSION OF BEDTIME STORIES."

Ms. Pang says, "That is touching. But I don't believe you."

>SHRUG

You shrug.

Ms. Pang says, "I think you chose this MUD for the software it uses."

Mr. Bungle is here!

Appearing seemingly out of nowhere, Mr. Bungle leaps onto the carousel, dressed in a heavy trenchcoat. "Check out MY trophy!" he cries, ripping open the coat to reveal a truly stupendous penis. You gape at it, awestruck, wondering how he manages to keep his balance while sporting such an enormous member. "But wait, there's more!" Mr. Bungle says. Opening up a jar of Turtle Wax, he anoints himself and begins rubbing the creamy wax into his foreskin. The truly stupendous penis becomes even more stupendous!

"We're gonna go a gusher!" Mr. Bungle warns. You scramble for cover but it's too late. He ejaculates, like a proverbial fire hose, spraying semen everywhere: onto the wooden horses, into the calliope, through the brass ring, and of course, all over you. Drenched from head to toe, you feel horribly violated, yet strangely aroused. If not for embarrassment about the inadequate size of your own manhood, you might even unzip your fly and join in.

Mr. Bungle's orgasm goes on and on. He begins to shrink and shrivel up as his entire body mass is converted into hot spunk. "Veni, veni, veni," he croaks, until at last, turning completely inside out, he vanishes into his own urethra, leaving you to enjoy . . .

Location: Cum-Covered Carousel

. . .

. . .

. . .

. . .

Ms. Pang says, "Your little hobby attracts some sick fucking people, you know that?"

>SAY, "YOU DON'T HAVE TROLLS IN THE PRC?"

Ms. Pang smiles at your pathetically transparent attempt to get her to divulge information about herself.

Ms. Pang says, "As I was saying. This MUD uses the MUDMAKER software suite. All versions of MUDMAKER have security flaws in the server, which is why griefers are so rampant here. But this particular build also has a critical client-side flaw that can allow hackers to gain root privileges on certain users' computers."

Ms. Pang says, "I believe you are aware of this. I

believe you brought Mr. Jones here so that you, or a confederate, can try to hack Mr. Jones's system. This hacking attempt is futile and reckless. If Smith notices, he will terminate your relationship with Mr. Jones. Do you remember how I told you not to disappoint me?"

>SAY, "I REMEMBER YOU PROMISED TO PAY ME TWO HUNDRED THOUSAND DOLLARS A WEEK. IS THERE A PROBLEM AT YOUR BANK?"

Ms. Pang says, "Your money is coming soon. In the meantime, you need to stop your foolish sleuthing attempts. Smith is not an idiot, and you are not nearly as clever as you think you are. The fact that I am here now should be proof enough of that. If you screw this up, I will make you very, very sorry."

>SAY, "I THINK IT IS WEIRD THAT YOU'RE TRYING TO SCARE ME LIKE THIS. IF YOU ARE WHAT YOU SAY YOU ARE, THE EASIEST WAY TO GET ME TO DO WHAT YOU WANT IS TO PAY ME WHAT YOU PROMISED. IF YOU WANT TO FREAK ME OUT TOO, THEN HAVE SOMEONE KNOCK ON MY DOOR AND HAND ME A SACK OF CASH. THAT WOULD MAKE AN IMPRESSION."

. . .

. . .

Ms. Pang says, "Very well. You will get your money. And regret your words."

Ms. Pang says, "He is leaving the funhouse. He is bored and wants to quit. I am having your double tell him to meet you back at the Game Lobby. Go now."

>SAY, "WAIT. HOW DO I CONTACT YOU IF I NEE

Ms. Pang leaves the carousel.

>FOLLOW MS. PANG

Ms. Pang is not here.

Mr. Bungle is here!

Appearing seemingly out of nowhere, Mr. Bungle bounds up to you, dressed in a heavy trenchcoat. "Who likes DONKEYS!?" he cries . . .

context fail — Confusing one social, political, or technological environment for another, with disastrous consequences. A popular, if apocryphal, example is the avid video gamer who gets hurt after forgetting that in real life there is no reset button. Other examples include acting as if you are anonymous when you are not; calling your spouse by your lover's name; telling a racist joke to the wrong group of friends; or expecting a stranger to show the same patience and understanding as someone who knows you well.

Context lag occurs when switching to a new environment after an extended period in an old one. Rapid switching or overlap between multiple environments can lead to **context collapse**. The practice of remaining continually aware of one's environment and the rules that apply there is **context vigilance**.

—*Lady Ada's Lexicon*

Three days later, I still don't have the money. And it's not just Ms. Pang who's delinquent—I haven't received my second week's payment from Mr. Jones, either, and neither he nor Smith is responding to my messages. I do have a brief conversation with Mom. She's kind enough to not say I told you so, but I can tell she's thinking it.

Mom sounds better rested than the last time we spoke, which makes sense—the culprit in the Delhi plane crash has been apprehended. Instead of a terrorist mastermind, he turns out to be an emotionally disturbed fifteen-year-old boy, Sunil Gupta. Sunil was angry at his parents for making him stay home while they went to Goa on holiday. He decided to get even by hacking into the air traffic control system at Indira Gandhi Airport and messing with their flight. Sunil has told authorities that he didn't mean to murder his parents; he just wanted to scare them, by engineering a near-miss between their small commuter plane and a much larger jet. But the commuter plane went down, killing all eleven people on board, and only quick work by the jet's pilots kept it from suffering a similar fate.

I would love to ask Mom for more details, but she can't even confirm that she was working on the case, so like the rest of the world I am forced to rely on news reports and net gossip. The big question on everyone's mind is, did Sunil Gupta act alone? On CNN, the pundits are reluctant to accept that a teenager could crack the ATC system's sophisticated encryption without help. But after consulting Wikipedia and discovering that India is in Asia, they grudgingly acknowledge that Sunil is probably a whiz at math.

There's a lot of wild speculation about how the hack worked—other than a vague pronouncement that they have "identified and fixed the problem," the authorities have no comment. But an unsourced rumor that goes viral says that the point of entry was a smart coffeemaker in the air traffic control tower. Rather than attack the ATC system directly, the rumor goes, Sunil used the insecure Bluetooth connection in the coffee machine to execute a "cyber bank shot" into the ATC computer. This strikes me as bullshit, but the CNN people love it because it sounds cool and raises a host of other questions that they can fill time blathering about: Should internet-connected appliances be banned from sensitive areas like air traffic control towers? What's a coffee machine doing in Delhi, anyway? Don't Indians drink tea? Does the presence of the coffeemaker suggest that some of the air traffic controllers are foreigners? From a Muslim country, maybe? What do people drink in Pakistan?

Idiots, I think, but the fact that I am watching this—and the commercials that come with it—means that it's not just the TV people who are stupid. By the time I log out of CNN, the virus has infected me: I spend another hour wandering the net, looking for evidence that the coffee machine story might actually be true. I don't find any, but my search leads me to Kowloon Bay Daily, a Hong Kong–based news site that specializes in virtual re-creations of crime scenes.

They have a 3D mock-up of the crash. A crude simulacrum of Sunil Gupta hunches over a computer desk, beaming radio waves out of the back of his laptop. The waves strike an air traffic control tower, causing a red coffeepot icon to flash ominously. Overhead, a jumbo jet and a prop plane converge. At the last second the jet increases power and pulls up; the backthrust from its engines forces down the nose of the prop plane and sends it spiraling into the ground. The cartoonish nature of the graphics makes this even more horrific and tasteless than it sounds, but I don't look away. When it's over, I decide to check out the rest of the website.

Which is how I end up in another airport, Suvarnabhumi International in Bangkok, watching a nervous Korean man enter the main terminal. A floating caption identifies him as General Han Yong-chol, "believed until recently to be a trusted member of Kim Jong-un's inner circle." As the general approaches the security line, a woman—"Unknown Female"—steps in his path and spritzes him in the face with the contents of a tiny spray bottle. The general clutches his throat and falls down convulsing. Unknown Female keeps walking, but she doesn't make it far—by the time security guards intercept her, she is limping and gasping, and before they can slap cuffs on her, she collapses. Unknown Female looks surprised by this turn of events, but she shouldn't be: The stuff in her spray bottle is VX nerve agent, one of the deadliest poisons on the planet. Though it was designed as a weapon of mass destruction, VX has been used in at least three political assassinations tied to North Korean intelligence, including the 2017 murder of Kim Jong-un's half brother, Kim Jong-nam.

I ask Googlebot to find me a more sober news report about the murder of General Han. I send Mom the link, along with a note. If we assume Kim Jong-un ordered the hit on the general, I ask her, could that be a sign of bigger problems inside the regime? And if there is some sort of palace intrigue going on in Pyongyang, could that be the reason I haven't heard from Smith or Mr. Jones?

Forty-five minutes pass before Mom sends back a one-word response: "Creative."

IT'S AFTER MIDNIGHT. I'M ABOUT TO LOG OFF WHEN I get an instant message from Anja, asking me to meet her in the Game Lobby.

I find her at the bar. "What's up?"

"I have a game in a few minutes," she says, "and I was hoping you could come along."

"Dungeon run?"

She shakes her head. "*Habitual Offender.*"

I smile. "Going to do some crimes?"

"Going to rob some banks. We're trying for the Butch and Sundance achievement on the South American server."

"Is this a paying gig?"

"No, just for fun . . . But I'd *really* appreciate it if you'd come."

From the way she says this I know she doesn't want me along for my bank-robbing skills. "Is this about a guy?"

She nods. "Javier," she says. "I met him when I was leveling up that cleric for Ray."

"You want my read on him?"

Another nod. "If you don't mind. He seems really nice, but . . . you know."

When Anja first joined the crew, she was dating a guy who went by the name of Hans Steuri. They'd met through Reboot, a virtual support group that helps severely disabled people adjust to life online. Hans claimed to be a nineteen-year-old from Switzerland, a one-time Olympic hopeful who, like Anja, had been paralyzed in an accident—in his case, a ski jump gone wrong.

Anja brought Hans along on a level grind one day. I took an instant dislike to him. He was friendly, but aggressively so, like a used-car dealer desperate to make a sale. He also played badly and didn't listen to advice. But Anja seemed smitten with him, so I did my best to make nice.

Then Hans got a phone call. He tried to take it in private but screwed up the b-channel. His voice changed: He suddenly sounded older, and American. The woman he was speaking to, who was obviously his wife, seemed to think he was out showing a house to someone. When Hans realized we could hear him, he hung up on her in mid-sentence. He made a half-hearted attempt at bluffing, but between my Googling and Anja's pointed questions, we soon got the truth out of him.

Hans's real name was Harvey Gladstone; he was a forty-eight-year-old Realtor from Miami. He confessed that he had never been on skis in his life, and aside from "a touch of sciatica," he was completely able-bodied. Listening to him struggle to explain himself, I couldn't quite work out whether meeting girls at Reboot was just a creepy pickup strategy, or if there was some additional kink involved. But that was more information than I needed.

Anja was mortified. She pronounced Harvey dead to her. But the next day she came to me in a panic. Harvey had gotten a new online ID to get around her block, and had approached her in the Game Lobby, wanting to talk things over. She pronounced him dead again. Half an hour later he was back, disguised in a new avatar; she recognized him by his body language.

She didn't know what to do. Harvey knew her routine and her favorite online hangouts; she didn't want to have to change all that, or get a new ID herself. And even more so than for most people, leaving the internet entirely wasn't a reasonable option for her.

I told her I'd take care of it. I reached out to Griefnet, the cyber-vigilante group, and called in a favor. I don't know what they did, but less than twenty-four hours later, Anja got an email of a recording in which a scared-sounding Harvey swore he would never bother her, or anyone else at Reboot, ever again.

Anja was relieved. She was also grateful. I tried to discourage the latter sentiment, because I guessed where it might lead, and I didn't want the responsibility of vetting all her future boyfriends. But some jobs fall to you whether you want them or not. It has become a thing, when Anja meets a guy she likes, that she asks for my impression. Is he as nice as he seems, or should she be wary? And while we're on the subject: Do I think he likes her, too?

As Jolene is quick to remind me, I take advantage of Anja's good nature and her willingness to work overtime—more than I should. But I try to treat that as a two-way street. If Anja wants something from me, even something I'm not comfortable with, something I wouldn't ordinarily say yes to, I do my best to accommodate her. To maintain the karmic balance between us.

That balance was thrown out of whack when I infected her computer with Smith's malware package. According to Mom's tech people, the malware is primarily spyware. Like all code that operates at a root level, it has the potential to be destructive, but its main function is surveillance: to keep tabs on what Anja sees and says and does, and to open her files to inspection. Even if Smith decided to turn the malware into a weapon, there are limits to what damage it could do. Google was right: Anja's life support is controlled by a separate, independent computer system. The malware can't touch it. Unless, maybe, there's a coffeepot in the room.

So I haven't put Anja's physical safety at risk. But I have sold out her privacy, which is still bad, even with Mom's tacit approval. Focused on the mystery of Mr. Jones—and the money—I managed to avoid acknowledging this until after I got Anja to download the software. Now I'm feeling guilty. Which, like apologizing when you're not sorry, is self-indulgent bullshit.

But I can still try to address the balance. And if Anja wants to know whether some guy she met on the internet is genuinely trustworthy, or only seems to be, I suppose I can provide some insight into that.

"You're sure Javier won't mind you bringing someone else along?" I ask.

"We're going as a group," Anja says. "Javier's bringing his sister and her boyfriend. We've got this cool SUV, too," she adds, "all tricked out for the bank run. You could be the driver, if you'd like."

"No, that's OK," I say. "You really want to know if this Javier is worth your time? Then *you* need to be the driver. And you need to pretend you're not very good at it."

WHILE I WAS ANJA'S GO-TO FOR SCREENING POTENTIAL boyfriends, there were other romance-related topics she couldn't discuss with me—or with Ray. Darla wouldn't have been my choice for sex counseling either, but I can see why Anja picked her.

A few days after the second Zuul'titlan raid, we arranged to meet up for a level grind in the House by the Crossroads. I was late, and when I got to the meeting place I found Ray harvesting magic herbs by the roadside. He was alone, but judging by the irked look on his face, he hadn't been for long.

"Because poop," Ray said, before I could ask.

"What?"

"We were coming down from Lookout Point," he explained, gesturing towards the hill I had just descended, "and we passed the spot with the outhouse quest, you know, the one with the goblin?"

"Proctor." Proctor the Traveling Salesgoblin, who has gotten himself trapped in an outhouse. He wants you to kill owlbears in the surrounding woods and collect the scraps of soft parchment they are carrying. Bring him eight scraps and he will reward you with a handful of warm and smelly diamonds. "Yeah, I remember that quest."

"Everyone remembers it, it's disgusting," Ray said. "Anyway,

Darla sees the outhouse, and she starts riffing on all the different quests that involve poop."

"It's true, there are a lot of them." Spend time leveling up characters in *Call to Wizardry* and you realize that someone on the design team has a thing for scatological humor. There's even a poop-related fishing quest, where you have to use a lump of unicorn dung as a lure to attract a sea monster.

"Yeah, so Darla's going through the whole list. And then she looks over at Anja and she's like, 'Hey Anja, how do you poop?'"

"Oh God," I said. "Was Anja upset?"

"No, actually, she was cool with it," Ray said. "Now that Anja's had time to get used to her, I think she kind of likes the fact that Darla doesn't tiptoe around her condition the way most people do. So that's fine, but the thing is, I don't want to know how Anja poops. I mean, if it's one question, OK, I can close my ears and ignore it. But of course it's *not* one question, it's a whole goddamn topic of conversation: What sort of container does it go into? Who empties it? How often? Are there *hoses*? And then, and then, Darla starts talking about this fashion model she heard about who's got Crohn's disease, and her thing, right, her signature, is to be photographed with her colostomy bag showing.

"And hey"—he put up his hands defensively—"I think it's great, you know, that we live in an enlightened time when people with gross medical issues can have fulfilling careers and feel empowered and whatever. OK? But I don't want to hear about it. I don't want to have to dwell on it. Especially since I know the gross-out factor is the only reason Darla's even interested.

"So I don't *want* to hear about it, but I don't *say* that, because it'll make things worse, and also, I don't want to hurt Anja's feelings.

But that doesn't matter either, of course, because Darla's like a god-damned bloodhound for stuff that bugs people.

"So I've got my head down, I'm minding my business, I'm praying for a change of subject, and suddenly Darla is like, 'Hey, Ray, why so quiet? You don't like to talk about pooping? Pooping's natural, Ray. The *Pope* poops. *Jesus* pooped—in fact, I'll bet He shit Himself while He was up on the cross . . .'"

"Yeah, OK," I said. "I get the picture."

"Do you?" Looking at me pointedly. "I'm *so glad* . . . So anyway, I told Darla to fuck off. Which wouldn't have worked either, but Anja took pity on me. She got Darla to go take a walk with her. So that's why I'm here all alone with this pissed-off expression on my face. Because poop."

"I'll have a talk with Darla."

Ray laughed. "Yeah, like that's going to make a difference . . . Have you got an answer to my question, yet? The one about how long?"

"I'm working on it, Ray."

"Work faster."

"ATENÇÃO, VADIA!" THE MOTORCYCLIST YELLS AS ANJA cuts into his lane. Then he swerves onto the sidewalk, hits a woman pushing a stroller, and gets catapulted into the side of the Ministério do Turismo. The federal police in the cruiser behind us look over at the crash but otherwise don't react—Anja didn't actually hit the guy, so the accident does not count as vehicular assault. When she runs a red light, forcing an old man in the crosswalk to drop his cane and leap for the curb, the cops yawn.

We are westbound on the Eixo Monumental, a massive twelve-lane thoroughfare that runs through the heart of Brazil's capital, Brasília. This stretch of the Eixo is lined with government office buildings—ministries of trade, finance, culture, energy, planning, defense. Our first bank is a kilometer away, in the commercial sector on the far side of the Eixo Rodoviário.

Anja's date, Javier Messner, rides shotgun in the front seat of our armor-plated SUV. Javier presents as a slim young white guy with blue eyes, brown hair, and a neatly trimmed beard. Both his appearance and his story—he's a twenty-year-old barista who lives and works in Buenos Aires—check out on social media. A cross-check on Ancestry.com shows that Javier's family emigrated to Argentina from Bavaria before the Second World War—so no, he is not descended from fugitive Nazis.

Javier and Anja converse in a mix of Spanish and German. Even in the latter tongue, Javier sounds completely laid-back, and he is untroubled by Anja's driving. A few kilometers ago, just after we left the garage where we picked up the SUV, he suggested that Anja make a left turn, and she instead pulled a hard right, directly into the path of an oncoming semi. Javier stayed calm, waited for Anja to finish swerving around the truck, and then said laughing, "Das andere links." *The other left*.

Javier's sister, seventeen-year-old Blanca, is more intense. She sits behind Javier, fiddling with the submachine gun in her lap in a way that suggests she is eager to get on with tonight's crime spree. But Blanca is also disciplined: Despite her impatience, she does not take potshots at pedestrians the way Darla surely would in the same situation.

Blanca's boyfriend, sixteen-year-old Bruno Ribeiro, is originally from Brasília, though he moved to Argentina with his mother after his parents divorced. Bruno marvels at what a great job the game designers have done of modeling his native city. To Blanca's embarrassment, he keeps pointing out landmarks and commenting on how well-rendered they are. "My God," Blanca says finally. "Why not just tattoo 'I'm a newbie' on your forehead?"

I sit all the way in the back with an assortment of heavy weapons. There's a roof hatch directly above me, so if need be I can stand up and shoot rockets at pursuing vehicles. But for now I just sit quiet and listen to Anja and Javier. I'm using subtitles for translation so I can hear the actual sound of their voices. So far my gut is telling me that Javier is an OK guy. A little too mellow for my taste, maybe, but Anja seems to like that.

After several more traffic violations we reach the street where the bank is located. From a block away we hear gunfire—a robbery is already in progress. Following standard in-game etiquette, Anja pulls over and waits for the other crew to finish. Javier takes advantage of the delay to go over the plan one more time.

The amount of cash in the bank's vault varies depending on how often it's been looted in the past hour, but it will always contain a special money sack made of red cloth. Stealing that starts a clock on the Butch and Sundance achievement. We'll then have ninety minutes to collect four other red sacks from banks in Argentina, Chile, Bolivia, and Peru. *Habitual Offender* squeezes South America's geography into a few hundred virtual square kilometers, creating a sort of greatest-hits version of the continent, which is what makes this grand tour possible. Brasília to Buenos Aires, for example, a three-thousand-kilometer journey in reality, is just a fifteen-minute commute in the game world—though if you're being shot at by police, it's a long fifteen minutes.

You can hit the banks in any order. We have tentatively decided on a clockwise route of Brasília to Buenos Aires to Santiago to La

Paz to Lima. Javier double-checks that everyone is still cool with this. Everyone is. "Let's get on with it," Blanca says.

At the bank, the gunfire has ceased, and ambulance crews are hauling away bodies. They work quickly. "OK," Javier says. "John, do you mind standing guard while the rest of us go inside?"

"No problem." There are griefers here too, of course, and the last thing you want when you're pulling a heist is to have some clown take off with your getaway car.

Anja parks in the bank's front lot, and she and the others get out. Anja and Javier, like Blanca, are armed with submachine guns; Bruno wields a combat shotgun. In the real world this would tend to draw attention, but *Habitual Offender* is an open-carry universe. So long as you don't aim your gun directly at someone, security guards will ignore it.

While the others proceed inside the bank, I stand up in the roof hatch of the SUV. I am holding a minigun—a heavy, six-barreled rotary machine gun that can fire five thousand rounds a minute. I keep the barrels pointed skyward. A beat cop walking by on the sidewalk smiles and tips his cap to me. "Boa noite," he says. *Good evening.*

"Foda-se a polícia," I reply. *Fuck the police.*

"FUCK YOUR MOTHER," DARLA SAID. "IT'S YOUR LIFE."

I walked through the woods in the direction Ray told me Anja and Darla had gone. I found them on the edge of the zone, on a cliff overlooking the Jurassic Swamp to the south. They were facing away from me as I came out of the trees; I was just about to announce myself when I realized what they were talking about.

"So you don't have any feeling in your clit at all?"

"Nothing below the neck," Anja said. "At least, not when I'm awake. It's like my brain still remembers, so when I dream, sometimes . . ."

"Remembers," Darla said. "So before the accident, you—"

"Oh yeah, sure. And there was a guy on the men's team, Rolando, we did things. Never all the way, but, you know."

"You and Rolando aren't together anymore? Because of the accident?"

"No, we broke up before then. Rolando got impatient. He kept wanting to do more, but I wasn't ready yet. I'm kind of sorry, now, that I didn't say yes."

"Nah, fuck that," Darla said. "If you weren't ready, you weren't ready."

I'd begun backing up, slowly. Then Darla started to turn around. I was about to dive for cover when I remembered I was playing a ninja and hit the stealth mode toggle.

"Anyway," Darla continued, looking my way now, "the fact that it's all in your head makes it a lot easier. You don't have to mess around with hardware at all, so your mother doesn't need to know what you're up to. She doesn't watch what you're doing online, does she?"

"No, we have a deal about that," Anja said. "But there is this tech guy who comes in once a month, and he can be nosy. If I've downloaded a piece of software he doesn't recognize, he'll ask about it."

"I can show you how to hide the software so your tech guy won't see it. Or if you want to be extra safe, you can just delete it before he comes and reinstall it afterwards."

"And this software, it lets you—"

"Enough to keep a guy interested," Darla said, "and then some."
I faded back into the trees.

"ON THE RIGHT," JAVIER SAYS CALMLY, AS A BLACK GOV-
ernment van with tinted windows appears along a side road. The
van tries to T-bone us, but Anja gives the SUV more gas and gets
out in front of it, while Blanca fires a full clip from her submachine
gun. The driver of the van is hit and loses control; a pair of llamas
grazing by the roadside watch as the vehicle goes plunging down
the mountainside.

We are crossing the Andes, en route to Santiago. Our notoriety
level is currently four out of a possible five, which means it's not just
the local and provincial cops who are after us, but the Argentine
equivalent of the FBI and the Secret Service. We're OK on time,
though, and the SUV is still mostly intact. Anja has dropped the
pretense that she can't drive and is doing a good job of swerving
around the spike strips that the feds keep throwing on the highway
in front of us, while Javier, Blanca, and I deal with the pursuit.
Bruno on the other hand is useless at the moment. It turns out he
really is a newbie, not just to *Habitual Offender* but to VR games in
general, and he's got a newbie's case of motion sickness: Every time
Anja whips the SUV around another switchback, he groans and
clutches his stomach.

We crest a high point in the mountains and pass a sign reading
BIENVENIDOS A CHILE. Crossing a national border instantly
knocks a level off our notoriety. This is good, but not good enough:
We want a clean slate before we hit the next bank. If we weren't on
a clock, we could detour down to Patagonia and drive around the

wilderness until the cops lost interest in us, but our current situation requires a quicker solution. Anja knows this.

The highway turns sharply into a long straightaway. The Chilean-Argentine border is above us now, on a steep slope to our right, running parallel to the road. "Bruno," Anja says, "you probably want to close your eyes." She floors the accelerator and cuts across the soft shoulder. The SUV tilts at a fifty-degree angle as we climb the slope, but the high-traction tires cling like magic and Anja slaloms back and forth across the border—Argentina, Chile, Argentina, Chile—zeroing out our notoriety. As we thunk back down onto the highway, a motorcycle cop who was out for our blood just seconds ago breezes past without even a glance.

We race downhill into the Chilean Central Valley. As we near the outskirts of the capital, we are treated to an amazing sight: A jumbo jet has just taken off from the Santiago Airport, and there are people riding on the outside of the plane. They run around on the roof and the wings, shooting at one another. Competing teams of hijackers, maybe, or perhaps a group of players have made up their own achievement, a guns-and-grenades version of the Mile High Club. Whatever the motivation, the outcome is predictable: A stray round knocks out one of the jet's engines. The plane rolls over and starts to nose-dive.

I am reminded, inevitably, of Sunil Gupta's hack. But I also know the difference between real mass murder and a video game, so what I feel in this case is not horror but annoyance: It looks like the plane is coming down onto the main road into the city. This could delay us.

"Don't worry," Anja says. "I know a good detour." She swerves right again, plowing through a barrier onto an unfinished highway exit that is perfectly angled to serve as a jump ramp. We enter Santiago in midair.

Bruno makes retching noises.

"DID YOU ENJOY THE SHOW?" DARLA SAID.

The griefers had caught me on my way back to Ray. I'd uncloaked once I got clear of Darla and Anja, which turned out to be a mistake. As I passed a particularly large tree, a troll warrior jumped out at me, screaming and swinging a battleaxe. I wasn't flagged for PvP, so he couldn't actually hit me, but I reacted by reflexively slashing with my katana—and then I *was* flagged for PvP. A gnome sorcerer popped out from behind another tree and started hitting me with frostbolts, which slowed me down while the warrior hacked me into slabs.

After I was dead, they camped on my corpse. I came back from the graveyard, resurrected, and tried to use my ninja smoke bomb to make a quick exit, but the sorcerer set off a freezing sphere to stop me turning invisible. They killed me again. And again.

I was debating whether to call for help or just quit the game and get a job at McDonald's when Darla showed up. She was playing a druid tank—an armored grizzly bear—which made her the opposite of stealthy, but she ran up on the sorcerer and mauled him to death before he knew what was happening. Then she took out the warrior, dancing around him with a nimbleness no real grizzly will ever possess. It was quite the show, all right—but I knew that wasn't what Darla was talking about.

"You saw me."

"Of course I saw you. Pro tip, if you're going to sneak up and eavesdrop on somebody, you want to turn invisible *before* you step out in the open."

"Where's Anja now?" I asked.

"Back with Ray. Helping him get his ass unchapped."

"Yeah, about that. I really need you to stop poking at him."

"Ray needs to get a thicker skin, is what needs to happen."

"The problem isn't Ray being thin-skinned," I said. "It's you, shit-stirring because you're bored."

Darla shrugged. "That's just how I'm wired. My mom says I get the devil in me whenever I don't have enough to do."

"Is that what's going on with you and Anja?"

"What do you mean?"

"I wasn't eavesdropping, before, but I did hear what you were talking about."

"Yeah? Did it get you hot?"

"It got me wondering. Are you trying to help Anja, or are you pretending to be helpful, so you can stir up some kind of trouble between her and her mom?"

"Wow," Darla said. "First of all, fuck you. And second of all, what the fuck do you think of me, that you'd even ask that?"

"I'm not trying to be an asshole, Darla. But I do pay attention."

"If you really fucking paid attention, you'd know that I *like* Anja. She's not a pussy, like Ray. Or like you."

"So when you ask her whether her family knows the Mengeles, or if they ever had Adolf Eichmann over for dinner, that's just you being friendly? Or the other day in Zuul'titlan, when you made that crack about how all the corpses must remind her of the old country . . ."

Darla rolled her eyes, like she couldn't believe I was uncool enough to judge her by her actual behavior. *"Fine,"* she said. "Maybe

I do tease her, sometimes. But this is different. She *asked* for my help, OK? She wants a sex life, the same as any normal girl would. You have a problem with that?"

"No, I don't. But it's not my opinion that matters. Anja's parents are religious—especially her mom. I don't know the whole story, but it's caused problems for her before."

"So what, because her mom has a thing for Jesus, I'm supposed to tell her tough luck?"

"I'm not saying don't help her. I'm saying, don't get bored and forget. If you get into a fight with your mom, you can walk away. Anja can't."

Darla sighed in exasperation. "Fine," she repeated, and looked away frowning. But then the frown became a smirk. "You know she's into you," she said, turning back to me. "Anja. She told me she had a big crush on you when she first joined the crew."

I did know that. It was another reason I'd agreed to vet Anja's dates for her—becoming her confidant was a diplomatic way to take myself out of the running.

"Yeah," Darla continued. "She said you told her you don't date coworkers. So is that, like, a blanket policy, or just something you say to girls you don't have the hots for?"

Now it was my turn to be bored. "Where are you going with this, Darla?"

"Where am I going?"

"It's no secret I'm attracted to you. And I think the feeling's mutual, but what I can't tell is whether you're really interested or just like pretending because it's fun to wind me up."

"Well," Darla said, "if you have to ask . . ."

"The answer's probably no, I know. But I'm asking."

"Why, so you'll know who to cut from the crew, me or Ray?"

"I just want to know where I stand, OK? Tell me you're not interested, and it'll never come up again."

But of course that would have been way too simple, and no fun at all for her. "Maybe I haven't made up my mind yet," Darla said shrugging.

"Well, is there something I could do to help you decide?"

Enjoying herself now, Darla stroked her chin and made a show of thinking it over. "What about a bullet?" she said finally. "If you're serious."

"You want a bullet? From me?"

"No, from the Duke of Luxembourg . . . Of course from you. Give me ten minutes, in PPML 4.2 format, with full audio and visuals—good ones."

"Uh-huh," I said. "And what do I get?"

"Well, I'm not making *you* a bullet," Darla said. "I could offer you a hundred bucks, I guess, but that'd probably be some kind of interstate felony. Just make me the bullet. Make it good. Then we'll see."

"I'll think about it."

She laughed. "Oh yeah—I know you will."

"I NEED MORE BULLETS!" BLANCA SHOUTS.

"Forget bullets, get the rocket launcher!" replies Javier, who has finally lost his cool. "A tank is coming!"

Like the original Butch and Sundance, we have come to grief in Bolivia. We'd hit the bank and were about to make our getaway when another group of players decided not to wait their turn and drove up shooting. Bruno was killed by the opening round of gunfire, and a lucky grenade toss blew the back wheels off the SUV. I got busy with the minigun and made short work of the attackers, but in the process I accidentally vaporized a procession of nuns in front of the cathedral across from the bank. This instantly maxed out our notoriety and put the Bolivian Army on crash alert.

Blanca grabs the rocket launcher out of the crippled SUV as the tank rumbles into view at the end of the block. She takes aim and fires before the tank can bring its cannon to bear; the tank explodes and its turret goes flying. Javier and I target the Army snipers who are trying to set up on the surrounding rooftops.

Anja meanwhile searches for a new getaway vehicle. She runs over to an armored car parked in front of the bank, hauls out the driver and executes him, then shouts, "Come on!"

Bad idea. If our notoriety were lower, sure, but that armor won't protect us against military weapons. We need high speed and maneuverability. "Get the Lobini!" I tell her, indicating a yellow sports car farther down the street.

"It's a two-seater!" Anja says.

"I know," I reply. "You and Javier get inside, while Blanca rides on the roof! I'll stay behind and try to keep the soldiers occupied!"

"Fuck that," says Blanca, standing over Bruno's body as she reloads the launcher. "I'll stay too."

"No!" says Javier. "We all go together!" He and Blanca start arguing, faster than the subtitles can keep up, but I get the gist: Javier believes in teamwork and fair play, and doesn't want to win the achievement at someone else's expense. But Blanca doesn't really give a shit about the achievement; she's just as happy to go out in a blaze of glory.

Their debate is interrupted by the arrival of a helicopter gunship. Blanca nails it with a rocket; the chopper spins out of control and crashes into the cathedral's main steeple, killing another sniper. "Take your girlfriend and get out of here while you still can," Blanca says, as fiery debris rains down all around us.

"It's OK, Javier," I add. "I can get the achievement another time." I can tell he's still not happy about it, but the flaming tail rotor that comes whizzing past his head appears to decide him; he gets moving. I glance over at Anja and give her a nod: As best I can tell, Javier is a keeper. Anja nods back, mouthing, "Thank you," and gets in the car. She and Javier speed away.

"Shit!" Blanca exclaims. Two more tanks have appeared at the end of the block. She fires a rocket at the one in front, turning it into a flaming roadblock. "I'm out!" She tosses the empty launcher aside and grabs an M-16 from the SUV. "Now what?"

"Back inside the bank," I suggest. "We can hold them off for a while from in there." Blanca nods and retreats into the building. Burdened by the weight of the minigun, I follow more slowly, continuing to pick off snipers as I go. Another gunship appears above the cathedral and I empty my last few hundred rounds through its windshield.

I drop the minigun and unsling my backup assault rifle. At the end of the block, the second tank pushes past the wreck and fires. The cannon shell zips by a few inches in front of my face and hits the armored bank truck, blasting it into shrapnel. I quickly duck into the bank.

Inside it's much quieter. The only sound is the whimper of terrified customers cowering in the corners. This would be disturbing if they were real people, but they're not, so I ignore them.

"Blanca?" I call. She doesn't answer. I walk slowly forward, scanning for security guards. I don't see any, but I do find Blanca. She is lying on the floor in front of the open bank vault. Her avatar's eyes are glazed and unmoving, and there is a bullet hole perfectly centered in her forehead.

"Don't shoot!" a man's voice calls, in English. I take cover behind a pillar. A figure emerges from the vault with both arms raised. His right hand is empty, while his left clutches a money sack. His only visible weapon is a Taser in a holster on his right hip. "Don't shoot," he repeats. "I just want to talk, John."

I recognize him then. It's the white guy from the CIA Factbook. The one I thought was a reporter, who seemed to be following me and Mr. Park around virtual Pyongyang. His *Habitual Offender* avatar is dressed in black body armor rather than street clothes, but the face is the same.

I lower my rifle and step out from cover. "Who the hell are you?"

"Ms. Pang sent me," he says. He waggles the money sack. "I have your payment."

I'd laugh if I weren't so confused. "You're going to pay me in play money?"

"No. It's real." The heels of his combat boots click against the marble floor as he walks towards me. But then I hear another sound, an incongruous sound—the creak of a floorboard. A wooden floorboard, like the ones in my apartment.

"Here," he says, and tosses the money sack at me. I make no move to catch it, so in the game world, it passes right through me.

In the real world, a cloth bag filled with soft bricks hits me in the face. I stumble backwards, more startled than hurt. I lift my hands to pull off my goggles and that's when he tases me. The synchronization is off this time: His avatar is still pulling the Taser from its holster when the real-world darts hit me in the chest and pump fifty thousand volts into my nervous system.

The two realities diverge as my avatar topples over backward while I pitch forward. The money sack breaks my fall, but the pain of involuntary muscle contractions keeps me from appreciating it.

When the current shuts off, I am blind. My headset was knocked askew in the fall. Once more I reach to pull it off, but he says sternly, "Don't."

He nudges the money sack. A stack of bills pokes me in the cheek. "Four hundred thousand dollars," he says. "Two weeks' pay. Ms. Pang wants you to know she's good for it. But she also wants you to start taking her seriously. If she tells you to do something, you need to do it. If she tells you to not do something, you need to not do it. Do you understand?"

"Yes." My voice is shaky and I'm short of breath.

"I hope so, John," he says. "You really don't want me coming back here for another visit. Trust me on that." A pause. "This is so we're absolutely clear."

He must have upped the voltage. The second shock is more painful than the first, and it goes on longer. I think I scream, though maybe that's just inside my head. I definitely piss myself. When it's over, I still can't see, but colors are blooming behind my eyes. Through the headphones pressed to the side of my skull, I can feel as well as hear the sound of raised voices in Spanish—Bolivian Special Forces have entered the bank. Their shouted commands mingle with the sound of his footsteps moving away, and a bang that registers dimly as a door slam. Or maybe the bang is a soldier executing my avatar—I can't really tell, and anyway it doesn't matter. The absence of pain, that's the important thing.

I lie on the floor, grateful that the pain has stopped, and while I wait for my nervous system to reboot, I drool on the money.

W hen Men on the Internet built the first fellatio machine, they called their bullet encoding scheme Blow Job Markup Language, or BJML. This inspired a fair amount of mockery from Women on the Internet, as well as two semi-serious attempts to create a female-friendly version of the code: CML, and the functionally equivalent but more cleverly named PTBML, in which PTB stands for "petting the bunny."

All of these encoding schemes were designed for solo playback of prerecorded sex acts, but of course once you got that working, the logical next step was figuring out a way to allow couples—or groups—to have cybersex in real time.

Men on the Internet once more took the lead—and proceeded to bungle the job. The problem was emotional, not technological: They wanted the convenience of quick, no-strings sex with strangers, without the potential downside of discovering that the hot woman they'd hooked up with was actually a guy. (Yes, there were also gay men who feared being tricked into having sex with girls, but let's be serious: It was freaked out straight boys driving this particular bus.)

The obvious solution—getting to know people before you fucked them—didn't fit with the "quick, no-strings" part of the program, so the Men opted for a brute-force approach instead. They created male and female versions of the software, and went to absurd lengths to try to ensure that only people with actual vaginas could use the female version. Saner members of the community pointed out that this was an impossible goal, but it was like trying to convince politicians that there's no such thing as a crypto back door that only good guys can use: The fanatics kept insisting that with enough nerd power, *anything* is possible.

The Men nerded as hard as they could, but none of the vagina-recognition schemes they came up with was close to foolproof. They did manage to make the software so bloated and cumbersome as to be essentially unusable, even for gay sex—so in that limited sense, they were successful. But the project was a bust.

It was a Berkeley grad named Martha Hollenbeck who wrote the first practical cybersex software. She called her creation PPML: Polymorphous Perverse Markup Language. One version fit all genders, which made sense from a technical perspective. Whether designed for men or women, the vast majority of computerized sex toys are simple vibrators, with the same limited set of functions: Speed up. Slow down. Buzz. Pulse. Hollenbeck wrote a standardized command code that allowed different devices to communicate, and added modular support for more advanced sex toys.

PPML combined an intuitive and newbie-friendly interface with a wealth of customization options. Say you'd decided to give a blow job to someone halfway around the world. If sucking on a sensor-equipped dildo was really your thing, PPML would of course allow you to do that. But you could also use a cyberglove, a game pad, a keyboard, a microphone, or some other input device. Or if you were feeling lazy and just wanted to phone it in, you could activate PPML's "white noise" feature and have it convert any handy string of ones and zeroes—an MP3 of your favorite Stones track, say, or a PDF of the Song of Solomon—into blow job commands.

The software also enabled a unique form of faceting. In the real world, if Alice gives Bob a blow job, Bob receives a blow job. But because PPML used the same code for different sex acts, a receiver in cyberspace could, if they wanted, turn the blow job inside-out, and experience it as an act of penetration. With larger groups of people and a bit of imagination, much wilder combinations were possible: Alice gives a blow job simultaneously to Bob, Carol, Donna, and Edgar; Bob receives a blow job, while Carol, Donna, and Edgar are licked, fisted, and fucked, respectively, and the combined bucking of their hips feeds back to Alice as anal. The accompanying sounds and visuals could be faceted too, of course: While Alice, Carol, and Donna share a prison rape fantasy, Bob sees himself as part of a living, breathing Rubens painting, and Edgar indulges in some hot furry action.

No surprise, this offended some people: Spectacle ensued. And to those inclined to be outraged by PPML, the fact that Martha Hollenbeck was trans just added fuel to the fire. For mainstream pundits, she became a metaphor for whatever they thought was wrong with contemporary cyberculture. Conservative feminists damned her as a not-so-secret agent of the patriarchy. To homophobic Men on the Internet, she was a gay guy in drag, trying to put one over on the vagina detector.

She got a lot of death threats. She stopped appearing in public early on, after San Francisco SWAT responded to a hoax 911 call by driving a tank through the wall of the auditorium where she was speaking. But her software was popular, even among people who publicly wished her dead, and by the time PPML 2.0 was released, it had become a de facto standard, the lingua franca of cybersex.

I was an early adopter, thanks to my girlfriend, Wendy Williams. Wendy was a Zero Day kid, and she was gear queer. Late one night we met up in an empty server room to fool around, and she told me about this new software suite she'd downloaded that she wanted to try out. She asked if I was up for being a guinea pig. I said that I was.

We were stationed in Osaka at the time. We went to a special computer store in Tobita Shinchi, the red light district. While Wendy chatted with the women behind the counter, I stood with my arms folded and tried to project an air of mature sophistication. My attention was drawn to a display case full of vibrators shaped like brightly colored animals. Their English-language names read like the product of an excitable machine translator: SURPRISE FANTASY CAT! TORRID HEDGEHOG! BACK DOOR MONKEY! INEXHAUSTIBLE PRICKLY HORSE!

We spent around forty thousand yen on toys—including a SURPRISE FANTASY CAT!—and went back to base. There was a delay while Wendy configured PPML's encryption. Once she was satisfied that our parents *probably* couldn't spy on us, we put on the gear and booted up the software.

It was a little strange, but a lot of fun. Which, at that early point in my sexual history, is also how I would have described regular fucking. And though with time and experience my tastes have become more refined, even now, if you ask me which is better, real sex or virtual sex, I'll tell you it's a question of what you're in the mood for.

It was the late *New York Times* columnist David Brooks who famously observed that "you can't kiss in cyberspace." Like a lot of declarative statements made by old people, this isn't strictly true: If you and your partner are in the same physical space, you can kiss all you like, though you do need to be careful not to smash your headsets together in the heat of passion. At long distance, your tactile options are more limited. There are full-body haptic suits, but they are very expensive and have a tendency to overheat. More likely, the sense of touch will be focused on your genitals, or whatever other part of your anatomy the vibrator is attached to. This strikes some people as cold and emotionless, but it's worth remembering that vibrators are a nineteenth-century invention, and Victorians probably used them while reading steamy love letters. So the concept isn't exactly new.

The store in Tobita Shinchi sold a "smell synthesizer" that looked like a piece of medical fetish gear. I thought about buying it, but I didn't really believe it could mimic Wendy's scent, and I wasn't going to spend fifteen thousand yen to have patchouli blown up my nose. Not even the Japanese make a sex toy that can reproduce taste, so if that's important to you, you'll want to stick to doing it in the flesh.

It's in the realm of sight and sound that cybersex really gets interesting. People have always fantasized during sex, but computers do the heavy lifting for you, and let you keep your eyes wide open. You can look like anyone or anything, anywhere. And the soundtrack can be dynamic, reacting to what you are doing: Marvin Gaye into *Led Zeppelin IV* into the climax of the *1812 Overture*.

Which brings me back to the subject of bullets. You can knock out a no-frills blow job in a couple of minutes, but crafting a polished fantasy with 3D visuals and surround sound is a much bigger undertaking. Thanks to Wendy, I know a lot of programming tricks and shortcuts, and of course PPML has tools that can help, but still, I worked my ass off on Darla's bullet.

One decision I had to make was whether to use my default avatar. Playing yourself in a bullet shows confidence, but it also risks embarrassment if the bullet's recipient decides to share it with the rest of the internet. The alternative is to use a stand-in avatar: Celebrity look-alikes are popular.

In Darla's case, I could think of two strong arguments against using a stand-in. First, she would rightly regard it as a sign that I didn't trust her, which in turn would make it less likely that she'd choose to hook up with me. And second, it might not actually protect me from being publicly humiliated. With PPML, you can also edit bullets that people send you, so even if I did use some other avatar, Darla could always reskin it to look like me before uploading to a revenge porn site.

Since being chicken wouldn't save me, I decided I might as well be bold—at least that would allow me to pick the most flattering version of myself. I set to work, creating a ten-minute scenario that I thought Darla would enjoy, based on various things she'd said and other little hints that she'd dropped. It took me three days to put together, and another couple days to polish. Once I had it just the way I wanted it, I encrypted the bullet and attached it to an email.

Then I paused, before hitting send, and asked myself whether I *really* wanted to do this. But the question was rhetorical: I'd made up my mind the moment Darla had asked for the bullet. And while I understood I might not be happy with the consequences of my actions, I didn't for an instant believe that I'd be sorry.

"WHO *WOULD* YOU HAVE PICKED AS A STAND-IN?" DARLA asked me, afterwards. "If you'd decided to pussy out?"

"I don't know. Keanu Reeves, maybe?"

"Keanu Reeves?" She made a gagging expression. "He's older than my grandfather."

"Real Keanu is older than your grandfather. Fantasy Keanu is whatever age you decide to skin him as. I'd have cloned the avatar from *Point Break* footage if I'd decided to go that way."

"Yeah, well. I'm glad you had the balls to play yourself."

So was I—although, all things considered, I was surprised that it had worked. After I'd sent her the bullet, I didn't hear from Darla for two days, and when she reappeared, she immediately picked another fight with Ray. I arrived in the middle of that, so I wasn't even sure what it was about, but for Ray it was the last straw. "Either she goes, or I do," he told me, before logging out.

It was then that I read Darla the riot act. Or tried to—it's hard to effectively chastise someone when you're waiting to find out if they'll sleep with you. Darla took full advantage of the situation and proceeded to tease the shit out of me, even as I insisted that no, really, I was serious: Whatever I might wish for, if she forced me to choose between her and the business, I'd pick the business. In the end, I did get the point across—or maybe Darla, having had her fill of fun, got tired of hearing me repeat myself. Fine, she said, if Ray's going to be such a huge pussy about it, I'll leave him alone. *And* Anja. *And* the customers.

I was still deciding whether to believe this when Darla grinned and asked me if I wanted to go someplace more private. She gave me the IP address of a mystery website and a password I'd need to get into it. And so now here we were, wherever here was.

It was a barren rock in outer space, the pronounced curve of the horizon making me think of the planetoids in *The Little Prince*. Someone had built a love nest inside a shallow crater, tucking a four-poster bed and a heart-shaped jacuzzi under a geodesic dome. UV lights in the dome struts made the naked skins of our avatars glow, and when I came, a supernova flared in the sky.

"So I've been thinking more about what I'd want in a dream game," Darla said, stretched out beside me on the bed.

"And?"

"What about something like this?"

"You mean a science-fiction setting?"

"No, genius." Darla turned towards me and propped herself up on an elbow. "I'm talking about fucking."

"There already are games about fucking. There are even games about fucking that won't download malware onto your computer."

"Not *about* fucking," she said. "*With* fucking. Like, what if you did a quality MMORPG like *Call to Wizardry*, and included an option for players to hook up between dungeon runs?" She considered. "Or during dungeon runs?"

It sounded like a terrible idea. But I remembered how our last discussion about game design had ended, and since I wanted this hookup to be more than a one-time deal, I kept my mouth shut and pretended to think it over.

Darla burst out laughing.

"What?" I said.

"What's the name of that mod you use, to keep your eyes focused on the person you're talking to? 'You So Interesting'?"

"Yeah. Why?"

"You should call up the ex-girlfriend who wrote it and ask her to code another one for the rest of your face," Darla said. "Because for someone who wants to get ahead in business, you are *way* too easy to read."

Wendy had made a similar observation, on more than one occasion; the last time was on the day we broke up. "I don't know if I'd want a mod like that."

"Why not?"

I shrugged. "Because I'm selfish but not a sociopath? Or maybe it's a pride thing."

"What, like, 'Real men should be able to lie without help?'"

"When it really matters, yeah."

"That's a retarded way to think," Darla said, leaning hard on "retarded." But I didn't rise to the bait, and after a moment she sighed and said, "So tell me why my idea about putting fucking in an MMORPG is stupid. It's OK, I promise I won't get pissed. You've got me in a good mood."

That was nice to hear, but I thought I'd better proceed cautiously anyway. "It's not stupid," I said, "just complicated. An Adults Only rating on a game makes everything ten times more difficult. Investment money is a *lot* harder to come by, and there are lots of companies that won't do business with you. PayPal, for example."

"Fuck PayPal."

"What about Superego? You know, the guys who did the physics engine for *Reign in Hell* and *Camp Blood Killing Spree*?"

"Duh, I know who Superego is."

"Do you know about their new terms of service? As part of the settlement for the sexual harassment lawsuit against their CEO, they added a new rider to their standard contract. If you want to license their software, you have to promise you won't use it to make a game that promotes sexism or misogyny."

"Oh, Jesus Christ!" Darla said. "Fucking is not sexist!"

"I agree," I said, putting my hands up. "But it doesn't matter what we think. What matters is what Superego thinks. What their lawyers think, and what their lawyers think the plaintiffs in the settlement will think. That's what an AO rating gets you. You can have the purest heart and the best intentions in the world, and other companies will still treat you like a leper.

"And that's *before* you finish the game," I continued. "Once you're ready to start marketing, you've got advertising restrictions. A lot of game sites won't review you, and the ones that do will tend to be stupid about it, because nerds and sex."

"Stupid reviews are fine, as long as they mention the sex part," Darla countered. "That's enough to get people interested. And there are other ways to get the word out. I mean, think of the hot takes."

"Yeah, you could probably gin up a controversy. Of course, Spectacle attracts politicians . . ."

"More free advertising."

"Lawyers to defend you from obscenity charges aren't free. But you're right, that could work as a guerrilla marketing strategy. Once you've got people's attention, though, you need to deliver. And to make up for the extra hassle, the game would need to be really popular."

"Well, why wouldn't it be? MMORPGs are popular. Fucking is insanely popular. And two great tastes . . ."

"Don't necessarily go together," I said, as gently as I could. "You're thinking chocolate and peanut butter, but what if this is more like chocolate and shrimp? And that leads me to one more point, which is that even people who are into that particular combination don't really need new software. I mean, right now, if you want to spice up your raid on Zuul'titlan with an orgy, all you have to do is find a quiet spot between fights and fire up PPML."

"Yeah, but that takes two different programs."

"Is that a problem, though? It might be, if PPML didn't play well with other VR software—but it does. And if you're into cybersex, you have PPML, so integrating its features directly into an MMORPG doesn't add anything. But if you're *not* into cybersex, the last thing you want is to give griefers the ability to literally fuck with you."

Despite her promise, Darla had been starting to get pissed off again, but this last remark struck her funny. "I suppose that *would* be pretty bad for business," she acknowledged. Then, smirking: "Chocolate and shrimp."

"I'm not saying it couldn't work. But there's got to be some kind of synergy, something extra you get from putting the two things together. We can brainstorm it if you like, try to come up with an angle . . ."

"No, that's OK," she said. "It's just an idea I pulled out of my ass. But you're right, it's dumb."

"We can still talk about it."

"No, it's all right. I told you, you've got me in a good mood." All smiles again, she tilted her head back and gestured at the dome and the dark sky above us. "So what do you think of this?"

"I like the lighting effects," I said, staying focused on her avatar.

"Perv."

"Where are we, anyway?" I asked. "Is this your site, or some secret online club I don't know about?"

"You've got the IP address. Look it up."

I opened a pop-up window. The IP address was registered to a company in southern California called Cumulonimbus. I didn't recognize the name, but guessed it was a reference to cloud storage. "Are you renting space on a server farm in L.A.?"

"It's in Los Angeles, but it's got nothing to do with me. Keep looking."

I ran the company name through BusinessTrak. Cumulonimbus turned out to be a subsidiary. It *was* a data center, and it did rent out storage space to other companies, but most of its servers were reserved for use by its parent corporation: Tempest.

Darla laughed as she watched me put it together. "This is one of Tempest's servers?" I said. "We're inside . . . We just . . ."

"We fucked in their corporate data core," Darla confirmed.

Staring at her under the lights a few moments ago, I'd started to get hard again, but now my erection shriveled away to nothing. I nervously scanned the horizon, imagining an army of blue-gloved EULA cops converging on us from all directions. Though of course that was wishful thinking. Breaking into a private corporate server isn't a EULA violation—it's a felony.

"Relax," Darla said. "We didn't break in. We used a password."

"News flash, it's still burglary if you use a stolen key."

"There's no reason for the sysadmin to think we don't belong here. And even if they did get suspicious, it's not like they can trace . . . Wait. You *are* using the PPML proxy server setting, right?"

"Of course I am, but that's not foolproof. If they wanted to backtrace us badly enough, they could—"

"Oh my God!" Darla said, looking suddenly stricken. "What if they're recording us right now? What if they digitize our faces, and then send image-recognition bots to scour the internets?"

"I know you think you're being funny, Darla, but if they wanted to identify us, that's exactly how they'd—"

"Attention, Tempest corporate overlords!" Darla cupped her hands to her mouth as she shouted up at the stars. "JOHN CHU and DARLA JEAN COVINGTON are FUCKING inside your computer!"

She cracked up, clutching her stomach and rolling around on the bed. I decided to be fatalistic. I mean, she was probably right: The fact that we hadn't been booted off the site meant it was unlikely we'd tripped any alarms. And if the system administrator *had* noticed us, there was nothing we could do about that now.

"Where did you get the password from?" I wanted to know.

"Orville," Darla said, still laughing. "A hacker friend. Don't worry, I'm not fucking him," she added, though in fact that was the last thing I was worried about.

"And what is this?" I asked, scanning the horizon again. "Concept art for a new game?"

"Think TempestCon, two years ago," Darla said. "It'll come to you."

I did, and it did. *"Call to Infinity."* That was the working title of an MMORPG that was, or would have been, a sci-fi sibling of *Call to Wizardry.* Tempest had shown a teaser trailer for it at one of their annual conventions, but there'd been no further news about it since then. The consensus in the gaming community was that the project had been canceled, probably because it was a little *too* similar to *Call to Wizardry*; most people only have time for one MMORPG in their lives, and it made no sense for Tempest to spend hundreds of millions of dollars on a game that would cannibalize their existing player base.

"This isn't just concept art," Darla told me. "It's a virtual studio for level design. This planet is hollow; there's a hatch a few craters over that leads down inside, and they've got all kinds of assembly tools stashed in there. It's what I used to build this dome. I thought you might want to check it out for yourself." She laughed again, watching my face as the words "intellectual property theft" flashed through my brain. "I'm not saying *steal* the tools—although we could. But you should at least play with them, maybe learn some tricks to use for our game."

"*Our* game?" I said. "Are we partners now?"

She shrugged. "I know everybody and his brother talks about making a game, but you actually started a business, so I know you're not just hot air. But you'll never do anything cool without someone to kick your ass and get you out of your comfort zone . . . And I suppose it wouldn't kill me to have someone practical to rein me in now and then. As long as you're not a patronizing dick about it. Of course," she added, "that's assuming we even have a future together."

"Why wouldn't we?"

"Because you already got what you really wanted from me. Now you can cut me from the crew and keep Ray. And not that I even care that much about the job, but you know I'm going to be pissed, right? This time next month, you'll probably be dead to me."

"Jesus, Darla . . . I don't want to cut anyone from the crew. I want you and Ray to get along."

"Yeah, well, like I said before, there's what you want, and what you can have."

"What I *need* is for the business to be successful. It takes capital to start a game company."

She snorted. "You think you can finance an MMORPG with the money you make as a sherpa?"

I shook my head. "It's not about the profits. It's about the contacts."

Give Darla credit, she got it right away: "You mean like the Kwan brothers? You're going to ask them to invest?"

"They'd be on my short list, yeah. When I'm ready."

"Huh. That's . . . actually not stupid."

"Gee, thanks." I started to smile, but then this image came into my head, of walking into a meeting with the Kwan brothers with Darla at my side. Easily bored, extremely volatile Darla.

"What is it?" she said. "Your face just did something weird."

"Nothing," I said, thinking, Change the subject. "You and I should meet up in person."

The suggestion caught her off guard. "You couldn't handle me in person."

"I'm willing to risk it. I'll even come to you, if you want."

"Gosh, that's so generous."

"I'm between cars right now," I explained. "But that's OK, I'll rent something and drive up to . . . what city are you in?"

"Nice try," Darla said. Then: "I'll think about it . . . If I did decide to meet you, it'd have to be after I get back from my trip."

"Where are you going?"

"Family reunion back east, at my mom's place." She raised an eyebrow. "Cousin Earl will be there."

"You'll have to shoot him in the ass for me. How long will you be gone?"

"I'm not sure. It depends what level of psychodrama Mom and I get into." Then she looked at me, dead serious, and said: "You'd better not disappoint me, if I do let you visit. Me pissed off online is nothing compared to me pissed off in person."

"I won't disappoint you," I said. "Promise."

"All right . . . So, you want to go check out those software tools?"

I eyed her avatar again. "In a few minutes . . ."

We stayed on Tempest's server for another four hours. The next day we came back again. And the next.

We were going to go there once more, the night before Darla left on her trip. But earlier that same day I got the call from Janet Margeaux's CAA agent. By the time I met Darla in the Game Lobby that evening, I'd decided to cut her out of the gig and not tell her until afterwards. I was comfortable with that choice—or told myself I was—but it would have felt wrong to have sex with her, with that between us. It's weird, the lines we draw.

Instead of going with her to the Tempest server I told Darla I was tired and asked for a rain check. She was immediately suspicious.

"Rain check? Are you bored with me already?"

When you don't trust yourself to lie effectively, the best way to do it is by telling the truth. "I'm definitely not bored with you, Darla."

"Hmm . . . Fine then, suit yourself. But if my plane crashes tomorrow, you're going to kick yourself for passing up a last chance with me."

"I will be sad if that happens," I said. Which was also true.

"If my plane *doesn't* crash," Darla continued, "I might have a surprise for you when I get back."

"Your home address?"

"Maybe. But I meant something bigger. Something you'll like." She paused, studying my expression. "You sure you don't have anything you want to tell me?"

"I'm sure," I said. "Have a safe trip, Darla."

tort of wrongful seduction — A **cause of action** in a civil lawsuit in which the plaintiff claims to have been enticed into sex by false pretenses, such as a fraudulent promise of marriage.

In the tort's earliest incarnation, the right of action belonged to the father of a dishonored woman, and the alleged harm was loss of services to her family. In time, the right to sue was extended to the woman herself, and the harm was recognized to be moral and personal rather than strictly economic. Ironically, this liberalization of the tort undermined it, as changing sexual mores and attitudes about women's honor—as well as the perennial reluctance of juries to take women at their word—made such lawsuits much harder to argue and win. By the end of the twentieth century, the tort of seduction appeared to be extinct. But the 2020s saw a revival of the tort, as another shift in mores inspired a new generation of plaintiffs—men as well as women—to attempt to rewrite the rules of love.

—*Merriam-Webster's Law Dictionary*

S o this guy breaks into your apartment, tases you, and hits you in the face with a bag of money?" Jolene says.

"The tasing came last," I correct her. "Hurt like hell, too."

"It's supposed to. Are you all right?"

"I'm fine. Once I could stand up again, I was more worried about my rig. The goggles and earphones are OK, I think, but the gloves are a little twitchy. The good news is, I can afford to buy replacements."

Our avatars are in a private chat room in the Game Lobby. In real life, Jolene is outdoors. When I reached her, she was at home, and I asked if she had a yard or patio she could go out to while we talked. I can hear the faint buzz of a lawnmower in the background.

"How much money are we talking about?"

"Four hundred thousand dollars. Two weeks' pay from Ms. Pang. The electricity was her way of saying I need to be nicer about how I ask for it, next time."

"I take it you didn't call the cops."

I shake my head. "What would I have told them?"

"You *did* call your mom, though."

"Eventually," I say. "First I made sure the guy was really gone, locked the door and moved some furniture in front of it. Then I counted the money. Then I checked that my rig was OK."

"And then you called your mom."

"No, then I went to sleep for a few hours."

"Jesus Christ!"

"I was tired. I was *already* tired, before, and being electrocuted takes a lot out of you. Anyway, I didn't feel like I was in any immediate danger. If they'd wanted to kill me, they could have."

"It's the money, isn't it?" Jolene says. "You were thinking of not telling your mother about it. That's what you needed to sleep on."

"No, I had to tell Mom about the money. What I needed to sleep on was whether to tell her it was four hundred thousand or just two."

"You're an idiot."

"I know," I say. "But have you ever seen four hundred thousand dollars? Not virtual cash, but real bills you can hold?"

"I've seen people get stupid for a lot less than that," Jolene says. "Stacking the money higher doesn't make it less stupid."

"Well, look, I wouldn't really lie to Mom. I just needed to think about it."

"So when you woke up, you called her?"

"After breakfast, yeah. She wasn't available, but I left a message with her assistant, Ensign Kim."

"OK," Jolene says. "So now you're going to hole up in your place with the door locked until she calls you back, right?"

"No, I decided to get out of there."

"Why?"

"After I spoke to Ensign Kim, I started thinking about what else Ms. Pang's people might have been up to in my apartment. I don't think the guy who broke in last night did anything after he zapped me, but if he had access, who knows how many times he was in there before?"

"Your computer?"

I shrug. "The anti-tamper seals on the case are intact, and as far as infecting the hard drive, I don't think there's anything they could do in person that couldn't be more easily done remotely. But I was looking around the room, and I saw my old Companion Cube up on a shelf. You ever have one of those?"

"No, but I know what they are." A Companion Cube is like a hardware version of Googlebot—an interactive digital assistant that you can query or give commands to. And like all internet-connected devices with microphones, it can be turned into a remote listening device if someone hacks it.

"I got the Cube as part of a game promotion," I tell Jolene.

"I never even put batteries in it. But seeing it made me realize, it doesn't matter how secure my computer is if someone has a bug in my apartment. They can just listen to me talking on my headset."

"And this is why I'm out on my lawn? You think my place is bugged too?"

"I don't know. But it's possible."

"Well, I've got good news," Jolene says. "The people I work for, they're paranoid about security. I get my house swept for bugs once a month. Last check was just a few days ago."

"A law firm does that?"

Jolene pretends not to hear the question. "Where are you now?" she asks.

"In a motel. At first I had this crazy idea about going to the Hilton downtown and renting out the penthouse, but I realized that even if they were willing to take cash, they'd want to log my ID and credit card into their system."

"So you went to a no-tell fleabag instead?"

"It's not a fleabag," I say. "It's clean, and they've got high-speed broadband. The neighborhood's remote, but it's safe."

"You hope. How'd you get there?"

"Loaded my gear and the money into a backpack and rode around on BART for a few hours. Changed trains a dozen times. Then I caught a cab."

"Hmm." She frowns. "That *might* be good enough."

"Can I ask you something, Jolene?"

"What?"

"You told me once that the firm you work for specializes in estate planning. Why would a law firm like that need to sweep an IT person's house for bugs? Are they worried you're going to take the clients' wills home and read them out loud?"

Jolene stares at me, lips pursed. She's annoyed, but not with me—with herself, for breaking character.

Before she can say anything, a pop-up window appears at the bottom of my visual field:

HE DESIRES A SESSION, TO BEGIN IN 30 MINUTES. ASSEMBLE YOUR CREW. — SMITH

This is followed almost immediately by a second pop-up:

CONFIRM THAT YOU ARE AVAILABLE. THEN SEE YOUR EMAIL FOR FURTHER INSTRUCTIONS. DO NOT DISAPPOINT ME. — PANG

"What is it?" Jolene says.

THE ENGLISH TRANSLATION OF THE NEWS CHYRON reads: MARRIAGE OF NORTH AND SOUTH TO BE CON-SUMMATED AT NOON TOMORROW.

Over the airplane's loudspeaker, the pilot announces that we have begun our descent into Pyongyang. It is raining in the capital, with scattered thunder and high winds; there will be turbulence during the landing, so we are advised to remain seated for the du-ration of the flight. But Mr. Jones ignores the warning. He stands in the aisle, staring at the TV at the front of the passenger cabin, which is now showing scenes from the recent unification summit: While crowds cheer outside South Korea's Blue House, President Sunwoo shakes hands with an elderly Kim Jong-un.

"What year is this supposed to be?" Mr. Jones asks.

"Two thousand and fifty-two," I tell him. Nodding at the TV screen: "The Supreme Leader just celebrated his seventieth birthday."

Mr. Jones tugs experimentally at the skin beneath his chin. "And this game—"

"*D.M. Zed.*"

"—it is from the Republic of Korea?"

"Yes. The company, GangnamSoft, is based in Seoul."

"And the government permits this? A game about reunification?"

"There's been some controversy about the content," I say, which is true enough. "But no calls to ban the game, so far. And the sale preorders have been through the roof."

The first turbulence jolts the plane. I look out the window. It is night, and we are descending into an unbroken bank of moonlit clouds. The photorealistic rendering is almost perfect, but as the plane bounces, a software glitch sends a silver squiggle cascading across the cloud tops.

D.M. Zed is in its final week of beta, and GSoft's programmers are working around the clock to get the last bugs out before the release date. Ms. Pang's email contained the address and password for this playtest server. My instructions are to keep Mr. Jones logged in for as long as possible. Ms. Pang didn't explain why she wants this, but my guess is that the game has an unpatched client-side security flaw that she means to take advantage of.

The view is obscured as we enter the clouds. The turbulence increases; I grip the imaginary arms of my seat and glance around the cabin. Jolene, Anja, and Ray are in the row directly behind me. Our avatars are dressed in United Nations uniforms, with insignia and equipment signifying our different roles. Mr. Jones, who has a big badge on his chest, is an envoy, empowered to give orders to non-player characters and call for help on his satellite phone. Anja is an engineer. Ray is a medic. Jolene is a computer specialist.

I'm security. The 9mm pistol on my hip is our only weapon at the moment, though I already have my eye on a possible upgrade. The rest of the passengers are NPCs; most of them are UN staff and reporters, but seated at the back of the cabin are two soldiers—one North Korean, one South Korean—armed with futuristic assault rifles. I've got dibs on one of those, the moment something happens to its current owner. Which, I predict, will be very soon now.

"Beginning final approach," the pilot says. The cabin lights go out, and the TV image is replaced by static and then a solid blue screen. As we break through the cloud layer, the plane banks sharply to the left, and this combined with the darkness in the cabin draws everyone's attention to the view of Future Pyongyang below us.

The city looks very different than it did in the CIA Factbook. The completed Ryugyong Hotel is surrounded by a forest of lesser towers, all of them as brightly lit as the skyscrapers in a normal metropolis. Across the Potong River on Mansu Hill, more lights ring the three Kim statues, which look like toy soldiers from this altitude.

"Beautiful," Mr. Jones murmurs, leaning across the seats in front of me. He sounds like he might cry.

"Check out the monorail." I indicate a string of lights stretching southwards from the Ryugyong. "That's the cross-DMZ express. Pyongyang to Seoul in under an hour."

"Beautiful," Mr. Jones repeats. But as we circle the city center, we start to see other lights—the flashing lights of emergency and police vehicles racing through the streets—that hint not all is well on the ground. Then, without warning, a massive explosion erupts from the side of the Ryugyong Hotel, provoking gasps from the NPCs. Seconds later, an even larger blast topples the statues on Mansu Hill.

The plane levels out. The cabin lights flicker back on and the TV transmission resumes. The chyron now reads: BREAKING NEWS! ". . . reports of violence from Pyongyang as well," the announcer is saying. "It appears the terrorist group Red Wolf has launched a coordinated assault on both capitals."

Mr. Jones looks up at the TV screen before turning to me. "Red Wolf?"

"A radical separatist group opposed to unification," I say, quoting from the official game wiki.

"And our goal is to crush them?"

"One goal, yeah." There's also the matter of the Zed referenced in the game's title, but I opt not to spoil that for him.

"We must get on the ground as quickly as possible," he says.

"I wouldn't worry about it," I say. Though in fact, the plane is no longer descending.

The pilot comes back on the loudspeaker: "Attention, passengers. Owing to the state of emergency in Pyongyang, we must abort our landing and return to Beijing."

"No!" Mr. Jones says, starting towards the cockpit. "I forbid—"

Lightning hits the plane, or maybe it's some sort of energy weapon. There's a blinding flash. The cabin lights go out for good this time, and the TV goes black. The plane's nose dips sharply and a female NPC starts screaming.

Mr. Jones steadies himself in the aisle and faces me, his expression only visible because of the flames streaming from the left-side engine.

"Like I said." I shout to be heard above the screams. "Don't worry about it."

RIGHT BEFORE THE CRASH, I GET AN INSTANT MESSAGE from Smith: YOU ARE LOGGED IN FROM A NEW IP ADDRESS. WHERE ARE YOU?

The game has seized control of my POV and plastered my face to the window. As lightning illuminates the ground rushing up towards the plane, the sound of my character's panicked breathing fills my ears.

HOUSE-SITTING FOR A FRIEND, I reply. As I hit send, it occurs to me that Smith may not know what "house-sitting" is.

I hear the pilot's voice, echoing as if down a long tunnel: "Brace! Brace! Brace!" The plane's left wing clips a power pylon. The wing shears off and the plane shudders and starts to roll. Everything goes black.

Out of the darkness, Smith messages: WHERE?

SAN BRUNO. NEAR THE AIRPORT.

WHAT STREET ADDRESS?

On the way to the motel, I had the cab detour through a nearby residential neighborhood, and picked out a house with a spiked fence and a Great Dane guarding the front yard. I type in the address, adding, BE CAREFUL OF SCOOBY IF YOU COME BY.

SCOOBY? Smith responds.

The darkness is lifting. GAME IS ON. GOT TO GO.

I am standing in a field strewn with burning wreckage. The rain has stopped, but lightning continues to flicker in the sky. My motion control comes back slowly: At first all I can do is stagger drunkenly, while my vision goes in and out of focus. Then things sharpen up and I'm able to look around.

The plane's fuselage broke into three pieces on impact. The front end of the passenger cabin, where we were sitting, stayed mostly intact, but the tail and the rows behind us completely disintegrated—so much for grabbing one of the soldiers' rifles. The detached nose of the plane continued onward, plowing through the perimeter fence of the Kim Jong-il International Airport. It looks like we almost made it to the runway.

Jolene, Ray, and Anja stumble towards me out of the gloom. Mr. Jones appears, leading a pair of shaken-up NPCs. He waves his satellite phone triumphantly. "I have made contact with another UN team," he says. "They say they can transport us to the city center. We are to rendezvous with them in the main terminal." He turns and looks back past the flames at the Pyongyang skyline, and I can tell there's a part of him that would like to just start walking. But the burning jet fuel and fragments of the tail section have formed an impassible barrier.

We go through the hole in the fence and sprint towards the terminal. Nothing else is moving on the airport tarmac, and as we pass a darkened hangar, the female NPC—the same one who was screaming on the plane, I think—starts whimpering with fear. "Be quiet, woman!" Mr. Jones says. Jolene, beside me, mimes sticking a finger down her throat.

As we near the terminal building we hear the sound of automatic weapons fire and see muzzle flashes behind some of the windows. Mr. Jones breaks out his satellite phone again, but before he can call the UN team for an update, there is a loud *crack!* of a rifle shot and the female NPC goes down. "Sniper!" the other NPC shouts helpfully.

We take cover behind a stalled baggage trailer. The trailer's driver was shot, but survived; we find him sitting with his back against one of the trailer carts, fighting to draw breath. His sucking chest wound serves as a tutorial for Ray's medic skills. Once he's been patched up and can speak, he tells us where the nearest entrance to the terminal is. It's close, but we're going to have to cross an open stretch of tarmac to reach it.

"You," Mr. Jones says, turning to our other NPC. "You go first." The NPC balks, but Mr. Jones pulls rank, tapping his envoy badge for emphasis.

The NPC makes a dash for it. He's barely out of cover when the sniper blows his head off.

"Running will not work," Mr. Jones observes. "What shall we try next?"

I nod at the trailer carts. "Maybe there's something in here we can use."

There is. The center cart contains several tall metal cases on wheels bearing the name and logo of a K-pop band. Anja uses her engineering skills and some scrounged bungee cords to string the cases together into a rolling ballistic shield. We crouch behind it and duck-walk across the tarmac. The sniper fires half a dozen bullets at us, but the shield holds until we are out of his line of sight.

We reach the door into the terminal. The lock is controlled by an electronic keypad; the baggage car driver gave us the code in exchange for a promise to send back help. But when we punch in the number, the keypad emits an angry buzz and a robotic voice informs us that the airport is on emergency lockdown.

Jolene goes to work hacking the mechanism. The door unlocks and Mr. Jones hauls it open. "Wait," I say, and remind him that of all the characters, I'm the only one who hasn't gotten to use my special ability yet.

"Good point," Mr. Jones says. "Lead the way."

I step through the door into a broad stairwell. Sprawled at my feet is the body of another baggage handler; it looks like he broke his neck falling down the stairs. Looking up, I glimpse another corpse on the half-landing above me, with a uniformed figure hunched over it. I hear grunting noises and the sound of tearing flesh.

"What is that?" Mr. Jones says, entering the stairwell behind me. The figure in uniform looks up at the sound and turns towards us. Its face is covered in gore, and in its eagerness to feed, it has bitten its own lips off, leaving its teeth horribly exposed.

"It's Zed," I say. The uniformed zombie growls at us.

I draw my pistol and aim for the head.

WE FIND MORE BODIES INSIDE THE TERMINAL. THE STAIR-well exits into a passenger waiting area that's been hit by a bomb blast; corpses and severed limbs are draped over the shattered seats. Slumped against the far wall is a flight attendant who is missing the top of his skull; his brain matter is spattered across a floor-to-ceiling poster that shows a grinning Kim Jong-un arm-in-arm with his old pal Dennis Rodman. There's a lot going on here, visually, but the detail that jumps out at me is that Rodman, who broke his back in a skydiving accident while I was still in grade school, is shown standing on two good legs. Like Kim's, his image has been artificially aged—at ninety-one, he looks like a mummy with facial piercings—but he's upright. This could be a nod to political realism on the part of the game designers: Physical handicaps are taboo in the DPRK, and it's unlikely that a friend of the dictator would be portrayed in a wheelchair. On the other hand, this is the future, so maybe the idea is that the medical establishment has finally gotten spinal cord regeneration to work. I notice Anja is staring at the poster too; when she sees me looking at her, she shrugs a shoulder as if to say, It'd be nice if they did figure it out.

Mr. Jones finishes talking on his sat phone. "This way," he tells us, pointing. "The UN team is in a restaurant across from boarding gate twenty-three. They have just beaten back an assault by the Red Wolves."

The gate is at the other end of the terminal. Along the way we pass more scenes of carnage, all exquisitely rendered; the Red Wolves, and GSoft's art department, have clearly put in a lot of work. "Jesus," I hear Ray say, as he averts his eyes from a particularly gruesome death scene.

Near gate fifteen we find the bodies of several DPRK soldiers. They've been stripped of their weapons, but one of them is carrying a couple spare clips of pistol ammo.

"Tell me about the Zed," Mr. Jones says, as I search the other corpses.

"They're infected with a genetically engineered virus," I tell him. "Later in the game, you find out that the Red Wolves recently infiltrated a bioweapons lab, looking for anthrax. They were caught and killed, but the Zed virus got loose, and one of the members of the tactical response team was infected before the lab could be sterilized. He brought the virus back to Pyongyang and it's been spreading ever since. Tonight's the night the zombie plague reached critical mass, just in time for the Red Wolves' big assault . . ."

The lights in the terminal go out. I stand up slowly in the

darkness, and since there are no NPCs around to state the obvious, I say: "The Red Wolves must have hit the local power station."

The emergency lighting kicks in. The backup lights are dim and strategically positioned to leave large portions of the terminal in shadow.

"Gate twenty-three," Mr. Jones says, sounding more annoyed than frightened. "Let's go."

The ambush happens at gate twenty. A man in civilian clothes steps out of the darkness in front of us; he has a black bandanna with a red wolf's head tied mask-like over his mouth and nose, and he is carrying a submachine gun. I drop to a crouch and raise my pistol, but before I can get off a shot, a zombie emerges from the shadows as well. The Red Wolf screams as the zombie bites him on the shoulder. As the two of them grapple, a gunfight erupts in the near distance behind them, more black-clad figures opening fire on a barricaded restaurant.

"Give me your weapon," Mr. Jones says.

"Remember our ammo is limited," I say, handing him the pistol.

"I know what I am doing," Mr. Jones says. He strikes a gunslinger pose, one eye shut and arm extended. He spends a long moment shifting his aim back and forth. Then he pulls the trigger, twice. The zombie's skull explodes, while the Red Wolf's head snaps sideways. As their bodies hit the floor, the nearby firefight culminates in a massive explosion that rattles the terminal and sends a wall of smoke billowing towards us.

Silence descends. We wait. The smoke has just begun to dissipate when we hear coughing and approaching footsteps. A figure stumbles into view with its arms in the air.

"Halt!" Mr. Jones commands. "Identify yourself!"

"Corporal Chen Li-jun of the United Nations peacekeeping force! Don't shoot, I am unarmed!"

Mr. Jones lowers the pistol and taps his envoy badge. "Report, Corporal Chen."

"The rest of my team is dead, sir! One of the Red Wolves set off a satchel charge."

"Did you say you are unarmed?"

"Yes sir! I am a mechanic, sir, not a fighter."

"What about your security people? Can we use their guns?"

"Their weapons were all destroyed in the explosion, sir. And the terrorists' weapons."

"How inconvenient," Mr. Jones says dryly. He hands me back my pistol and takes the submachine gun from the Red Wolf he killed. It looks like it's in working order; there's only one forty-round clip, but it's full. "This will do for now," he says. "Corporal Chen, I was told you could arrange transport to the city center."

"Yes sir." Corporal Chen explains that there is—or rather, was—a monorail line linking the airport to the central station at the Ryugyong Hotel. The Red Wolves have knocked out a section of the rail near the airport perimeter, but three kilometers to the south there is another station that is still connected, and soldiers and police are reported to be rallying there. "We must find a vehicle and drive there. Then you can take the monorail into the city center."

"No," Mr. Jones says. "I wish to get to the city center as quickly as possible. We will drive there directly."

Corporal Chen blinks and looks momentarily confused. Then he repeats his previous statement word for word, with the exact same intonation.

Mr. Jones sighs in exasperation. "We can try driving straight to the city," I say. "But if we're supposed to take the monorail, a car trip may not be possible."

"Ridiculous," Mr. Jones mutters. Then he says, "Very well. Corporal Chen, get us out of here and find us a vehicle."

"Yes sir! Sir, I must also inform you that there is a Red Wolf sniper on the roof of the terminal . . ."

"Yes, we know."

"Before we leave, you may wish to go up to the roof and deal with him. It will safeguard our departure, and his weapon could be useful."

"I have no interest in acquiring a sniper rifle," Mr. Jones says. "I am impatient to get to the city. Find us a vehicle." He waits, frowning, to see if the corporal will repeat himself again.

"Yes sir!" Chen says. "This way, sir." He turns and starts moving. Mr. Jones, Jolene, Ray, and I all follow him, but I turn back when I notice Anja isn't with us.

She is standing over the Red Wolf and the zombie Mr. Jones shot. It looks like she's staring at something, but this time there's no poster in her line of vision, and as I get closer I see that her avatar is not just still but completely motionless.

"Anja?" I say, reaching out. My hand doesn't just pass through her, it erases the portion of her avatar that it touches. I wave my arm back and forth, and her entire upper torso disappears, leaving her head hanging frozen in midair. Creepy.

"John Chu!" Mr. Jones calls back to me. "What is the problem?"

"Anja's glitched," I tell him. "She must have disconnected."

"Can she rejoin the game?"

"I don't know."

"We will proceed without her," he says. "If she logs back in, she will have to catch up to us. Now come on!"

As we make our way through the terminal, I send Anja an instant message, asking her what happened. I get no answer. But I do get a message from Ms. Pang. LOOK FOR AN OPPORTUNITY TO ISOLATE MR. JONES, it says.

WHAT DO YOU MEAN, "ISOLATE"? I write back.

LOSE THE OTHER MEMBERS OF YOUR PARTY. KILL THEM IF YOU HAVE TO, BUT TRY TO BE SUBTLE. ONCE YOU AND JONES ARE ALONE, KEEP YOUR EYES OPEN. WHEN YOU SEE ME COMING, DISTRACT HIM.

I HAVE QUESTIONS, I write.

YOU HAVE YOUR MONEY, she replies. NOW DO AS YOU ARE TOLD.

In baggage claim a pitched battle is underway between a Red Wolf, a squad of North Korean soldiers, and a big pack of zombies. The Red Wolf tries to make a fighting retreat along a stalled conveyor belt; he gets grabbed from behind and dragged out of sight, along with his weapon. The zombies swarm the soldiers' position. The squad leader screams something patriotic and sets off a belt of grenades; the blast brings down a big chunk of the ceiling, burying the squad and most of the Zed. While Mr. Jones and I shoot the few zombies that are left, Jolene spies a golf bag among the scattered luggage and arms herself with a nine iron.

Outside, the passenger pickup area is another scene of carnage. In addition to the bodies, there are enough cars to constitute a traffic jam by DPRK standards, but none of them are drivable: They are all shot or smashed up, or on fire. Off to our right, though, in the clear and conspicuously undamaged, is an idling passenger bus. "There is our ride," Corporal Chen says.

"I will drive," says Mr. Jones, but Corporal Chen sprints ahead, and by the time we board he is already behind the wheel. No amount of envoy badge-tapping will convince the corporal to move, so Mr. Jones takes a seat across from him and glares instead.

Jolene, Ray, and I move towards the back of the bus. A zombie pops up and I shoot it in the head. We sit.

"What's up with Anja?" Jolene asks me.

"I don't know. I messaged her, but she's not answering. Maybe her internet is out."

"Lucky girl," Ray says.

"What's your problem?" says Jolene.

"My problem is I don't like seeing people with their faces chewed off. I mean, if it's cartoon gore, OK, but *this* shit . . ." He gestures at the downed Zed, whose left eye has come out of its socket and now dangles from a stalk, jiggling with the motion of the bus.

We've cleared the terminal. The road curves to merge with a broader thruway. As Corporal Chen makes the turn, we hear a familiar *crack!* and the side window behind Mr. Jones shatters. The bullet hits the corporal in the head and his brains spray across the front windshield. "Great," Ray says. As the bus swerves out of control, Mr. Jones tries to grab the wheel. But the crash that follows is scripted—our penalty for declining the sniper side quest.

The bus plows through a guard rail and plunges down a steep embankment. Our characters don't black out this time, but the simulated whiplash as we hit bottom is enough to make even a veteran VR player queasy.

We stumble out of the wreck and regroup by the light of the one surviving headlamp. We've come down onto a two-lane road that runs beneath the thruway. To our left the road is blocked by a jack-knifed tractor trailer. To our right is a dark tunnel; a blinking pair of hazard lights is visible at the far end. Our next ride, probably, if we can get to it.

"I'm sure there aren't a million Zed hiding in there," Jolene deadpans. She glances towards the embankment, but without even trying she knows it's impossible to climb back up. We *have* to go through the tunnel.

Mr. Jones, impatient as ever, is already marching into the darkness. Jolene hefts her nine iron and starts to follow him, but I stop her and say, "You and Ray wait here."

"Excuse me?"

"Just do it," I say. "Please?" She frowns but doesn't argue. Neither does Ray, who I think at this point would be just as happy to get killed off.

I run to catch up with Mr. Jones. We are in the middle of the tunnel when the first Zed come shambling out of the dark. They are few in number and they are slow movers, so it would be easy enough to just dodge around them, but I choose to deliberately fall into the game designers' trap and fire my pistol. The gunshot echoes loudly in the tunnel, and as the echo fades I hear the crash of a metal door slamming open, followed by a chorus of growls.

We are close enough now to see that the hazard lights belong to a white airport security jeep that is sitting with its front doors open. On the other side of the road is a sedan that has been flipped onto its roof. The guys in the jeep must have stopped to investigate the wreck, and you can guess what happened next.

Sure enough, as Mr. Jones goes to climb in the jeep, he is ambushed by a Zed in a tattered security uniform. While he's busy shooting it, I step past him and slip behind the wheel. The jeep's keys are in the ignition and the motor starts on the first try. "I will drive," Mr. Jones says, but instead of sliding over I pull the driver's door shut and motion for him to go around. This gets him glaring again, but the rest of the Zed are almost on us.

"What about the other two?" Mr. Jones asks, as he climbs into the passenger seat. I look up at the rearview mirror. The mob of approaching Zed must number in the dozens now, and they are jammed shoulder to shoulder, snarling furiously. I doubt even Darla could break through that with only a golf club for a weapon.

"Don't worry, they'll catch up to us," I say. Then I step on the gas.

THE ROAD CURVES LEFT AND UP. AS WE REJOIN THE THRU-way, I brace for more gunshots, but it seems we are out of sniper range.

I get a terse instant message from Jolene: WTF???

LATER, I reply.

The rain comes back with a vengeance. I put on the windshield wipers. Downtown Pyongyang still has power and the skyline remains hazily visible through the deluge, but it doesn't seem to be getting any closer. The blacked out landscape around us, as revealed by intermittent lightning flashes, is a mix of open farmland and concentrated apartment housing. The monorail line is on our right, running roughly parallel to the road, which confirms that we're going in the right direction—not that we actually have a choice. "The rally point can't be far," I tell Mr. Jones, but he only grunts impatiently, so I give the jeep more gas.

I get another instant message:

INTRUSION DETECTED — SECURICAM/A1

When I was searching my apartment this morning, something I found, in addition to my old Companion Cube, was the nanny-cam I bought for my previous apartment when I thought one of my roommates was stealing from me. It occurred to me that it might be useful to get footage of Ms. Pang's white guy if he came back, so before I left I set the camera up and programmed the motion sensor to send me alerts.

Keeping one eye on the road, I open a pop-up window and check out the video feed. It's not Ms. Pang's white guy. The three people in my apartment—two men and a woman—are all Asian. I want to say Korean, though they could be Chinese. Agewise I'd guess they're in their late twenties, though the tougher-looking of the two guys could be older.

Thanks to my thousands of hours of experience in first-person shooters, I have a much easier time IDing their guns. The tougher-looking guy is holding a 92 series Beretta semiautomatic, the default handgun for Hong Kong movie gangsters. The woman is armed with a Beretta 21A pocket pistol that has been fitted with a silencer—a common accessory in video games and films, but one that I've never actually seen on a real concealed-carry weapon. Staring at it, I think: WTF???

"Look out!" Mr. Jones says. A makeshift barricade of sandbags and concertina wire stretches across the road in front of us. Even if I weren't distracted, there's not enough time to avoid a collision, so instead of slamming on the brakes I just try to steer through the crash. This works for a few seconds but then the tires blow and we go into an uncontrolled skid.

The jeep comes to a stop with its front bumper and grill wrapped around a lamppost. The motor is dead but the headlights are some-how still working, so I can see the sign hanging askew from the post. MONORAIL STATION 0.6 KM, it reads. I try the ignition and confirm we'll be walking.

We climb out of the jeep and a series of closely timed lightning flashes gives us a sense of our surroundings. We've entered one of the suburban housing complexes, the thruway now a boulevard with rows of identical six-story apartment buildings lining either side. Behind us at the wrecked barricade I spot the remains of a blown-up machine-gun nest with uniformed bodies scattered around it.

Another sniper opens up with an automatic rifle from the other end of the street. I take cover behind the jeep. Mr. Jones ducks down beside me, but not before firing a long burst from his submachine gun.

"Hey," I remind him, "careful with your ammo!"

"Sorry!" he replies, sounding uncharacteristically abashed. Then he says: "The shooter is in a third-floor balcony about forty meters away."

"Stay here." I crawl around to the back of the jeep and peek out carefully. I quickly spot the shooter, and I also see how I'm supposed to deal with him. Parked on the sidewalk almost directly beneath the balcony is a military supply truck. Its tailgate is open, and lying beside it are two more dead soldiers who must have gotten shot as they were about to unload the truck's cargo: big red steel drums with flame icons on their sides.

Why would the North Korean Army be unloading barrels of fuel in the middle of a housing complex during a zombie apocalypse/terrorist uprising? Don't ask me, I just work here. I draw my pistol and wait for the next lightning flash. It's a long shot and my first bullet goes wide, but the second is dead-on, and the fuel is as volatile as nitroglycerin. The whole truck goes up, sending a huge gout of flame up the side of the building; the sniper is caught in it and dies screaming.

I salvage a grenade from one of the dead soldiers by the barricade. Mr. Jones and I proceed along the boulevard, the now-blazing apartment building lighting our way. We go about three hundred meters before our progress is blocked by a pair of buses parked nose-to-nose across the road. In real life this would be a surmountable obstacle, but the game won't allow me to give Mr. Jones's avatar a boost, or let me climb on his shoulders.

We are forced to detour into a small plaza to our left. At the center of the plaza, a life-sized portrait of Kim Jong-un has been placed atop a concrete pedestal. The pedestal is ringed by brightly burning torches, so despite the blackout and the storm, the Supreme Leader is clearly visible, a beacon of Juche strength in the darkness. At his first sight of it, Mr. Jones does a funny little dip, almost like he's genuflecting.

My own attention is focused on the edges of the plaza. I look for an open alley or a breezeway but don't find one; the surrounding buildings form a solid wall, and the doorways are all blocked with piles of sandbags. It's a dead end.

"How do we get to the station?" Mr. Jones asks.

I shake my head. "We don't. Not yet. Something has to happen first."

"I do not understand."

I approach the Kim Jong-un shrine and check out one of the torches. It's cast bronze, about three feet long, the flame fueled by a reservoir in the handle. I lift it from its sconce and swing it experimentally; it should make a decent club.

Growls echo from the direction of the boulevard. Mr. Jones and I turn to see the zombified citizens of Pyongyang emerging from the shadows. Whatever their social rank in life, they are members of the Hostile Class now, starving and eager to feast on our entrails. Mr. Jones tenses up and raises his weapon.

"Single shots to the head," I remind him.

"Yes, I understand," he says, nodding.

There are fifteen Zed in the first wave. Mr. Jones shoots ten of them; I shoot one and use the torch to bash out the brains of the other four. I load a fresh clip into my pistol and do a quick spin around to make sure there aren't more zombies sneaking up behind us.

I spot a lone figure standing on the far side of the shrine, but it's not one of the Zed. It's Ms. Pang. She is dressed all in black with a Red Wolf bandanna tied beneath her chin. She locks eyes with me and puts a finger to her lips.

"More of them!" Mr. Jones cries, still looking towards the boulevard.

The second wave is massive, more Zed than I can count. Mr. Jones is soon out of ammo; I toss him the torch and grab another for myself. We fight the mob hand to hand and are nearly overwhelmed. In desperation I use the grenade, taking out a dozen zombies at once and nearly killing us in the bargain. This buys us a moment's rest but it isn't enough; we can hear more of them coming.

Something big slams into the bus barricade. We hear a monstrous roar, and the growls of the Zed abruptly fall silent. One of the buses slides forward as the new arrival makes an opening for itself. Lightning flashes as it breaks through.

It's some kind of mutant Zed, grown to troll-like proportions. The sight of it makes me regret having used up my grenade, but there's no point crying about that now. I slam my last clip into my pistol and open fire on the monster. I can tell I hit it in the head because I see bits of skull flying off it, but this only seems to piss it off. Then my gun is empty, and the Zed pounds its knuckles on the ground and roars again.

Mr. Jones roars too—a kind of Rebel yell, the loudest sound I've ever heard him make—and charges the beast with his torch. The Zed swipes at him with both fists, but Mr. Jones dodges the blows and brings the torch down like a sledgehammer on the top of the Zed's skull, once, twice, three times. The monster's head comes apart and its body crashes to the ground, even as Mr. Jones continues to pound on it. He hits it until he is certain it's not getting up again, and then he hits it some more.

"Good *job*," I say, when he's finally finished. I say this not to praise him—although I am pretty impressed—but because Ms. Pang is walking up behind him now, and I want him to look at me instead of her. But he doesn't look at either of us, just stands there catching his breath.

Then Ms. Pang is right on top of him. She raises a hand, and I see blue sparks dancing over her palm and her fingers. This is a fairly cheesy visual effect—the kind of thing an amateur might whip up at home—but whatever computer process it signifies appears to be more sophisticated. Mr. Jones grunts and stiffens up, and his avatar turns one hundred and eighty degrees, rotating as if he were standing on a turntable. Ms. Pang shoves her hand into his face and the sparks wrap around his skull, for a moment seeming to form an almost solid band, like a VR headset made of lightning. Then the sparks go out and she draws her hand back. Mr. Jones's avatar is now frozen, just like Anja's avatar was frozen. Ms. Pang thrusts her hand forward again, and erases Mr. Jones's head.

"Excellent," she says. She turns to me smiling. "Well played, John Chu. You did not disappoint me."

Somehow I don't hear this as good news. "What did you just do?"

"A good question," says Ms. Pang. "The answer depends on how clever Smith is. But with a bit of good fortune, you will hear about it on the news very shortly. In the meantime—"

The rest of her words are drowned out by a sudden whine of static in my headphones. I start lagging like crazy, my visuals breaking up into a stuttering series of still images shot through with junk pixels. Whatever this is must be affecting my avatar as well, because right before I disconnect I hear a quizzical "John Ch-ch-ch-chu?" break through the static. Then my goggles go dark. The static drops to a hum, then nothing.

I spend a long moment in the silent void waiting to see if the words ACCOUNT TERMINATED will appear. They don't. But even without that confirmation, I can tell I'm down another name.

THERE'S A COMMON SCI-FI MOVIE TROPE WHERE A CHARacter thinks they've logged out of virtual reality, only to discover later that they've been tricked: They're still in the simulation. It's a believable scenario, because all of us have experienced something like this, in dreams. But when it comes to VR, the technology isn't quite there yet.

As I pull off my headset, I can smell something burning, and since I haven't bought any new Japanese sex toys, I know this must be real life. The Venetian blinds on the motel room window are drawn, but enough light is coming through the slats that I can see my computer on the dresser in front of me; it's not actually on fire, but when I pick it up the case is warm, and the glow of fried components is visible through the air vents on the back.

It's not just my game rig that's dead. The alarm clock and the lamp on the nightstand are both out, and when I flip the wall switch for the overhead lights, nothing happens.

I go to the window and peek out through the slats. It's evening and the sun has just set. The motel parking lot looks empty—no pistol-packing mystery Asians lying in wait. But when I step outside, there's a shoebox sitting on the doormat with my name written on the lid.

As I'm staring at the shoebox, the door to the motel room on my left opens and a shirtless white guy with dreads and a scraggly beard stumbles out. "Hey," he says, throwing me a confused look, "did you just lose power?"

I nod. We both turn and look at the Texaco station across the street, which is lit up and open for business. The streetlight on the corner is still working, too. "Weird," says the white guy.

Not really, I think. I've spent enough time browsing griefer forums to know there are lots of ways to cause a localized blackout, if that's your thing. For example, if you wire a Taser to an extension cord and plug it into a wall socket, you can melt down a building's electrical system as effectively as you can a human nervous system. I doubt that Ms. Pang's enforcer is to blame in this case, but here in America, where electroshock weapons are covered by the second amendment, he's not the only one with access to Tasers.

A phone starts ringing in the shoebox at my feet. The dreadlocked white guy, helpful as any NPC, nods at the box and says, "Sounds like you got a call."

"Thanks," I say. I take the shoebox back into my room and set it on the bed and open it. The smartphone inside is a Xiaomi 2035, a Chinese brand that according to my research is very popular in North Korea. Its screen reads: SMITH CALLING.

I pick it up and answer it. "How did you find me?"

"You have more important things to worry about," Smith says.

"Look, I don't know what just happened, but—"

"Don't you? Your confederate—who I believe to be an agent of the People's Republic of China—just tried to assassinate my boss."

"Assassinate?" I say. "What is this, *The Matrix*? You can't kill someone by—"

"I knew you were a security risk," Smith says. "My error was assuming that the danger was purely informational. I did not expect a physical threat."

"What physical threat?" Remembering the light show in the game: "Did something happen to Mr. Jones's VR headset?"

"As if you did not already know. You can be sure we will be looking much more closely at our foreign hardware sourcing, going forward."

"Is Jones all right?"

"Yes, he is quite well. Fortunately, we detected your confederate's incursion into our system, and as a precaution I had one of my own agents take over for Mr. Jones in the game. That agent will be honored as a hero."

I step to the window and scan the parking lot again. "Look, I don't know if you're bullshitting me here," I say, "but I don't know anything about a plot against Mr. Jones's life."

"You are not working for the PRC?"

"I *was* working for someone else. She calls herself Ms. Pang, and she could be PRC. But she wasn't just paying me, she was threatening me."

"Ah," Smith says. "'Carrot and stick,' is that the expression?"

"Yes."

"Well, John Chu, *I* have no more carrots for you. Your contract with Mr. Jones is terminated. You will receive no more money—but you will perform one last service. Do you see the envelope in the box I left for you?"

Nestled in the bottom of the shoebox is another, smaller box, rectangular and relatively flat. Resting on top of it is a letter-size envelope. The envelope contains a train ticket, a coach seat on to-morrow morning's Amtrak Coast Starlight to Los Angeles. "You want me to go to L.A.? What for?"

"You will find out when you get there."

"I don't think so."

"I do," Smith says. "There is a message with a video attachment on this phone's email app. Open it now and watch it."

The video clip is from the feed of another nannycam that is fo-cused on a long white medical pod. The head of the pod's occupant is enclosed in a special VR helmet, so I cannot see her face, but on the wall behind the pod are several shelves full of trophies, and a big poster of Anja performing at the Pan American Games.

A red light flashes on the side of the medical pod, and a robotic voice begins shouting: *"Achtung! Systemfehler!"* Within seconds, a woman I recognize as Anja's mother runs into view. She goes to a computer terminal near the foot of the pod, but even as she reaches it, the alarm ceases. Anja's mom snatches up a headset from beside the terminal and puts it on. "Anja?" I hear her say. "Alles OK mit dir?" She pauses to listen and then continues talking; by the time Anja's father appears, she is calmer. "Falscher Alarm," she tells him.

"Do we have an understanding now?" Smith says when I get back on the phone.

"You hacked Anja's iron lung."

"No, John Chu—*you* did. But so we are clear, if you force me to terminate her life support, there will be no alarm to warn her parents."

"OK," I say. "I understand the rules."

I find myself looking into the shoebox again, at the second box nestled inside it. Something tells me that whatever it contains, I'm not going to like it.

It's as if Smith can read my thoughts.

"Yes," he says. "Open it."

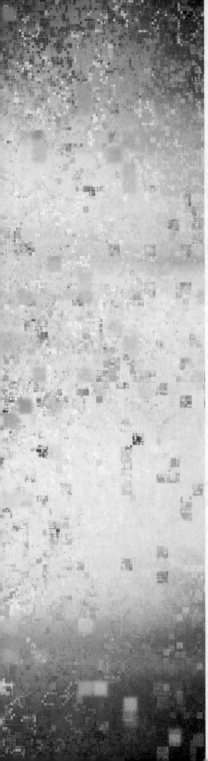

PART THREE

RL

You can play with your friends
in the Realms of Asgarth, but
remember to play with them
outside Asgarth as well.

    —*Call to Wizardry* loading screen tip

prohibition — A popular blood sport in which a government attempts to tame desire by passing a series of ineffective and increasingly draconian laws.

—*The New Devil's Dictionary*

Yesterday must have been protest day in Sacramento. The southbound Coast Starlight is carrying scores of anti-gun activists, and an equal number of anti-abortion protesters. Amtrak, hoping to avoid a riot, has seated the two groups at opposite ends of the train.

I get put in a car with the anti-gun crowd. At twenty-one I am an old man among them: Most are high-school age or even younger. They wear blood-red T-shirts, adorned on the back with the names of places where mass shootings have occurred. On the front of the shirts, above a graphic of a fist smashing an AK-47 into pieces, is the name of their movement: Repeal the 2nd.

Given how my grandparents died, you might assume I'd be all in favor of this, but as usual, I get hung up on the practical shit. When I think about gun control, I think of my aunt Emma, an Army surgeon who served four tours in Iraq. Retired now, she lives on a ranch outside Carson City, Nevada, with her wife, Yoko Hayashi. Aunt Yoko has a sad story about her grandparents, too: They were interned at the Tule Lake Segregation Center during the Second World War. Her grandmother was raped by one of the guards there.

Em and Yoko own a lot of firearms: a shotgun to deal with coyotes and human trespassers; a rifle for hunting; an assortment of pistols for mostly sentimental reasons (they met at a shooting range); and hidden behind a false wall in the bedroom closet, a pair of AR-15s and several thousand rounds of ammunition, their insurance against history repeating itself. Emma is mechanically gifted and Yoko can perform sorcery with a 3D printer, so in the event of a fascist takeover, I imagine they would have no trouble converting the AR-15s to full auto.

This makes them sound like doomsday preppers, which they kind of are, but they are also two of the sweetest people I know, and funny as hell. They are on a very short list of relatives who I enjoy arguing politics with. But good luck trying to change their minds about anything. When I first heard about the secret arsenal in the closet, I suggested to Emma that even machine guns would be useless in a fight against the government: Mom's got drones that could incinerate the entire ranch from fifty thousand feet in the air. Aunt Em replied that America had drones in Iraq, too, but the insurgents still managed to inflict enough pain that we eventually gave up and went home. "Don't get me wrong," she added good-naturedly. "I'm sure your mother could kill me if she wanted to. But I'm not making it a freebie."

Emma and Yoko raise Cavalier King Charles Spaniels for competition. This is relevant because the ATF has a standing policy to shoot any dogs they encounter during a raid. The agency does not discriminate: Even obviously harmless pets are treated as vicious attack animals and put down. My aunts regard their Spaniels as their children, and if a bunch of men and women in black showed up at the ranch and started murdering their babies, it doesn't take a genius to guess what would happen next. I would feel like a huge asshole if I were in any way responsible for that.

None of which changes the fact that America has a gun problem. If I could wave a magic wand and prevent all future Columbines, stop people from shooting each other in domestic disputes, and make it harder to commit suicide on a whim—yeah, sure, I would do that. But there is no magic wand, only the blunt instrument of the law versus the endless adaptability of the human heart in pursuit of what it wants.

Maybe these kids will come up with a strategy to make prohibition work at a reasonable cost in innocent lives. On another day, I might ask them about it, kill some time shooting the breeze on the way down to L.A. But at the moment, I'm dealing with too many distractions to feel like chatting.

Distraction number one is the collar around my neck. To a casual observer it must look like bondage gear, or some sort of science-fiction cosplay: a two-inch-wide band of black plastic ribbon cable, secured by a chunky metal buckle beneath my chin. There's an LED light on the front of the buckle that turned green when I locked the collar in place. If I try to undo the buckle or cut the ribbon cable, or if I fail to follow Smith's instructions to the letter, the light will turn red, and then something very bad will happen to me. Smith wasn't explicit about the nature of the bad thing, but it undoubtedly has something to do with the little glass vial at the back of the collar. The vial is filled with an amber-colored liquid, and sits in a metal bracket attached to the outside of the collar; on the inside of the collar, riding flush against the nape of my neck, is a tiny grommet with a hole a couple of millimeters wide. Feeling it there, I imagine a spring-loaded needle poised to jab me in the spine. That's probably wrong, though: VX, a topical nerve poison, doesn't need to be injected. A single drop on exposed skin is all it takes to kill you.

This makes it hard to get comfortable. The collar chafes, and I can't lean my head back against the seat rest for fear of breaking the glass. I sit up straight, stiff-necked, studying the faces of the people around me.

Distraction number two: Figuring out which of my fellow passengers is a DPRK sleeper agent. Smith told me that he'd have someone on the train keeping an eye on me. I assume the watcher is the same person who delivered the box to the motel.

I doubt it's any of the protesters. They were already on the train when I boarded, and besides, they're mostly white kids. Caucasian teenage North Korean spies seems like a stretch. I can probably also rule out the Sikh family who got on in Oakland. It could be the Asian guy in the business suit: He boarded the same time I did, and he has a pissed off resting expression that reminds me of Smith. But he's Japanese, not Korean, and while that doesn't rule him out, it does make me feel guilty about racially profiling him. Aunt Yoko would be disappointed.

Maybe it's none of these people. The collar buckle is big enough to contain a GPS tracker and a microphone, so there's no reason for the watcher to be in the same car as me. He, or she, could be sitting with the pro-lifers at the front of the train, remotely monitoring my GPS signal. And listening.

Which brings me to distraction number three: Finding a way to call for help. My computer got fried, and I left my cell phone back in my apartment because I was worried about being tracked with it. I have the Xiaomi phone that Smith provided, but for obvious reasons I can't use that. I need to borrow another phone, without asking for it out loud.

The girl in the window seat next to me has an iPhone, but unfortunately she has decided I am some kind of weirdo. She took one look at my collar as I was sitting down and immediately put in earbuds and assumed a defensive posture that says, "I will tase you if you so much as tap me on the shoulder." I could try passing her a note anyway—"I NEED YOUR PHONE. PLEASE DON'T RESPOND VERBALLY."—but I doubt that would end well.

Looking through the gap between the seat backs, I can see that the boy in front of us is using his phone to watch a video. A two-second glimpse of the footage is enough for my nerd brain to identify it as an episode of the original *Star Trek*. It's the one about the guy named Lazarus who's caught in an eternal feud with an insane twin from an alternate universe. One Lazarus is made of matter, the other of antimatter, and if they ever meet outside a special interdimensional corridor, the resulting explosion will destroy all of existence.

I am thinking about this when the conductor announces that the dining car in the middle of the train is open for lunch. It gives me an idea.

JUST AS SOME PEOPLE ASSUME I MUST BE IN FAVOR OF gun control, there are others, including several members of my own family, who argue that I ought to be in the anti-abortion camp. Their logic is straightforward: As the unplanned child of an ambitious single mother, I am lucky not to have been killed in the womb.

This is true as far as it goes, but I don't think it goes very far.

Because I paid attention in sex ed class, I know that a lot of things had to go right in order for me to be born. Not getting aborted is actually pretty far down on the list.

For example: The average male ejaculate contains hundreds of millions of sperm. They are not identical; each carries a random combination of half the man's DNA, further altered by mutation. And their race to fertilize the egg is governed by the rules of chaos theory, in which outcomes are highly dependent on initial conditions—a nerdy way of saying that if your parents had had sex a few minutes earlier or later, they'd have conceived a different child.

This is another case where a magic wand would be useful. I happen to think being alive is great, and if I could I'd happily give the gift of life—a good life—not just to all the kids who got aborted, but to those millions of potential brothers and sisters whose existence was precluded by my own conception.

That's a fantasy, of course. And so is the idea that you could have stopped my mother from getting an abortion, if she'd wanted one. Granted, at the time she became pregnant, she didn't yet have access to Hellfire-equipped drones. But she was already a badass, confident in her own judgment, and she knew how to stand up for herself. If you'd told her she didn't have a choice what to do with her own uterus, she'd have tossed you into a swimming pool—and if that didn't get the point across, she'd have shot you.

When the thing standing between you and your heart's desire is another person with their own wants and needs, the answer is never as simple as just laying down the law. We all understand this when someone else tries to tell us what we can and can't do, but conveniently forget it when it's our turn to give orders. This blind spot is common to people on all parts of the political spectrum, which is one reason why I don't like arguing politics much.

Another thing we all have in common is that we all need to eat. So now, in a bid to save my own precious life, I head for the dining car, the interdimensional corridor where the matter of Repeal the 2nd mixes with the antimatter of Overturn Roe.

The car door opens on the sound of raised voices. Looking down the aisle as I step inside, I see a teenage girl in a blood-red T-shirt going nose-to-nose with an older woman whose blouse is patterned with sonogram images. Standing beside them, trying to play ref, is a nervous looking Amtrak attendant.

The woman and the girl aren't so much arguing as exchanging bumper sticker slogans; you could write their dialog yourself if you really wanted to. The Amtrak attendant's dialog consists of a single phrase, which he repeats over and over again: "Ladies, please!" This is completely ineffectual, but he keeps saying it anyway, like a sorcerer's apprentice trying to get his Charm of Silence to work.

Everyone else in the car is focused on the woman and the girl, waiting to see if they'll go full PvP on each other. The girl's back is to me, so I can't read her expression, but the Overturn Roe woman looks like she's enjoying the verbal sparring too much to start throwing real punches. Which is fine. I don't want anyone to get hurt here, I just need a distraction.

I turn my attention to the nearest tables. I spot what I want almost instantly: A guy sitting alone just ahead and to my left has a phone. It looks like he was scrolling through Twitter when the live-action version broke out behind him. Now he's set the phone down on the table and turned around in his seat to watch the fireworks.

Thinking will only cause trouble here, so I will myself to just act: Grab the phone as if I have every right to take it, turn, and go. But even as I step forward, a teenage boy in a red T-shirt gets up from a table on the other side of the aisle. It looks like he intends to provide backup to the girl, whether or not she actually needs his help. But having gotten to his feet, he just stands there, in my way.

I need to get the phone before it goes to sleep and locks itself. I could probably get away with saying "Excuse me" here, but my sense of urgency inclines me to more forceful methods, and because this is the real world, chest-bumping is allowed. The train car jolts over a rough spot on the tracks and I pretend to lose my footing, shoving the boy forward. He shoots me an angry look over his shoulder, but when he sees I'm not wearing a sonogram shirt, he turns back towards the girl.

I can reach the phone now. I've got my hand on it when the train gives another big jolt. This time it's the boy who stumbles. He falls into me. More worried about losing the phone than my balance, I tip over backwards. When my head hits the floor, the bracket on the back of the collar jams painfully against my spine, and as my teeth click together I swear I hear the crunch of breaking glass.

My body goes numb. This is panic, but it could also be the VX starting its attack on my neurotransmitters. I jerk my head up, reach around to the nape of my neck.

Yes, I know, this is dumb: using my bare hand to check for leaking contact poison. But if the vial is broken, I'm almost certainly doomed; the only real question is how many other people will die with me. Better to find out fast, so I can start agonizing about whether to throw myself heroically from the train.

I touch the bracket. The vial is intact. I feel for cracks in the glass, pressing hard enough as I do this that, if it were cracked, it would probably shatter. But as best I can tell, it's undamaged. The only moisture I feel is the cold sweat on my fingertips. I am still alive.

The boy, who landed on top of me, is trying to get up; my sense of relief is cut short as he elbows me in the balls. I grit my teeth again. As I cup my wounded testicles, I see the phone, lying on the floor within easy reach and still unlocked. I grab it. The boy steps on my hand.

It's OK, I needed to get my blood pumping again after that scare. I wait for the boy to get off me and haul myself to my feet. Then I try to make a quick exit. I get as far as the door at the end of the dining car.

When the door slides open, the surly Japanese guy in the business suit is standing on the other side. He glances at the phone in my hand, then looks me right in the eye, scowling. I start to go numb again, but not before I feel my face compose itself into a perfectly guilty expression.

He doesn't kill me. He stares at me unblinking for a few seconds, then tilts his head and looks past me to where the woman and the girl are still going at it. "What's that all about?" he asks.

Even if I were free to speak, I'm not sure what I'd say to this. I answer with a shrug. Then I duck my head, and make good my escape.

I FIND A VACANT LAVATORY AND LOCK MYSELF INSIDE. Holding up the phone, I carefully close Twitter and open the dialing app. Then I stare at the screen and realize I don't know what to do next.

Normally I contact Mom through my computer. There's an emergency number I can call if I get into trouble when I'm away from my PC. I'm supposed to have that number memorized, and I do, sort of—it's programmed into my cell phone. I had optimistically assumed that the act of programming it into my cell phone would also imprint it in my brain, but now, try as I might, I cannot recall a single digit.

I don't know Jolene's phone number either. Or Ray's. I do know Darla's, but reaching out to her is one of the few things I can think of that might conceivably make my situation worse.

The answer, when it comes to me, is so blindingly obvious that I feel stupid: Duh, of course. I'm traveling to his city, after all, and not only can he relay a message to Mom, he's got resources of his own that could help me.

I punch in his number, start composing a text.

DEAR DAD, it begins.

apophany — A false epiphany, in which a person perceives a meaningful connection between things which are in fact unrelated. The term, coined by German psychiatrist Klaus Conrad in the 1950s, originally referred to a type of delusion suffered by schizophrenics, but has since come to apply broadly to any misfire of human pattern recognition.

—*Lady Ada's Lexicon*

The Coast Starlight arrives at Los Angeles Union Station just after eleven p.m. Everyone on board is cranky. At the start of the dinner service, after another shouting match between protesters ended in a food fight, the crew shut the dining car down and sent the passengers back to their seats without supper. Now, as we roll to a stop, I see Amtrak security and LAPD out in force on the platform.

When the train doors open, I'm one of the first to disembark. I keep my head down and walk swiftly past the cops. Inside the terminal, I fake towards the Metro subway escalators but instead go up and out. A black limousine is waiting at the car service pick-up; the driver sees me coming and the back door opens automatically. I duck inside, and before I've even got my backpack on the floor, the door clanks shut and we are moving.

"Hi John," the driver says, turning to flash me a quick smile. "How was your trip?"

"Exciting," I tell her, reluctant to say more until I'm sure we can't be overheard.

"It's OK," she says. "Faraday's on." She points to the bright green shield that has lit up on the dashboard, a telltale signifying that the limo's Virtual Faraday Cage has been activated. All electronic transmissions into and out of the vehicle should be blocked; GPS trackers cannot transmit, cell phones have no bars, and booby-trapped death collars cannot be remotely triggered. So for the moment I am safe, and if we are lucky, Smith will interpret the loss of GPS signal to mean that I've taken the subway.

My chauffeur's name is Bamber Holtz—"Bambi," inevitably, in the trades. Originally from Oklahoma, she did a stint in the Army after high school and then came to Hollywood to do FX work, specializing in pyrotechnics and demolition, skills she'd honed defusing IEDs in Syria. She's won two VES awards and was nominated for a Visual Effects Oscar, but to heterosexual men of a certain age she's most famous for her one on-screen role, body-doubling Sandra Bjorn during the nude motorcycle chase in *Death Race 5000*. After the original stunt woman suffered a bad case of road rash during a test shoot, the director, desperate to keep the film on schedule, turned to the only other woman on the crew and asked how she'd like to take her clothes off and ride a vintage Harley. Bamber agreed to do the scene in exchange for the bike.

We met on one of my previous trips to L.A. Dad had told me he had a new girlfriend, but hadn't said who she was. The first night of my visit, I got up at two a.m. to get a snack from the kitchen and found Bamber raiding the fridge. We were both in our underwear, and even without a motorcycle helmet, I recognized her instantly. Which was awkward for about five seconds, but then we got dressed and made fajitas, and Bamber told me about the exploding hovercar she was building for *Fast & Furious 17*. We've been friends ever since. And of all the women I've seen gratuitously naked, she's the one best suited to help me with my current predicament.

"Where's Dad?" I ask her.

"Picking up your friend Jolene." She steers with one hand and keeps an eye on the rearview screen in the dashboard, watching to see if anyone's following us. "Her plane landed at LAX about an hour ago."

"What about Mom? Were you able to get through to her?"

"Your dad talked to her on the phone earlier today. She had him put me on for a few minutes at the end."

"What was that like?"

"Awkward, for him. I don't think they'd spoken since they broke up. With me she was all business." Bamber smiles. "Reminded me of my old squad leader in Damascus."

We're on Sunset Boulevard now, near Dodger Stadium. It doesn't look like anyone's tailing us. Bamber pulls the limo into the parking lot of an Arby's. "OK," she says, "let me see this famous collar of yours." I climb through the partition and sit in the front passenger seat. She checks out the buckle under my chin first, then has me tilt my head forward so she can examine the vial in its metal bracket. "Someone told you this was loaded with VX?"

"Smith didn't tell me what it was, only that I'd be sorry if I tried to take the collar off. If it is VX, though, or something like that, shouldn't you be—"

"Wearing MOPP gear? Yeah, probably. Your mom gave me an address to take you to if I decided to go the full hazmat route, and

I've got a couple auto-injectors of atropine in the glove box. But I don't think we'll need those."

"No?"

"No . . . Keep your head down and hold still a second." She takes a knife from a side pocket in her jeans and flicks it open. I hold very still. I feel the blade slide up against the back of my neck, and there's a tug, and then the collar pops loose and falls away.

I straighten up, rubbing my neck. As Bamber turns the collar over in her hands, I see that the LED light on the buckle is still green, despite the ribbon cable being cut.

She holds up the glass vial so I can take a close look at it. "VX isn't bright orange like this," she says. "It's more of a pale brown, and it's viscous, like motor oil."

"So what do you think this stuff is?"

"Probably ethanol, with some dye mixed in."

"Ethanol?" I say. "Alcohol?"

She nods. "That's why they call it a spirit level." She balances the metal bracket on her palm; with the vial lying on its side, I can see the bubble in the fluid, watch it move as she waggles her hand back and forth. When her palm is perfectly horizontal, the bubble comes to rest between two thin black lines painted on the glass.

"Oh," I say, and as I belatedly recognize the level for what it is, I can feel my cheeks get hot.

Bamber smiles, not unkindly. "I'm going to go out on a limb here and guess you never worked a summer job in construction."

"I was more of a *Minecraft* guy," I tell her.

THE NEW SONY PICTURES HOTEL IS ON HOLLYWOOD BOU-levard, across the street from Grauman's Chinese Theatre. Dad, who is doing some script-doctoring for the studio, has arranged the use of one of the top-floor executive suites. The suite is equipped with a version of the same signal-blocking technology as the limo.

I have the North Koreans to thank for this. Back in 2014, as retaliation for a Seth Rogen comedy that disrespected the Supreme Leader, the DPRK hacked Sony's corporate network and used the stolen information to embarrass the studio. Those studio execs who survived the resulting scandal became obsessed with data security. To say they are paranoid about leaks is like saying Kim Jong-un has a problem with satire.

Bamber and I take a private elevator from the hotel parking garage to the penthouse level. Dad's waiting for us at the door to the suite. "What's the verdict?" he says.

"False alarm on the deadly nerve agent," Bamber tells him.

"Well, that's good!" Dad says. "Are you hungry, John? We ordered Lebanese."

One of the things I like about my father is that it's almost impossible to freak him out. I suspect he was always like this, but life in Hollywood has given him lots of practice taking weird shit in stride. And as a professional artist, he is inherently sympathetic to trains of thought that my mother would deride as "imaginative," so he's not going to try to make me feel dumb for believing a carpenter's level was a weapon of mass destruction. Which is good, because I'm doing a fine job feeling dumb on my own.

Jolene is inside, finishing up a plate of kafta and rice. I approach her almost shyly, and we both do that staring thing you do, the first time you meet an online friend in the flesh. The close-cropped hair is the most obvious difference between Jolene and her avatar, but it's little details that really jump out at me: the corkscrew threads of gray at her temples, and the crow's feet at the corners of her eyes.

That Jolene is old enough to be my mother is not news to me. But at this point in history, video games have conquered every demographic, so when you play online, you routinely interact with people of all generations, and granting a certain base level of maturity, age just doesn't matter that much. I mean, not to exaggerate: The internet, as we know, did not eliminate prejudice. But it did create an environment where shared interests can easily count for more. And what strikes me now is how unlikely it is, in a world without the net, that Jolene and I would ever have spent time hanging out with each other.

Score one point for living in the future.

"Thanks for coming," I say.

She smiles, exposing the gap between her teeth. "Don't mention it."

"No, I mean it. I just hope I didn't get you out here for a prank."

"No matter if you did. Your mom's got me on loan from my regular job, so my travel and expenses are covered. And besides, I'm as curious as you to find out who Mr. Jones really is."

"I'm curious who *you* really are," I say. "Is Jolene even your real name?"

"My middle name. My first name's Karen, but only my parents ever call me that."

"And you're some kind of federal agent, right? The Colorado law firm is just a cover. What are you, FBI?"

"Treasury," she says.

"Treasury?"

"It's a fascinating story," says Dad, returning from the kitchen. He hands me a plate. "Jolene has been working undercover, investigating the black market economies in online role-playing games.

Looking for ties to organized crime." From his tone, I can tell he is already cooking up a screenplay pitch on this subject.

"It's not an official investigation," Jolene clarifies. "Just one of my boss's crazy pet projects. She saw this *60 Minutes* piece about gold farming, and some other report—or maybe it was a Tom Clancy movie—about narcoterrorists using game chat to send secret messages to each other. And by adding two and two to make five, she concluded that the drug cartels might be laundering money through *Call to Wizardry*."

Unlike my father, I am quite capable of astonishment. "That's . . ."

"Batshit, I know. Welcome to *my* reality . . . Anyway, she'd caught me messing around in VR on my lunch break often enough to know I'm a gamer, so she called me into her office, and long story short, I got drafted into this off-the-books undercover op. It's not a bad gig, really: She covers my monthly subscriptions and lets me play on the clock when I'm not busy with other things. In exchange, I file reports about any 'suspicious activity' I come across."

"And have you found much?" I ask. Thinking not of money laundering, but tax evasion.

Jolene grins knowingly. "Nothing *too* suspicious, until recently. My investigation had about run its course when the Mr. Jones thing popped up. My boss was thrilled about that—and she was over the moon when your mom reached out to her. I'm like her star agent, now. So like I say, don't apologize about getting me out here. I may get a promotion out of all this yet."

The suite's doorbell rings. "That'll be Ray," Jolene says, as my dad goes to answer it.

"You invited Ray?"

"*I* didn't." This one's on you, her expression says. Which it is, in a roundabout way: Because I forgot mom's phone number, Dad, who was still ghosted, had no way to contact her directly. But he'd met Jolene on one of our monthly game nights, so in my texts from the train, I told him to go the Game Lobby and look for her. "Ray was there when your dad found me," Jolene explains. "We'd both been looking for you and Anja, to find out what the hell happened in *D.M. Zed*. When your dad showed, I tried to tell Ray to get lost—among other things, his computer's compromised—but, you know, good luck with that."

"Dad told Ray everything?"

"He told him enough. Ray got really pissed when he heard about the threat against Anja." She says this somewhat grudgingly, as if Ray getting angry on Anja's behalf contradicts her own poor opinion of him. "He wanted to help, and I guess he doesn't live that far from L.A., so . . ." She trails off, her eyes widening as she looks past me.

I don't know if this is racist, but I'm much less surprised to learn Ray is a woman than to discover she's Hispanic. Brown skin notwithstanding, I immediately see the resemblance to her avatar. She's got the same build, the same eyes. The same hair, too, only longer and with bangs. "Renata," Ray says, in answer to my opening question. "Renata Calveros."

"You're undocumented." This from Jolene, who's spent the last thirty seconds trying to work out why her law woman's intuition pegged Ray as a malefactor. And she's using the polite term, rather than "illegal," because she's worried she'll be wrong twice.

If Ray appreciates the courtesy, she doesn't show it. "I don't have a birth certificate, if that's what you're asking."

"Are you a desposeída, Renata?" my dad asks. I'm not familiar with the term, but later when I Google it I'll learn that it refers to someone who is legally an American citizen but who, for reasons beyond their control, can never prove it.

Ray answers with a shrug. "My mother *says* I was born here, and the midwife just forgot to register me. I don't really know. But I grew up in San Bernardino. It wasn't until I started applying to colleges that I found out I had a problem, and by then, it was a little late to do anything about it." She looks at Jolene. "Why do you care? You have a day job with ICE you haven't mentioned?"

"I'm a Treasury agent," Jolene says.

Ray laughs. "Well then, you've got no beef with me. I pay my taxes."

"And I'm going to pay mine," I put in. Just to get it out of the way.

THE SUITE HAS A SECURE LANDLINE THAT ALLOWS YOU to make calls even when the signal blocker is active. The five of us gather around a conference table and get Mom on speaker. Jolene recaps what's happened since my arrival. Then Bamber, who has completed an autopsy on the collar, takes a turn.

"John was right about the microphone and the GPS tracker," she says. The good news, she adds, is that the microphone is only equipped to transmit, not record—which means that what we say now will remain private.

"Tell me about the manufacture," Mom says.

"The electronics are all off-the-shelf components. Made in China, but nothing you couldn't get here—it's what I'd use, if I were building something like this."

"What about the spirit level?" I feel a twinge of embarrassment as she asks this.

"The logo was sanded off, but I recognize the brand," Bamber says. "American."

"So it would be reasonable to conclude the collar was constructed locally," Mom says. "Does it seem like something an amateur could build?"

"They'd need some technical know-how, to set up the GPS and mike transmitter, but a skilled amateur could do it, sure."

"OK," I speak up, feeling more than a twinge of embarrassment now, "the collar seems like a prank, but what about the money? And what about—"

"What about Anja?" Ray interjects. "Do we know if she's OK? Have you tried to warn her?"

"Something's blocking internet access to her house," Mom says. "My people are working on it."

"Her parents' cell phones are down too," Jolene adds. "Their numbers are both listed, but if you call you get a message saying they're not in service."

"What about the local police?" Ray says. "Their phones have got to be working, right?"

"Smith told me he'd have someone monitoring the emergency channels in Paraná," I say. "If we send the cops or the fire department to Anja's house, he'll shut down her life support."

"That could be a bluff," Mom says, "but I'd rather not take the risk if we can avoid it."

"Well, is there someone else you can call?" Ray says. "What about the CIA? They've got people all over South America, don't they?"

"There's a CIA station in Buenos Aires," Mom replies. "But I've dealt with them before, and they're not going to want to help with this."

"I bet I know someone in Buenos Aires who'll help," I say. "Anja's new boyfriend, Javier Messner."

"Is he a tech guy?" Jolene asks.

"No, he's a barista. But he's not stupid. If we send him to Anja's house, you can talk him through whatever he needs to do to deal with the malware."

Jolene nods, in tentative approval. "He still needs to get to Paraná from Buenos Aires. How far is that?"

"About three hundred miles, in the real world," I tell her. "I assume Javier's got a car . . ."

Dad speaks up. "I might be able to get him a helicopter. HBO's got a film crew in B.A. right now, shooting exteriors for their *Highlander* reboot," he explains. "I know the DP, and I think I can talk him into loaning us a chopper along with one of his tech guys. Then all Javier has to do is convince Anja's parents to let us in."

"Sounds like a plan," Jolene says.

On the phone, I can hear Mom sigh. "Not the way I'd normally do it," she says. "But."

"We should think about shutting down the Faraday soon," Bamber puts in. "Smith is going to be wondering where John's GPS signal went."

"In a minute," I say. "First, there's one more thing I need to mention . . ." I tell them about the nannycam I left set up in my apartment, and about the mystery trio of gun-toting Asians.

"Well," my mother says when I've finished. "*That's* interesting."

SMITH'S XIAOMI PHONE RINGS A FEW SECONDS AFTER Dad turns off the signal blocker. Bamber has handed me back the collar, and I hold the microphone up to my throat as I answer the phone. "Hello?"

"Where are you?" Smith says.

"I think you already know that," I say.

There's a pause, just long enough to glance at a pop-up screen. "Sony Pictures Hotel. Expensive."

"I can afford it."

"Enjoy your money tonight," Smith says. "Tomorrow, you go to work."

"Are you ready to tell me what I'm doing here?"

"I think you already know that."

It's true, I have a theory. I had plenty of time on the train to think about what a ruthless dictator and kidnapper interested in MMORPGs might want from Los Angeles. But if there's one thing this evening has taught me, it's that I shouldn't be so quick to trust my own conclusions.

"I'm too tired for games tonight," I say. "Just tell me." And he does.

S o who do you think these guys really are?" Jolene asks.

It's quarter of ten the next morning, and we are sitting in the limo on the second floor of a parking garage. Our parking spot has a clear view across the street to the world headquarters of Tempest, LLC.

Tempest HQ is a fourteen-story blue glass tower. Extending west from the tower's base, and occupying nearly twice as much ground space, is a two-story public amusement center and playtest space known as the Arcade. The Arcade opens at ten, and there is already a long queue of people on the sidewalk waiting to get in. Ray and Bamber are both in line. Jolene uses binoculars to scan the rest of the crowd.

Last night while I slept, Bamber performed a second autopsy, this one on my fried gaming rig. Though the motherboard and video cards were slagged, the military-grade hard drive was undamaged. By mounting the drive on another computer, Bamber was able to salvage the footage from my apartment nannycam. Mom's people are now running a facial-recognition search on the mystery trio, and in the meantime, Bamber printed out some nice mug shots for us.

But "I have no idea," is all I can think to say in answer to Jolene's question. I'm feeling much more clear-headed than I was last night, but that clarity just makes it easier to appreciate how little I understand what's going on.

At breakfast this morning, Bamber asked me whether the backpack I'd been using was the only backpack I owned. I told her no—like most nerds, I have a pile of old backpacks gathering dust in the bottom of my closet—but it's my newest backpack, and the one you'd expect me to use if I were taking my rig somewhere. "I thought so," Bamber said, and then she showed me the GPS tracker she'd found hidden in one of the pack's side pockets. It was the same make as the tracker in the collar.

So now we know how Smith found me at the motel. That business where he asked about my IP address must have been a head fake, or a test to see if I'd lie. But if he knew where I was all along, it does raise the question of why he'd send armed goons to break into my apartment. And if the mystery trio aren't his people, and they aren't Ms. Pang's—then yeah, who the hell are they?

Don't ask me, I just work here.

It's five minutes to ten, time for me to get ready. I open the glove compartment and take out the collar, which Bamber has patched back together. On Mom's instructions, she's also disabled the microphone in the buckle. This will likely make Smith suspicious, but it's a risk we need to take, as we are planning to pull a real-life version of a b-channel.

I snap the collar in place around my neck. Then I take Smith's Xiaomi phone, turn it on, and put it in my pocket. Next are a mismatched pair of earbud phones. The one that goes in my left ear

has Zero Day-approved encryption and will allow me to communicate securely with Jolene and the others. The one for my right ear is
a civilian model that connects wirelessly with the Xiaomi and will
let me talk hands-free with Smith while I am doing his bidding.

This second earbud was part of a package that a courier delivered to the hotel early this morning. The package also contained
a stolen ID badge and a prosthetic thumb. The badge belongs to
Jim Boden, a senior computer programmer for Tempest who has
worked on *Call to Wizardry* since its inception. I don't look anything like him, so if I tried to walk into Tempest HQ through the
front door I'd never get past security. But according to Smith, there
is a less well-guarded side door that connects to the tower from
the Arcade. By swiping the badge, and using the fake thumb to
spoof a biometric sensor, I should be able to enter through there.
I am then supposed to take an elevator to the floor where the real
Jim Boden works, and convince him to walk out of the building
with me. Smith's people will be waiting to grab him at street level.

To help with this last part, the courier's package also contained
a handgun—a .50 Desert Eagle semiautomatic. This is another
popular video-game gun, a fetish weapon that shoots bullets that
are half an inch in diameter. The Desert Eagle that the courier
delivered is unloaded, but the thing is so scary looking that just
pointing it in Boden's direction should be enough to ensure his
cooperation. If not, Smith told me, I will need to think and talk
fast. "If you fail your mission, I will trigger the collar, and I will
terminate your friend Anja's life support."

Thanks to Bamber, I know the first half of this threat is bullshit. We're still waiting to find out about the second half. The helicopter with Javier and the tech guy touched down in Paraná twenty
minutes ago, so they should be at Anja's house any moment now,

and once they talk their way inside, the tech guy's first priority will be to make sure the medical pod is completely disconnected from the internet.

Until we get the all clear on that, we are going to pretend to play along with Smith's plan—up to a point. I am not actually going to kidnap Jim Boden, and if Mom has her way, I won't even go so far as to breach Tempest's security. For a variety of bureaucratic and legal reasons, Mom's goal, as she puts it, is to maintain "the lightest possible footprint"—ideally, neither Tempest nor the local police will ever know we were here.

Partly for this reason, I will not be bringing the Desert Eagle into the Arcade with me. The only member of our group who will be armed is Jolene. If something happens that Jolene can't handle, Mom has "other assets" that she can bring into play, but, as she stressed in our pre-op conversation, she'd really, really prefer not to use those.

That's what she wants. We'll find out soon enough what she can have.

At ten o'clock sharp, the Arcade doors open and the line starts moving. Beside me, Jolene makes her own final preparations. Smith knows what she looks like, so to disguise herself, and to conceal her Kevlar vest and gun, she is wearing a gray USMC hoodie. She slides a big pair of tinted glasses onto her face and milks the drawstrings of the hood until her chin and forehead disappear. "How do I look?" she asks, flashing me a gap-toothed grin.

"Like the assassin who loses the knife fight to Quvenzhané Wallis in *The Bourne Resurrection*," I say. I reach for the button on the dash that turns off the Faraday Cage. "See you inside."

Thirty seconds later I am walking out of the parking garage. There's a subway exit just to my right.

As I wait to cross the street, the Xiaomi phone rings.

A TWELVE-FOOT-TALL TROLL STATUE STANDS JUST IN-
side the Arcade entrance. It doesn't move or speak, but you can sit
in the cauldron at its feet and have your picture taken pretending to
be boiled into gumbo. I pass.

Beyond the troll, spread out across the Arcade floor, are long
rows of stylish gaming booths chased with blue and purple neon,
each one containing a state-of-the-art VR rig. For twenty-five
bucks an hour you can play all your favorite Tempest games, and
take an advance look at upcoming titles and expansions. Forty
bucks an hour gets you a legendary booth—these are larger, and
decorated with orange neon—that will project your gameplay onto
an overhead holographic display, letting passersby admire your elite
skills.

Off to the right, past a long counter selling time cards and mer-
chandise, a sweeping crystal staircase leads up to a second-floor
gallery. I spot Bamber at the top of the stairs. She takes a moment
to admire a crossed pair of orcish scimitars that are mounted on the
wall, then leans on the gallery railing and looks out over the floor.

"Heads up," Ray says, her voice in my left ear. "There's a cop in
the building."

I raise a finger to my right earbud and make sure that the microphone is switched off before asking, "Where?"

"Cheapside." This is a region of the Arcade that, like the virtual
arcade in the Game Lobby, is devoted to vintage coin-op games
and pinball machines. The budget entertainment option, Cheapside is a big draw in its own right, but like the dairy case in a su-
permarket it is located a long way from the entrance—to get to it,
you must walk past the more expensive VR game booths, and a
concentration of legendary booths along Cheapside's fringe serves
as a constant reminder of what you are missing.

"What's he doing?" This from Mom.

"Fucking off on duty, looks like," Ray says. "Playing *Lethal Enforcers*."

"Keep tabs on him," Mom says. "But try not to let him notice you."

"No fear."

I reactivate the mike on my right earbud. Smith hasn't said a word since he first checked in with me on the street. He told me there would be a delay while he confirmed Jim Boden's exact whereabouts. I don't mind being patient; the longer this takes, the better it is for Anja. I go over to a nearby legendary booth, where a kid in a Repeal the 2nd T-shirt is tanking a run through the Temple of the Seven Lanterns. A group of older gamers go by, and I scan their faces, instinctively looking for Smith. But this is pointless: They're a diverse bunch, but none of them are Gray People.

Static crackles in my right ear. "It is time," Smith says. "Where are you?"

"Inside the building," I tell him. "Near the troll by the front door."

"Directly behind the troll as you come in, there is an aisle leading towards the far side of the building. Do you see it?"

"Yes." The aisle, a sort of Broadway spanning the width of the Arcade's first floor, is roughly divided into two lanes by a series of padded benches, snack and drink machines, and display cases filled with game world artifacts.

"Follow it to its end, to the back corridor where the restrooms are."

"OK, Smith," I say, for the benefit of my other listeners, "I'm headed towards the restrooms at the end of the big aisle."

But I've barely started walking when Bamber announces: "John's mystery Asians are here."

"Where?" I say, Jolene echoing the question in my left ear.

"Where what?" says Smith. I forgot to shut off his mike.

"Coming my way, up the stairs," Bamber says. "I think they want a bird's-eye view."

"Where do I go once I get to the restrooms?" I say, to Smith. I turn and look up at the gallery. I see the trio pass behind Bamber and move to the railing a few yards beyond her.

"Just keep walking," Smith says. "And keep your eyes in front of you."

I turn back to the aisle, take a few more steps. Even as I ask myself how he could know which way my eyes are pointed, I see, coming towards me down the aisle's other lane, a figure in a hoodie. It's not Jolene. This hoodie is black and bears the *Resident Evil* game logo, and though the hood is pulled forward over the wearer's head, the drawstrings are loose, so I can see the jaw and the lower part of the face.

His face: It's a white guy, and even this partial glimpse is enough to tell me that I know him. Then I see his lips move, forming words, and the gray monotone voice of Smith speaks in my ear: "That's right, John. Keep going. You're almost there."

I stop dead in my tracks, my head swiveling as he continues to walk forward. I feel like I've taken a hit of something, but it's what happens next that really floors me: A kid comes darting up the aisle, closely pursued by a couple of friends. They're on a collision course with the guy in the hoodie, but just as the lead kid is about to plow into him, the hoodie guy does this sideways pivot, dodging around the kid without even breaking stride. Then he does it again, and again, the kids zipping by heedlessly like paintballs flying across an open field.

Only when he's cleared the last of them does he come to a stop. He's directly across the aisle from me now; we are separated by about ten feet of space and a waist-high display case. I see his lips curve in a smile. He reaches up and slips off his hood and turns to face me. I know him, all right: The white guy from the CIA Factbook. The white guy who broke into my apartment. Ms. Pang's white guy. But he's someone else, too, and though he is flesh and blood, in a moment of total context fail I see him as an avatar, controlled by another person altogether.

"Darla?" I say, the word falling into a moment of perfect stillness that probably exists only in my imagination.

His smile broadens. He winks at me. "Perv," he says, and Smith, in my ear, says it too.

Then his right hand slips inside the front of his hoodie and comes out holding a Desert Eagle handgun. It's the same model as the one the courier delivered to me this morning, but where that one was finished in silver, this one is plated in gold. It is also, I feel quite certain, loaded.

I've been in more VR gunfights than I can count, so I know what I'm supposed to do here: Move. Even at point-blank range, it is amazingly difficult to hit a target that is ducking and weaving and jumping around. I *know* this, but like a newbie I just stand there with my mouth open.

He doesn't shoot me. He doesn't even point the gun at me, in fact, just says, "Cover your ears." Then he sidesteps, extending his arm and aiming up, towards the gallery.

I clap my hands over my ears. This probably protects me from at least *some* permanent hearing damage. Not that I really appreciate it in the moment. This is one thing video games, by necessity, get totally wrong: how *painfully* loud guns are. Even a small-caliber handgun can produce more decibels than a jet engine. When the Desert Eagle fires, I feel the shockwave in the bones of my face, and the muzzle flash—a three-foot-long column of hot gas and propellant—is blinding.

I am literally staggered. The second shot knocks me completely off balance; I am already falling when Jolene comes in from the side and tackles me.

As we hit the floor, the glass in the display case shatters, struck by return fire from the gallery. I shut my eyes and scream into the side of Jolene's neck. The Desert Eagle booms twice more. The last shot is from a different location, and I dimly surmise that he is on the move.

Seconds pass with no more shots fired. I open my eyes carefully. Someone goes running by, and I hear, through the ringing in my ears, the panicked commotion of scores of gamers fleeing towards the exits.

Jolene pushes herself up on one arm and sweeps her hood back. She draws her own gun and swivels her head around. She looks down at me and says, "Get your ass out of here," mouthing the words broadly so I'll be sure to understand. Then she gets up and sprints down the aisle in a crouch. Going after the guy in the hoodie.

I stand up carefully, brushing bits of glass from my shoulders. A logjam has developed by the base of the troll statue, people fighting one another to get out of the building. I look up at the gallery. Bamber and the trio have vanished. I can see where a fist-sized chunk was blasted out of the gallery railing, and three larger and more jagged holes are punched through the glass panels of the balustrade, but there are no bodies, and no blood.

At the Arcade entrance, the logjam breaks. The crowd surges out onto the sidewalk. I go the other way.

A grinning statue of Proctor the Salesgoblin stands guard outside the restroom corridor. From inside, just out of view, I hear two people shouting—it sounds like Jolene is one of them. Then I hear three gunshots in quick succession. Then nothing.

When I poke my head into the corridor, Jolene is on the floor in front of the women's room, clutching her right side. Slumped against a trash bin outside the men's is the person who just shot her—an LAPD officer, probably the same one Ray spotted earlier. The cop has been hit in the shoulder. In most video games this would barely count as a flesh wound, but the guy looks pretty bad—pale, sweating, in shock. He's got his other hand pressed to the wound, but there's a lot of blood seeping through his fingers.

Keeping a wary eye on the cop, I crouch beside Jolene. "Are you all right?"

She glares at me, infuriated by the question or by the fact that I'm still in the building. I take her anger as a good sign. "Ribs," she wheezes, wincing. "Busted."

"Jesus Christ," Ray says, appearing behind me.

"Hey," I say to her. "Jolene's going to be OK, I think, but that guy"—nodding at the cop—"could probably use some help."

Ray gives me a look. "You know I'm not a real cleric, right?"

"Yeah, of course, but . . ." I guess I assumed, given her affinity for playing healers, that she'd at least know first aid in real life.

Jolene takes a deep breath. "Pressure," she says, wincing again. "Put pressure."

I nod, and look up at Ray again. Ray looks back, like: Are you serious? But then she sighs and goes to put pressure on the cop's wound, so he won't bleed out before help gets here.

Past the men's room, the corridor we are in ends in a set of stairs, headed up.

"The guy in the hoodie," I say. "Did he go that way?"

Jolene shakes her head. Not saying no. Telling me not to do it. Which of course I'm going to. I glance at her gun, which is lying on the floor beside her, and she hisses through gritted teeth: "Touch it and I'll break your damn arm."

"OK," I say, putting my hands up. "OK."

Then I stand, and turn, and head for the stairs.

AS I'M CLIMBING THE STAIRS I TRY TO TELL MOM WHAT'S going on, which is when I realize I've lost my left earbud. I've still got the right one, though, and the microphone is still on.

"Sorry, perv," he says, "I'm not your mom." He's turned off the Smith voice filter, so he sounds like a real person now. Though still not the person I think of him as.

"Who the hell are you?" I say.

The question makes him laugh. "A badass," he says. "A *different flavor* of badass."

The Arcade's upper level is a huge food court. At the top of the stairs I pause and look around carefully. I don't see anybody, but that doesn't mean much—the sightlines are terrible, the floor space broken up by fast food kiosks and whimsical statues of NPCs eating and drinking.

"What about those guys you were shooting at?" I ask, keeping my voice low. "Who are they?"

"The kind of people who keep their money in Burmese savings accounts. They're pissed because I ripped them off."

"Gangsters? You stole the money from gangsters?"

"I *told* you I was going to have a big surprise for you when I got back from my trip."

Oh my God. "You ripped off a bunch of gangsters . . . to finance our MMORPG?"

"I was going to steal the money for that," he says. "Technically, the surprise was that I got my hacker friend Orville to show me *how* to steal it. I was going to talk it over with you before I did it, give you a chance to wet your pants and get used to the idea, then discuss how much we'd actually need. But before any of that could happen, you fucked me over. So I decided to steal the money to fuck you back, instead."

"Jesus Christ," I say. "I know you're mad I cut you out of the Janet Margeaux gig, but this . . . You think this is proportional?"

"Of course it's not proportional." He laughs. "But it is *awesome*."

"You're an asshole."

"Look, if you're worried about Anja, don't be. You know I'd never really hurt her. All I did was fiddle the alarm system on her medical pod. I had to, to get you to put on that collar . . . Which I can't believe you fell for, by the way."

As we've been talking, I've been making my way through the food court, staying low, moving from cover to cover. Listening. At the moment I'm hunkered down beside a Panda Express kiosk. Straight ahead is a dwarven longboat with some kid's tables inside it. When he laughs again, I don't just hear it in my right ear, I hear it in my left as well.

"You do have to admit it was an epic troll," he says. "One for the ages."

"Yeah, really epic," I say. "Do you know Jolene just got shot downstairs?"

Long pause. "Well, *I* didn't shoot her," he says, sounding offended by the implication.

"And if you're such a fucking genius," I continue, "how come the gangsters got onto you?"

"That was your fucking fault. The first withdrawal went smooth as silk. But you made me go back for more, and I guess that time they noticed. They've been on my ass ever since I picked up the cash at the bank."

I'm crouched beside the longboat now. Gripping the gunwale with both hands, I stand up, stick my head over the top. He's sitting on the floor inside, looking up expectantly.

"Boo," he says.

Ordinarily it would be unhealthy to think about punching a guy who has a gun, but having finally grasped the rules of the game he and I have been playing, I know that even if I broke his nose, he would probably just laugh. But before I can put this theory to the test, I glimpse movement out of the corner of my eye, and some late-arriving reflex of self-preservation makes me hop over the gunwale and squat down beside him.

Posed on the prow of the longboat is a figure of a drunken dwarf, dancing a highland jig. Peering out through the gap beneath his kilt, I see the male contingent of the trio headed our way with their guns out. The younger guy looks nervous—no doubt this has to do with the sound of approaching sirens outside the building—but the tough older guy just looks focused, like he's cool with being arrested as long as he gets to kill someone first.

My boat mate elbows me in the side. I turn to him, and he offers me the Desert Eagle, holding the gun in his left hand while showing me his right wrist, which is swollen and badly bruised. "Recoil," he mouths, by way of explanation.

"Idiot," I mouth back. I don't take the gun. I shift back in the boat and look over the gunwales, trying to decide if there's any way to run that won't get us instantly shot.

That's when I see Bamber. She's crouched by the corner of the Panda Express kiosk where I was a few moments ago, and she is holding an elvish longbow. The bow is a replica of Helios, a legendary loot drop from the Fields of the Sun. Bamber briefly makes eye contact with me. Then she nocks an arrow in the bow and fires it in a high arc over the heads of the approaching gunmen. The arrow lands with a clatter in the distance and the gunmen spin around at the sound.

Bamber nocks another arrow. Then she freezes, and I see a look of frustration come over her face. She tosses the bow and arrow to the floor and raises her arms. The female member of the trio, her pistol pointed at the back of Bamber's head, marches Bamber into the open.

"Everybody come out," the gunwoman says, "or I shoot her now."

I stand up and put my hands in the air. The boy in the hoodie stays crouched below the gunwale.

"*Every*body," the gunwoman says. I look down, scowling, and my boat mate rolls his eyes and says, "Fine." He gets up, leaving his own gun on the floor.

We exit the longboat and stand next to Bamber. By this point the gunwoman's confederates have joined us. The young guy keeps his Beretta out, but the tough guy holsters his pistol, and then, to my consternation, reaches into the other side of his jacket and pulls out a cleaver.

"Where is the money?" the gunwoman says.

Bamber answers: "In a safe in our hotel room."

"What hotel?"

"The Sony, on Hollywood."

"What room?"

"Suite 10A." Glancing down: "The key card is in my pocket."

The gunwoman makes no move to take it. "Tell me about the safe. Is it a number combination, or"—nodding in the direction of the guy with the cleaver—"a biometric lock?"

"It's a voiceprint lock," the boy in the hoodie says. The gunwoman points her pistol at him, but he looks back unblinking with a screw-you expression on his face that makes me wish I'd punched him when I had the chance. "Go ahead, shoot me," he says. "Shoot all of us. You won't get the cash back."

"Motherfucker." The young guy, really on edge from the sirens now, raises his own Beretta.

"Wait!" the gunwoman says. She turns back to Bamber, and then, reconsidering, zeroes in on me. "You," she says. "Is your friend here telling the truth?"

And I just gape at her, trying to think how to sell the lie, which of course means I've already blown it. In a moment of rising panic I see something flitting through the air behind her. I glance at it, look away, then look back again, even as my brain warns me not to.

The gunwoman sees it all in my face. Eyes narrowing in suspicion, she turns, pistol at the ready, but the drone is small, no larger than a pack of cards, and it's much faster than she is. The instant her gun is pointed away from us the drone fires, hitting her in the neck, dumping more voltage into her body than any civilian Taser would be allowed to. She does a jittering dance, and the men, each tasked with their own drone, dance too. All three of them go down.

The Taser drones settle into a protective hover, and a larger drone glides into view from behind the Panda Express kiosk. The big drone has a camera mounted inside a dome on its underside. It pauses to scan the trio, confirming that the Real Threats have been neutralized, then glides forward until it's right in front of me. As it comes to a stop, it does this little side tilt, the way a person might cock their head, and through this gesture I intuit who the driver is.

"Hi Mom," I say, and I tilt my own head towards the dude in the hoodie at my side. "I'd like you to meet my girlfriend, Darla."

88 Names

On the internet, nobody knows you're a dog.

—Mark Twain

"The Great Impostor" — Sobriquet of Ferdinand Waldo Demara Jr. (1921–1982), an American folk legend who used stolen identities and forged credentials to obtain work as a prison warden, college dean, sheriff's deputy, civil engineer, and numerous other jobs for which he was technically not qualified. In what became his most famous exploit, he assumed the identity of a Canadian doctor, Joseph C. Cyr, and served as a trauma surgeon aboard the destroyer HMCS *Cayuga* during the Korean War. Despite his lack of medical training, he performed several successful operations, speed-reading medical reference books to learn the necessary procedures. Demara's stated motivation for his many impostures was "Rascality. Pure rascality."

—*The Book of Lulz*

He wants to see me.

Darryl Joseph Carter (aka Darla Jean Covington, aka Smith, aka Mr. Jones, aka Ms. Pang, aka Nameless White Guy, aka Mr. Bungle) is being held in the John McCain Special Housing Unit at the Federal Correctional Complex in Victorville. The McCain SHU is an ultramax-security facility designed for the sort of prisoners who used to be held at Guantanamo Bay. Darryl's incarceration there has less to do with his alleged crimes than with the circumstances of his capture. The government's logic goes like this: Darryl was the target of a Zero Day operation; Zero Day exists to hunt down super-dangerous terrorists; QED, Darryl deserves the Al Qaeda treatment. Don't get on my mom's bad side, is the moral of the story.

The SHU does not have regular visiting hours. Even the prisoners' lawyers must apply in advance to meet with their clients. As a civilian with no security clearance, I require an escort to get inside the facility. For a while Mom talks about doing this herself—she'd love an excuse to fly in and spend some time with me and the other West Coast relatives—but other work duties keep intervening, so eventually she sends her latest Zero Day recruit in her stead.

Jolene picks me up at LAX. This is the first time I've seen her in person since the day she got shot. She's looking much better; her broken ribs have healed, and she's thrilled about the new job. "Almost worth taking a bullet for," she jokes.

Our appointment at the prison isn't until two, so we stop for lunch at a diner in the San Gabriel Mountains. Over burgers, Jolene asks me how the sherpa business is doing. Not well, I tell her. I'm working without a crew these days. "Anja left right after you did."

"You told her the truth about the malware?"

I nod. "I thought about pretending that Darryl hacked her medical pod without my help, but that just didn't feel right. So I came clean."

"Good," Jolene says. "How pissed off was she?"

"More sad than mad, I think. She didn't actually say she was quitting, just told me she was going to take a break and spend some time with Javier. Did you hear about Ray?"

"Oh yeah, I heard."

In the movie version of this story, Ray's reward for saving the life of the cop Jolene shot will be full recognition of her American citizenship. In the real world, Ray knew better than to count on that ending—after the SWAT team escorted her and the cop and Jolene out of the Arcade to where paramedics were waiting, she managed to slip away. But her face had been captured by Tempest's security cameras, and the LAPD IDed her as a fugitive with an outstanding ICE warrant. Mom tried to run interference by claiming that Ray was a Zero Day asset, but the local cops were upset that she hadn't told them about the op in advance, and ICE just didn't give a shit. Rather than back off, ICE demanded, and eventually got, Ray's home address, which Mom knew from having traced her internet connection.

Ray was living in a rented trailer outside of Barstow. ICE raided the place two weeks ago. The agents shot a stray dog on the property, but Ray herself was nowhere to be found. From the look of things, she'd cleared out just hours earlier, taking her computer and VR rig with her.

ICE is mad. They think Mom warned Ray that they were coming. I thought so too at first, but now, listening to Jolene say, "Oh yeah, I heard," it occurs to me that someone else might have given Ray the heads-up.

"So anyway," I say, "I'm working solo now, when I'm working at all. It looks like my fifteen minutes' of fame from that *People* article are over."

"That's a shame," Jolene says, not sounding too broken up about it. "Especially since you lost all that money."

Just as Mom predicted, the government confiscated the half million dollars Darryl had given me. Or as much of it as they could get their hands on: The ten thousand I paid Anja for her first week's cut is safe in her bank in Argentina, and Ray cleared out her

PayPal account before ICE could freeze it. I assume Jolene had to give up her share, but since she was working undercover all along, she never expected to keep it. "Yeah, I'm back in the poorhouse where I started." I shrug. "It happens."

"Don't worry, I'll pay for lunch," Jolene tells me, and she does. While we're waiting for the waitress to bring her change, she says: "So listen, it's none of my business but I've got to ask. You and Darla. When the two of you were having your thing together, whatever that was, did you ever . . ."

"Have cybersex? Yeah. A few times."

"Yeah, OK. So is it weird for you, to find out that she's . . . well, I want to say 'a guy,' but maybe that's making assumptions."

"I don't think Darryl's trans, in the traditional sense," I say. "And even if he was, I think he'd think it was funny that you were worried about the etiquette. You didn't watch the recording of his FBI interview?"

She shakes her head. "I was going to check it out, for today, but I didn't get around to it."

"His gender identity came up. One of the agents asked him if he felt 'like a woman trapped in a man's body,' quote-unquote."

"How'd he answer?"

"He laughed his ass off. Then he told them no, it wasn't like that, he just wasn't hung up on the whole male-female thing."

"Hmm. And you?"

"I'm a little hung up on it. I'm not going to pretend that Darla being a girl was irrelevant, because I liked the way her avatar looked—the way I thought she looked. But that was never the main attraction. The thing that got to me about her was her talent, and that was real."

"I don't know. I think I'd still be pretty upset, if it was me."

"It's the internet," I say. "Nobody's ever exactly what they seem like. You know what does freak me out, though? Unless Darryl erased it, the feds have the bullet I made for Darla."

"You worried they're going to send a copy to your mom?"

"Don't even joke about that."

We're at the prison at two o'clock, but it's closer to three by the time we make it past the gates, doors, ID checks, pat-downs, and scans. Near the end of the gauntlet, Jolene and I part company. She heads for a security office to watch on closed-circuit television while I go up to the interview room alone.

The room is like something out of the Combine interrogation center in *Half-Life 3*: an octagon assembled from poured concrete slabs, divided down the middle by a curtain of armored Plexiglas. Small circular grilles of titanium mesh are set into the Plexi to allow sound to pass through. On either side of the barrier, a broad strip of floor has been painted red, with signs warning of dire consequences if this no-go zone is violated; God help you if you actually tried to pry one of the grilles out, or messed with the cameras mounted on the ceiling.

The chair on my side of the Plexi is an expensively padded and ergonomic office number, the kind of thing you'd want under your butt if you were settling in for a marathon session of online poker. The prisoner chair is a hardback plastic seat that you might buy in bulk if you were shopping for an underfunded school district. This might seem like needless cruelty, and it is, but it's also logical from a business perspective: As much as any private corporation, the Department of Corrections knows the difference between its clients and its products.

I take a seat in the comfy chair. I've still got a few minutes to wait, so I have another look at the crib sheet on Darryl that Mom had prepared for me.

He is twenty-four years old, and he does not live in Oregon. It's true that his parents are divorced, but the whole family still resides, as they always have, in Palo Alto. Darryl's dad works for Apple. His mom is a deputy in the Santa Clara County Sheriff's Office.

Darryl's own occupation, which he seems to have pursued full-time for at least the past several years, is pretending to be other people on the internet. Principally Darla, whose stories about visiting Dad in Arizona or attending family reunions with her mother were a scheduling strategy to block out time for her different on-line relationships. The FBI and Mom's people are still working to compile a full list of contacts, but so far they've identified four individuals who Darla spent significant time with.

The first is Darla's hacker friend, Orville. A positive ID is still pending, but they believe he is Orville Slusarski, a forty-nine-year-old former NSA employee who quit the agency under a cloud of suspicion and took some stuff he shouldn't have when he left. Orville, an avid *League of Avengers* player whose favorite alter ego is Lex Luthor, was apparently tutoring Darla in the dark arts of cyberwarfare. The crib sheet doesn't say what Orville got out of the deal, but I think it's a safe bet that Darla lied when she told me she and Orville weren't fucking. Not that I care.

The second name on the list is Martin Duncan, a New Mexico schoolteacher and *Star Trek Online* devotee who'd been sending Darla gifts of cash—paying Darryl's rent—in hopes that she would one day agree to meet with him in person. Then there is Jason Hoyt, a physical therapist and *Call of Duty* leaderboard champ from Boston who used to send Darla gifts of cash, until he lost patience and decided to stalk Darla instead. Hoyt is undergoing some serious physical therapy of his own now, after tracking Darla to a house in New Haven that actually belonged to a Navy SEAL.

Individual number four is yours truly. Zero Day's psych profilers are divided on what my relationship with Darla meant to Darryl. One theory is that he was grooming me to be a replacement for Martin Duncan, which if true would be pretty funny, given the difficulty I often had paying my own rent. My preferred hypothesis is that Darryl saw me as a more age-appropriate version of Orville. I believe Darla's passion for game design was real, and that Darryl was sincere about wanting to go into business with me—however dim the long-term prospects for that might have been. Why else would his revenge have taken the form that it did?

Mom, after hearing me out at length on the subject, agrees with me. She thinks Darryl did regard me as a kind of peer, a friend even. But she also pointed out that being befriended by a sociopath, like being hired to work for a dictator, is not really something I should be proud of, or flattered by. And I know that she's right, but it feels a lot better than being taken for a sucker.

The door opens on the other side of the room and Darryl comes in. He is dressed in orange prison scrubs, and his arms and legs are shackled. His hair has gotten longer, and he is sporting a thick growth of beard whose unkempt nature gives him the appearance of a hermit. He stops just inside the threshold and looks around, taking in the dimensions of the room, which is significantly larger than the cell they've been keeping him in. Before sitting down, he does a brisk circuit of his side of the octagon. Despite the chain between his ankles, he doesn't shuffle, he *walks*, maintaining a short graceful stride, and in this, and in the way he comes right up to the edge of the red zone without going over, I see Darla's talent, that thing I found so compelling in her.

But I see him, too. At the Arcade that day, there was too much going on for me to ever really take a good look at Darryl, but now, as he takes his turn around the room, I have a chance to check him out. I think about that question Jolene asked me at the diner, and find myself wondering how things might have played out if Darla ever had given me her home address.

I identify as straight, and have never been with a guy in real life, but I like to believe I'm cool enough to be open to the possibility. The masculine physique isn't a problem for me. I'm attracted to athletic women, a polite way of saying I'm not a huge boob guy, and Darryl, from the neck down, could pass for a flat-chested Valkyrie. Kind of. The beard, though, really doesn't work for me.

And yes, I am aware of the absurdity of this train of thought. We're talking about someone who tried to blow up my life and my business. Who tricked me, tased me, and threatened to kill me. Who threatened Anja's life too, and nearly got Jolene killed, and started a panic in a crowded building that could easily have killed or injured many more people. Ostensibly he did all this to get even with me for lying to him, but really he did it to entertain himself. For the lulz. Mom's right, Darryl is a sociopath—and as sexual turn-offs go, what's a little facial hair, compared to that?

I don't know. Maybe I'm just shallow.

Done with his stroll, Darryl sits in the public-school chair and looks directly at me for the first time since he entered.

"Darla," I say, to break the ice.

"Perv." He smiles, but it feels perfunctory. Then he says: "I'm bored shitless."

As he would be. There are no video games in prison, of course, but inmates in the SHU don't get television, either. They are allowed reading material, but in a jailhouse version of the old desert island meme, they are limited to a maximum of five books at any given time. And if they tire of their current selection and want to swap out titles, they can't just run down to the prison library; they have to make a written request to the warden's office. The response time is measured in months.

"My mother can get you out of here," I tell him. "Agree to cooperate, and you'll be moved to a medium-security facility, with extra privileges. If the information you provide is valuable enough, you'll eventually be released to home detention, though you'll still owe restitution for the medical bills of that cop who got shot."

"What are they going to want for that?" he asks. "The bank in Burma?"

"To start with. They want to know how you hacked in, and everything you learned when you did."

"I can give you that. No problem."

"Also, your hacker friend Orville. Is his last name Slusarski?"

"He never told me his last name. But there can't be too many Orvilles who know how to tunnel past a Burmese firewall."

"The NSA wants to talk to him," I say. "They want to know where he is."

He shakes his head. "I can't tell you that."

"Because you don't know, or—"

"I'm not going to rat out Orville. He always played fair with me, and *I'm* no backstabber."

"Darryl, come on. You really want to stay in here?"

"Ask me something else."

There is nothing else. Finding Orville Slusarski is a top government priority, and Mom has made it clear that this point is non-negotiable—that it is, in fact, the only thing of real value that Darryl has to offer. But I do have some questions of my own that I'd like answered.

"The girl in the videos," I say. "The one you modeled your avatar on. Who is she?"

He grins like he was expecting this question. "You know those videos are fakes, right?"

I nod. Mom's tech people figured it out: The girl's image was added into pre-existing footage. The technique is basically the same one used to skin and reskin avatars; the editing software is widely available, and popular for making internet memes. Doctoring video crudely is easy, but to match the image to the background so that the fakery is hidden takes significant skill, along with lots of time and processing power—way too much effort for a typical prankster. But Darryl's not typical. "That was originally me, in the paintball video," he says. "And in the balloon. Most of the other clips were found footage, cool stuff I saw on the net that I thought Darla would be into."

"But the girl," I say. "Who is she?"

"Why do you want to know? So you can stalk her on Facebook? It's *me* you had the hots for," he says, and in his smirk, in the set of his shoulders as he leans forward, I see Darla again. I feel her. But the beard still doesn't do it for me. He picks up on this, and I can tell he's disappointed. "She's nobody," he says, sitting back in the chair. "I mean, literally nobody. I made her up, used morphing software to create a composite from a bunch of different images. Tweaked it for days, until I had it just the way I wanted. Then I put together a backstory for her, started building her Facebook page. I'd done that sort of thing before, made puppets, dozens of them, but Darla, she's my masterpiece."

"Why? What for?"

"You *know* why," he says. "Don't tell me you never pretended to be someone else online. It's *fun*, playing Darla. Getting people to believe in her and watching how they react. There are the ones like you, who fall head over heels for her, and that's fun in one way"—he winks—"and then there are the others, the assholes who try to grief on her, and that's really fun. That never gets old, taking someone who thinks they're a badass and teaching them who the real badass is. Darla, she's perfect for that."

"The bigger bitch," I say.

"Always." He smiles for real this time, enjoying himself.

"What about that day we met in the Jurassic Swamp?" I ask next. "Was that just a coincidence, or did you—"

"Come looking for you on purpose?" He laughs. "What are you thinking, that I saw one of your ads and said to myself, 'Gee, this one sherpa guy who sounds exactly like all the other sherpa guys must be super interesting, I guess I'll go pretend to bump into him by accident'?"

"OK, never mind."

"Aw, don't be hurt." He laughs again. "Who knows, maybe it was fate. I went to the swamp that day because I was bored and wanted to blow off steam, so I was definitely looking for *someone* to mess with, and there you were . . . I could tell how much you loved it when Darla kicked your ass, and when you offered me that job, I was like, OK, sure, let's see what kind of fun I can have with this. But then," and he hesitates, before continuing in a more serious tone, "then you showed me that eye thing, that mod you use, and your Mom-and-Pop switch, and there was just something about that, that made me think, I don't know, that maybe we were . . ."

"What? Kindred spirits?" I'm not buying it.

"I know you think I'm bullshitting," he says. "But it's true. I felt a connection, and I know you did, too." Scowling: "Of course if I'd known I could never trust you, I'd have cut your ass dead right there."

"That probably would have been the smart move," I say. "But if you had done that, you'd never have gotten the chance to play Mr. Jones."

"True." He brightens.

"What was the plan, with Jones?" I ask. "Did you always intend me to think he was Kim Jong-un?"

"It was never that specific. I assumed you'd figure out where the money came from—I was going to have Ms. Pang drop a clue-anvil on your head, if you didn't—so it made sense that Jones was some kind of powerful Asian dude, someone the PRC security ministry would be interested in. A dictator with a creative itch was an obvious choice, but I was open to other possibilities. A Chinese government official or spymaster gone rogue, or a drug kingpin, or even a pirate."

"Why would a pirate want to study MMORPGs?"

"I don't know. But that was the genius part of the plan—I didn't *need* to know, any more than I needed to know exactly who Mr. Jones was. I had you to figure it out for me. I knew you would, once the money got your imagination rolling. All I had to do was plant the seed, and let Mr. Profiler do the work." He grins. "It was amazing, watching you connect dots that weren't even there."

"Yeah, you really had me going. Well played, I guess."

"Oh, come on, don't be like that. I was pranking you, sure—I was mad—but don't pretend it wasn't fun for you too."

"Fun?" I say.

"OK, maybe not all of it . . . But solving the mystery? Thinking the Supreme Leader of North Korea had picked *you* to be his personal sherpa? Come on, that was fun."

I want to tell him he's wrong, but I remember how it felt, catching Mr. Jones out on the Juche calendar, and laying out my theories for Mom. "I suppose it had its moments."

"Moments!" He snorts. "It was the best fucking game you ever played. The best game I ever played, too."

"Well, I'm glad we both had fun, Darryl." Thinking as I say this that it is likely to be the last game he will play, for a long while.

He reads the thought in my expression. I watch him mull it over in silence.

"So," he says. "About Orville . . ."

"Yes?"

"What if I don't tell you exactly where he is, but I give you a really good hint? Enough for the NSA to figure it out on their own."

"Why not just give up the location?"

"I told you, I'm not a backstabber. But Orville likes to brag about how much smarter he is than the people he used to work for, always one step ahead, so as long as I leave him a chance to see it coming, it's not like I'm actually betraying him."

"Darryl."

"The odds will be stacked in your favor, don't worry. But I've got to leave him an out. A small one."

"Five percent?"

"Hey, that's all *I'd* need . . . So what do you say?"

"It's not my call," I tell him. "But I can talk to Mom about it, I guess."

"One other thing," he says. "Even if I do get home detention, there's going to be some pretty big restrictions on what I can do, right? Like, no computers?"

"I don't know. But I suppose so, yeah."

He nods. "Yeah, that doesn't work for me. Not being able to go online, that's worse than being locked up. I wouldn't mind staying in here if I had my rig."

"I understand," I say. "But you know they've got you flagged as a cyberterrorist."

"And that's totally cool!" he says. Like it's a badge of honor. "I get that they're not going to want to just turn me loose. But maybe there's another way to handle it, so everybody benefits."

He pauses, waiting to see if I'll figure it out on my own, which of course I do. We've seen a lot of the same movies.

"You want a job?" I say. "With Zero Day?"

"I know it sounds like a bullshit Hollywood plot twist," he tells me. "Black hat hacker gets caught and joins the good guys. But before you get all practical on me and say it's never going to happen, really think about it. That game I ran on you, I did that all by myself—well, except for the bank hack, but even that, I *convinced* Orville to tell me how to do it. And the rest of it, with you, I was playing all those different characters, sometimes two or three at the same time . . . Like, when you had your first meeting with Smith and Mr. Jones, I know you were suspicious, but did it even occur to you that the same person might be controlling both avatars?"

"I don't know. I don't think I thought that hard about the actual mechanics of it. And I mean, yes, OK, you did fool me. But—"

"And you're not stupid," Darryl says. "Gullible as fuck, sure, but even with the money, I had to work my ass off to make sure you bought it. And if I could do that with you, on my own, imagine what I could do with some support. You want to run a game on the real Kim Jong-un? Have your mom give me some resources, and I'll show her what I can really do."

He is delusional, I realize. The prospect of being stuck in prison has made him crazy. Or maybe he was nuts all along. I think this, but I try very hard not to let it show, because I know it will piss him off and make him uncooperative. But even as I struggle to control my expression, another thought comes to me, out of left field, and before I can stop myself, I laugh.

He thinks I'm laughing at him. He doesn't like it. All at once I see Darla again, at her most furious. "What?" he demands. "What's funny?"

"It's not you," I say. "I just . . ."

"What? What?"

"It just occurred to me . . . You're never going to apologize, are you? For any of it. You're never going to say you're sorry."

"I'm *not* sorry," he replies, indignant. "So why the fuck would I say I am?"

"No reason at all," I say. And as insane as it may sound, what I feel, in that moment, is a warm and genuine affection towards him.

Oh Darla, I think.

"OK," I tell him. "I'll talk to Mom about the job. I can't make any promises, but I'll talk to her."

"THE BABY DRAGONS POOP KRAZY GLUE?" MOM SAYS. "DID I hear that right?"

"The magical equivalent of Krazy Glue," I clarify. "The point is, if we break too many eggs, we can't maneuver, and then the mother dragon just kills us."

"Why doesn't she break the eggs herself, then?"

"Because she's a mindless drone, not a three-dimensional chess–playing badass like you, Mom."

"Ooh, flattery!" Mom laughs and looks over her shoulder at Jolene. "Are you hearing this?"

Tonight was supposed to be my monthly game night with Dad, but Sony moved up the deadline on his latest rewrite, so he's got to work. On a whim I messaged Mom and asked if she'd like to give *Call to Wizardry* a try, and to my surprise she said sure. After hearing a basic rundown of the different character roles, she decided she wanted to try tanking, so I gave her my best paladin and took her to the transmog parlor. There's something about the way Mom's head looks on top of a giant suit of plate mail that makes it seem like she's wearing power armor, so if she starts flying around like Iron Man, I won't be surprised.

I thought about inviting Anja along tonight as well, but it's still a bit too soon. So we're running the Caverns of Malice as a four-person team, which is easy enough if you've got a good healer. And we do: His name is Roy Wilson, and he presents as a thirtysomething white guy with a medium build, brown eyes, and short black hair. I haven't checked Roy out on social media, so I couldn't swear under oath that he is actually a white guy, nor could I hazard a guess as to his real-world location—but I think I might hire him.

"So don't break the eggs," Mom says. "Don't stand in the acid, and steer clear of the tornadoes. Anything else?"

"Nope. Just keep holding aggro, like you've been doing. We'll ace this."

"Cool," she says. Then, grinning mischievously, she tosses her shield into the air and catches it, spinning, on one finger. It's an impressive move—one that is not included in the paladin avatar's default repertoire. The only way Mom could do this is by turning off kinetic photoshopping. Which means that she knows what kinetic photoshopping is, and that it can be turned off, without me telling her about it. And if she's done that much advance research on her own, you can bet she's read up on the boss fights for this dungeon, too.

She's been humoring me again. But what can I say—it makes me happy when she does that. And in turn, I'll do what I can to make her happy too, to keep things in balance between us. Which, in a nutshell, is what I know about love.

Mom tosses her shield up one more time, catches it and grips it firmly. Twirls her sword for good measure.

"All right," she says. "Let's do this."

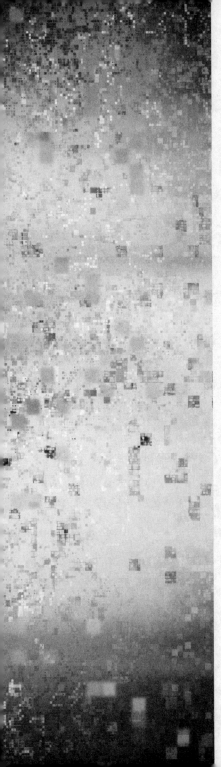

APPENDIX

This game client software is provided under license, and remains the sole property of Tempest, LLC . . . Player acknowledges that they have no ownership right to their characters or other in-game assets such as gold, magic rings, etc. . . . In the event that Player's account is suspended or terminated for violation of the Terms of Service, and it is later determined that such suspension or termination was made in error, Player agrees to indemnify Tempest, LLC for any and all damages, including, but not limited to, mental pain and suffering . . .

—*Call to Wizardry* End-User License Agreement

John Chu's *Call to Wizardry* Quick-Start Guide

IN TEMPEST'S *CALL TO WIZARDRY*, YOU PLAY A MIGHTY hero adventuring in the storied Realms of Asgarth. Below are some useful terms and game concepts to be aware of.

CLASS: Your character's profession, which determines your abilities and defines how you will play the game. Enjoy hand-to-hand combat? Become a warrior, paladin, or honorable samurai. Prefer to deal death from a distance? Try life as a sorcerer or an arrow-slinging ranger. Do you like ninjas? Yes, you can be a ninja. Can't decide? Talk to us, we'll help you choose!

RACE: The type of being you are: human, elf, dwarf, or something more exotic. The effects of race are mostly cosmetic. A dwarf cleric, for example, has the exact same healing powers as a goblin cleric, but the dwarf looks better in a kilt. Not all race/class combinations are available, but we will do our best to accommodate your preferences.

GENDER: All player characters are designated either male or female. Like race, this is a cosmetic choice, with no direct effect on gameplay. (Unfortunately, *Call to Wizardry* does not currently support non-binary as an option, but a trip to an in-game transmogrification parlor can provide your character with a suitably androgynous appearance, and of course we at Sherpa, Inc., will respect your choice of pronouns.)

LEVEL: A measure of your character's power and experience. A 100th-level warrior fights like the Roman gladiator Maximus, while a 10th-level warrior would be a guy who gets killed during practice warm-ups at the arena. The character we provide you with will be of sufficient level to handle whatever in-game content you wish to experience.

ROLE: *Call to Wizardry* puts a heavy emphasis on fighting. Each character in an adventure party is assigned one of the following combat roles:

DPS — The dps (short for "damage per second") characters do most of the actual killing. They hack, slash, and burn monsters to the ground. This is the simplest of the combat roles and a good choice for first-time players. In a typical five-person party, three characters will be assigned to dps duty.

TANK — The tank is a heavily armored character who typically deals less damage than the dps but can absorb a lot more punishment. The tank's job is to "hold aggro"—to keep the monsters' attacks focused on them while the more fragile dps and the healer do their jobs. Tanking effectively is a skill that requires practice, but it can be very rewarding. Let us know if you'd like to learn the ropes.

HEALER — The healer keeps everyone else alive. Like tanking, this takes significant skill, and gamers who prefer a more aggressive play style may find it is not to their taste. But the job is yours if you want it.

COOLDOWN: A powerful class ability that requires a lengthy recharge period between uses. We'll show you how to use these efficiently.

SECONDARY SKILLS: In addition to the powers granted by their class, characters can learn resource-gathering and crafting skills like mining, fishing, and smithing. If you just want a few hours' adventure, you don't need to worry about these, but if you intend to purchase your character or create one of your own, we can advise you on what secondary skills will be most useful to you. (We can also level up your secondary skills and/or gather resources for you, freeing you to focus on more interesting parts of the game. Please see Appendix B, Additional Services.)

DUNGEON: A scripted adventure zone featuring a fixed set of challenges, including several powerful boss monsters and their minions. You can think of these as violent theme-park attractions scattered throughout the game world; some are literal dungeons, but they come in many forms, including time portals to important events in the history of Asgarth. Each dungeon is designed to be tackled by characters in a specific level range, and most offer a "heroic mode" with increased difficulty and better rewards.

RAID: A special type of expert dungeon, intended for highly experienced players using max-level characters equipped with the best armor and weapons. Where normal dungeons are restricted to five-person parties, raids allow—and often require—much larger groups. Because of the extreme difficulty and the logistical challenges involved, we generally recommend that players interested in raiding join a guild devoted to that purpose. But if you've got money to burn, we can cater a raid for you. Email for a price quote.

LOOT: The spoils of victory. When you kill a monster, the game server generates a random number and consults a hidden "loot table" to determine what treasure(s) it was carrying. The loot tables of dungeon bosses and other elite foes often contain unique items, like powerful weapons, that cannot be obtained anywhere else.

ACHIEVEMENT: A challenge goal, like clearing all the bosses in a dungeon within a given time limit. Most achievements award only bragging rights, but some of the more difficult ones earn you special tokens or titles like "[Character name here], Destroyer of Worlds." An up-to-date list of achievements can be found on the Tempest website. Please let us know if there are any we can help you with.

PVE: "Player versus Environment." The default game mode, in which you fight, kill, and loot computer-controlled monsters and non-player characters (NPCs).

PVP: "Player versus Player." If the computer AI isn't challenging enough for you, you can also pick fights with other players. PvP combat is ostensibly optional—outside of designated PvP zones, players must voluntarily flag themselves for PvP before you can attack them—but there are ways around this restriction. Ask your guide for details.

PWNED: "Owned," as in totally dominated. What your enemies will be, when you adventure with Sherpa, Inc.!

ACKNOWLEDGMENTS

I was introduced to computer games in the late 1970s, while volunteering as a playtester for Simulations Publications, Incorporated. SPI made and sold tabletop wargames, but the company had a minicomputer that ran *Colossal Cave* and a text-based *Star Trek* simulator, and a couple of Radio Shack desktop machines that gave me my first taste of programming. It was SPI founder James Dunnigan who told me about this newfangled "role-playing game" called *Dungeons & Dragons*; intrigued, I ran out to the Compleat Strategist hobby shop and bought a copy, and nothing has ever been the same since. Thanks, Jim!

Julian Dibbell's 2006 book *Play Money* was a useful early primer on the subject of gold farming. Karen Glass and Caitlin Foito motivated me to turn my half-baked ideas on the subject into an actual story. My depiction of North Korea and the Kim regime draws from many sources, but Paul Fischer's book about the Shin Sang-ok kidnapping, *A Kim Jong-il Production*, was particularly helpful. Other people who provided inspiration and/or technical support include Neal Stephenson, William Gibson, Susie Bright, Raph Koster, Cory Doctorow, Monica and Jack Ruff, Anna Leube, Barbara Lehenbauer, Thomas Zenker, Nurri Kim, and Adam Greenfield.

As a career path, novel-writing may be even more impractical than game design. I am indebted to the people who continue to make it possible for me to earn a living this way: my wife, Lisa Gold; my literary agent, Melanie Jackson; Matthew Snyder at CAA; and Jennifer Brehl, Jonathan Burnham, and Lydia Weaver at HarperCollins. Thank you all.

About the author

About the book

Read on

Insights,
Interviews
& More . . .

Meet Matt Ruff

Matt Ruff decided he wanted to be a novelist at the age of five and spent his childhood and adolescence learning how to tell stories. His parents supported his ambition: Ruff's mother bought him a good typewriter and shared tales of her youthful adventures in the wilds of Brazil; his father passed along what he'd learned in the Lutheran ministry about reading people's motives and psychologies. The house where they lived in Queens, New York, was a stopping-off place for a succession of South American relatives who brought their own dramas—personal, cultural, and theological—that Ruff would later incorporate into his fiction. ▶

Meet Matt Ruff *(continued)*

Ruff wrote what would become his first published novel, the comic fantasy *Fool on the Hill*, while a student at Cornell University. With the help of one of his professors, Alison Lurie, Ruff found an agent and sold *Fool on the Hill* to Atlantic Monthly Press just months after his graduation. The book became a cult hit in both the United States and Germany.

By continuing to follow his inspiration wherever it led him, Ruff gradually acquired a reputation as someone who—to the delight of his readers and the chagrin of his publicists—never wrote in the same genre twice. His second novel, *Sewer, Gas & Electric: The Public Works Trilogy*, was a science-fiction satire of Ayn Rand's *Atlas Shrugged*. His third, the critically acclaimed *Set This House in Order*, was a literary exploration of the relationship between two people with multiple personality disorder. This was followed by *Bad Monkeys*, a paranoid thriller in the Philip K. Dick mold, and *The Mirage*, an alternate history of 9/11 in which the U.S. and the Middle East trade places. His sixth novel, *Lovecraft Country*, combined supernatural horror and the real-life terrors of racism in 1950s America; it has been adapted as an HBO series by Misha Green, Jordan Peele, and J. J. Abrams. With *88 Names*, he adds cyberthriller and "twisted romantic comedy" to his list of achievements.

Ruff's fiction has won numerous awards. He is also the recipient of a Literature Fellowship from the National Endowment for the Arts.

You can read more about Ruff and his work at his website, www.bymattruff.com. ❧

88 Names: A Theory of Mind

by Matt Ruff

I GREW UP AN ONLY CHILD IN NEW YORK City in the 1970s. I was what they called a latchkey kid: My parents both worked, so from what would today be considered a scandalously young age, I made my own way to school and fended for myself in the evenings until my folks got home. An introvert as well, I spent much of my free time alone, reading, writing, watching television, and playing board games.

The thing about solitaire play is that you always know what your imaginary playmates are going to do. Partly for this reason, I developed an early fascination with wargames. Whether they concerned the clash of vast armies or a desperate struggle between small groups of soldiers, the fun in playing them came as much from creating a story as from determining a winner. Which is not to say I didn't care about winning.

The late '70s was a lucky time to be a wargamer in New York; the city was home to Simulations Publications, Inc., a wargame company that held weekly open playtest sessions. At the age of twelve, I became a regular. Every Friday evening, I'd head to lower Manhattan and spend hours playing and critiquing whatever prototype the company was working on. SPI was best known for historically accurate games with names like *Terrible Swift Sword* and *NATO Division Commander,* but they also did sci-fi and fantasy titles. The first game I ever worked on, *The Creature That Ate Sheboygan*, simulated a fight between a giant monster and the Wisconsin National Guard.

Playtesting is important because real players, unlike imaginary ones, are perversely unpredictable. You may think you've designed a game about Godzilla slugging it out with tanks and howitzers, but then a precocious twelve-year-old comes along and says, "Wait a minute. If I *fight* the tanks, I might lose. But I see here in Section 14 of the rules that I get victory points for property destruction. So what I'm going to do is give my monster the Fire Breathing special ability, and then I'm going to run *away* from the tanks and scoot around the board, setting fire to all the buildings. I'm also going to give my monster the Jumping ability, so if the National Guard does manage to corner me, I can just leap over the burning buildings and escape. I'll be unstoppable!"

Strategies like this one can break an otherwise fine game. While the designer's first impulse might be to say, "You can't do that," a better solution is to tweak the rules—rewarding fewer points per building destroyed or increasing the effectiveness of firefighting units—until the strategy becomes fair. In the published version of ▶

The Creature That Ate Sheboygan, you can still be a high-jumping arsonist if you want, but it's no longer a guaranteed win. The National Guard player gets to enjoy the game, too.

My time at SPI was a formative experience in many ways. SPI president Jim Dunnigan introduced me to *Dungeons & Dragons*—the ultimate storytelling game. He also let me screw around on the company's computers, sparking a lifelong addiction to computer games. That could have proved disastrous, but fortunately for my nascent writing career, personal computers were very expensive back then, and it would be decades before I could comfortably afford state-of-the-art equipment. This became particularly important in the late 1990s, when a new generation of game designers figured out how to put *Dungeons & Dragons* on the internet. Like John Chu's father, I would happily have frittered my productivity away on MMORPGs, but you needed a fast internet connection to play, and I was still using dial-up well into the 2000s.

Since I couldn't play the games, I read about them instead, which is how I discovered the phenomenon of gold farming. That people were making real money selling virtual loot was intriguing in its own right, but what really caught my interest was the dilemma this created for the game companies. Even if they were willing to overlook gold farmers profiting off their intellectual property, the practice caused headaches for customer service. Players who couldn't afford to buy gold resented those who could. And when someone got cheated out of the money they'd paid for a magic sword, guess who they called to complain?

But unless you are willing to completely eliminate the in-game economy—which will make all of the players unhappy—shutting down the black market is just as difficult as it would be in the real world. More difficult, in fact, because you can't threaten gold farmers with prison. And just like griefers, they are remarkably adept at finding and exploiting loopholes in rules meant to curb their behavior.

I sensed a novel here. Very quickly I came up with a plot skeleton for what would eventually be *88 Names*. But my instinct told me that this was one of those ideas that would benefit from more time and thought. Gamers would eat this story up, I knew, but I wanted to find a way to appeal to non-gamers as well, and bring in themes and subjects from outside my little niche hobby. So I put *88 Names* on the shelf in my back brain where I keep novels that aren't done baking yet and turned my attention to other matters.

A decade passed. The internet, once the domain of nerds and fringe enthusiasts, became more and more central to public life. Every so often I'd take *88 Names* off its shelf and have another look at it. The creative ▶

About the book

tipping point came during the 2016 presidential election, when it dawned on me that everyone in America had become trapped in an online role-playing game—one in which the stranger you were arguing with on Twitter might well be a Russian bot. Or a precocious twelve-year-old.

The internet makes it easy to pretend to be someone you're not, but a bigger problem is that it encourages you to treat other people like imaginary playmates. It's not that we take strangers at face value online, it's that we assign roles to them—Hero, Villain, Fool, Whipping Boy—and naively expect them to stay in character. When they act unpredictably—by putting a reality show host in the White House, for example—we're dumbfounded and enraged.

Understanding people whose worldviews differ from our own has always been a challenge. The internet ramps up the difficulty level, even as it makes the effort more vital. The screen in front of me connects me to billions of other human beings. It also strips away context, rewards glibness, shatters focus and shortens attention spans, and provides a wealth of new tools for distraction and harassment. It turns minor differences of opinion into blood feuds, while making genuine atrocities seem no more consequential than cutscenes in a video game.

Writing *88 Names* offered a means of working through my feelings about all of this. It's my nature to be optimistic, and I've lived long enough to know that it's always two minutes to the apocalypse. If the threat seems more serious at the moment, I can take comfort in the fact that it's not just griefers who have a talent for adaptation. And of course there are also many benefits to living in the future. Those billions of human beings, for instance: Some of them are amazing people, and even an old introvert like me has forged friendships that wouldn't have been possible in any other era of history.

The point of understanding others is not just to make new friends, though. We are not all going to get along. You cannot play nicely with people who selfishly insist on winning every time. But branding someone a villain doesn't magically make them disappear. You still have to figure out how to deal with them, and the rules you propose for doing so will be more effective if you grasp that your antagonist has goals and motives of their own, and a mind that is not beholden to how you see the world.

The question "What are they thinking?" has an answer. The first step to finding it is remembering that other people are real. ᔐ

Have You Read?
Also by Matt Ruff

LOVECRAFT COUNTRY

CHICAGO, 1954. WHEN HIS FATHER GOES missing, twenty-two-year-old Army veteran Atticus Turner embarks on a road trip to New England to find him, accompanied by his uncle George—publisher of *The Safe Negro Travel Guide*—and his childhood friend Letitia. On their journey to the manor of Mr. Braithwhite—heir to the estate that owned one of Atticus's ancestors—they encounter both mundane terrors of white America and malevolent spirits that seem straight out of the weird tales George devours.

A chimerical blend of magic, power, hope, and freedom that stretches across time, touching diverse members of two black families, *Lovecraft Country* is a devastating kaleidoscopic portrait of racism—the terrifying specter that continues to haunt us today.

PRAISE FOR *LOVECRAFT COUNTRY*

"Lovecraft Country *takes the unlikeliest of premises and spins it into a funny, fast, exciting and affecting read.*"
—Neal Stephenson, *New York Times* bestselling author

"*At every turn, Ruff has great fun pitting mid-twentieth-century horror and sci-fi clichés against the banal and ever-present*

bigotry of the era. And at every turn, it is the bigotry that hums with the greater evil."
—*New York Times Book Review*

"Nonstop adventure that includes time-shifting, shape-shifting, and Lovecraft-like horrors.... Ruff, a cult favorite for his mind-bending fiction, vividly portrays racism as a horror worse than anything conceived by Lovecraft in this provocative, chimerical novel."
—*Booklist* (starred review)

"Lovecraft Country *rubs the pervasive, eldritch dread of Lovecraft's universe against the very real, historical dread of Jim Crow America and sparks fly.... Ruff renders a very high-concept, imaginary world with such vividness that you can't help but feel it's disturbingly real.*"
—Christopher Moore, *New York Times* bestselling author

"Ruff is sure to retain his cult following and certainly gain a wider audience with the thoughtful, fast-paced Lovecraft Country. Perhaps his greatest victory is giving his characters the space to live and breathe, even when their environment seeks to constrict them. The slippery dialogue and suspense-soaked prose make Lovecraft Country—a challenge to one of the most recognizable legacies in science fiction—worth every dime."
—*Chicago Review of Books* ▶

THE MIRAGE

11/9/2001: CHRISTIAN FUNDAMENTALISTS hijack four jetliners. They fly two into the Tigris & Euphrates World Trade Towers in Baghdad, and a third into the Arab Defense Ministry in Riyadh. The fourth plane, believed to be bound for Mecca, is brought down by its passengers. The United Arab States declares a War on Terror. Arabian and Persian troops invade the Eastern Seaboard and establish a Green Zone in Washington, D.C. . . .

Summer, 2009: Arab Homeland Security agent Mustafa al Baghdadi interrogates a captured suicide bomber. The prisoner claims the world they are living in is a mirage—in the real world, America is a superpower, and the Arab states are just a collection of "backward third-world countries." Other captured terrorists have been telling the same story.

The gangster Saddam Hussein is conducting his own investigation. And the head of the Senate Intelligence Committee—a war hero named Osama bin Laden—will stop at nothing to hide the truth. As Mustafa and his colleagues venture deeper into the unsettling world of terrorism, politics, and espionage, they are confronted with questions without any rational answers, and the terrifying possibility that their world is not what it seems.

PRAISE FOR *THE MIRAGE*

"A topsy-turvy tour de force, another winner from a truly inventive and unpredictable storyteller."

—San Francisco Chronicle

"An intriguing addition to the genre . . . Ruff keeps you reading, [out of] eagerness to see what twist he'll think of next."

—New York Times Book Review

"Both entertaining and provocative, exactly what the best popular fiction should be."

—Publishers Weekly (starred review)

"A unique and compelling read."

—Associated Press ▶

BAD MONKEYS

"So in your job with Bad Monkeys, what is it you do? Punish evil people?"

"No. Usually we just kill them . . ."

Jane Charlotte has been arrested for murder. She says she's a member of a secret organization devoted to fighting evil. She says she's working with the Department for the Final Disposition of Irredeemable Persons—aka "Bad Monkeys."

Her confession lands her in the jail's psychiatric wing and earns her countless hours of poking, prodding, and questioning by a professional. But is Jane crazy or lying?

Or is she playing a different game altogether?

PRAISE FOR *BAD MONKEYS*

"A science fiction Catcher in the Rye. . . . *Highly entertaining. It moves fast and keeps surprising you."*

—*New York Times Book Review*

"Rarely is a book that flirts with both the nature of reality and theories of good and evil so absolutely entertaining in a 'do-not-talk-to-me-until-I-am-done-reading' way."

—Associated Press

"Enough paranoia, double-dealing, plot twists, and mortal thrills to fuel a dozen le Carré novels."

—*Washington Post Book World*

> "A highly satisfying speculative thriller, intricate, unpredictable, and frequently laugh-out-loud funny."
>
> —*San Francisco Chronicle Book Review*

SET THIS HOUSE IN ORDER: A ROMANCE OF SOULS

"I suppose I should tell you about the house. . . . The house, along with the lake, the forest, and Coventry, are all in Andy Gage's head, or what would have been Andy Gage's head if he had lived. Andy Gage was born in 1965 and murdered not long after by his stepfather. . . . It was no ordinary murder: though the torture and abuse that killed him were real, Andy Gage's death wasn't. Only his soul actually died, and when it died, it broke in pieces. Then the pieces became souls in their own right, coinheritors of Andy Gage's life . . ."

Andrew Gage was "born" just two years ago, called into being to serve as the public face of a multiple personality. While Andrew deals with the outside world, over a hundred other souls share an imaginary house inside his head, struggling to maintain an orderly coexistence: Aaron, the father-figure, who makes the rules; Adam, the mischievous teenager, who breaks them; Jake, the frightened little boy; Aunt Sam, the artist; Seferis, the defender; and Gideon, the dark soul, who wants to get rid of Andrew and the others and run things on his own. ▶

Have You Read? Also by Matt Ruff *(continued)*

Andrew's new coworker, Penny Driver, is also a multiple personality—a fact that Penny is only partially aware of. When several of Penny's souls ask Andrew for help, he reluctantly agrees, setting in motion a chain of events that threatens to destroy the stability of his house. Now Andrew and Penny must work together to uncover a terrible secret that Andrew has been keeping from himself. . . .

PRAISE FOR *SET THIS HOUSE IN ORDER*

"Irresistible."

—*New York Times Book Review*

"Funny, wildly inventive, and emotionally astute."

—*Boston Globe*

"A stunning feat of literary craftsmanship."

—*San Francisco Chronicle*

Discover great authors, exclusive offers, and more at hc.com.

BOOKS BY MATT RUFF

LOVECRAFT COUNTRY
A Novel

"A funny, fast, exciting and affecting read."
—Neal Stephenson,
New York Times bestselling author of *Seveneves* and *Anathem*

Ruff makes visceral the terrors of life in Jim Crow America
and its lingering effects in this brilliant and wondrous work
of the imagination that melds historical fiction, pulp noir,
and Lovecraftian horror and fantasy—now an HBO series.

THE MIRAGE
A Novel

"A topsy-turvy tour de force." —*San Francisco Chronicle*

A mind-bending psychological thriller in which an alternate
history of 9/11 uncovers startling and harrowing truths
about America and the Middle East.

BAD MONKEYS
A Novel

"*Bad Monkeys* has wit and imagination by the bucketload. . . .
Buy it, read it, memorize then destroy it. There are eyes everywhere."
—Christopher Moore, *New York Times* bestselling author
of *Shakespeare for Squirrels* and *Lamb*

A page-turning psychological thriller about a secret organization of
vigilantes that will keep you guessing until the very last page.

SET THIS HOUSE IN ORDER
A ROMANCE OF SOULS

"A stunning feat of literary craftsmanship."
—*San Francisco Chronicle*

Andy Gage was born in 1965 and murdered not long after
by his stepfather. . . . It was no ordinary murder. Though the
torture and abuse that killed him were real, Andy Gage's death
wasn't. Only his soul actually died, and when it died, it broke
in pieces. Then the pieces became souls in their own right,
coinheritors of Andy Gage's life. . . .